He didn't want to go back to Esperanza.

He had sworn the day he'd left, over eight years ago, that he would never return, and so far he had kept his word. They couldn't send him back!

Esperanza. The word meant hope, but Cody had found little hope in the town. He had lost the only people he cared about there—his father to a better life, his mother to the booze and, later, to death . . . and Mariah.

He loved her name, just as he had once loved the woman who suited it so beautifully. It was soft, flowing, lyrical. She was soft, too, so soft. . . .

He swore viciously. Mariah had left him. She had made him wish he had never been born. She had almost destroyed him, and now they were asking him to go back to the town where he had met her, where he had loved her.

How could he do it and survive?

Dear Reader,

When two people fall in love, the world is suddenly new and exciting, and it's that same excitement we bring to you in Silhouette Intimate Moments. These are stories with scope, with grandeur. The characters lead the lives we all dream of, and everything they do reflects the wonder of being in love.

Longer and more sensuous than most romances, Silhouette Intimate Moments novels take you away from everyday life and let you share the magic of love. Adventure, glamour, drama, even suspense—these are the passwords that let you into a world where love has a power beyond the ordinary, where the best authors in the field today create stories of love and commitment that will stay with you always.

In coming months look for novels by your favorite authors: Maura Seger, Parris Afton Bonds, Linda Howard and Nora Roberts, to name just a few. And whenever you buy books, look for all the Silhouette Intimate Moments, love stories *for* today's women *by* today's women.

Leslie J. Wainger
Senior Editor
Silhouette Books

Marilyn Pappano
Cody Daniels' Return

Silhouette Intimate Moments

Published by Silhouette Books New York

America's Publisher of Contemporary Romance

SILHOUETTE BOOKS
300 East 42nd St., New York, N.Y. 10017

ISBN: 0-373-07258-9

First Silhouette Books printing October 1988

Books by Marilyn Pappano

Silhouette Intimate Moments

Within Reach #182
The Lights of Home #214
Guilt by Association #233
Cody Daniels' Return #258

MARILYN PAPPANO

has been writing as long as she can remember, just for the fun of it, but recently she decided to take her life-long hobby seriously. She was encouraging a friend to write a romance novel and ended up writing one herself. It was accepted, and she plans to continue as an author for a long time. When she's not involved in writing, she enjoys camping, quilting, sewing and, most of all, reading. Not surprisingly her favorite books are romance novels.

Her husband is in the navy, and in the course of her marriage she has moved all over the U.S. Currently she lives in South Carolina with her husband and son.

Prologue

Cody Daniels changed into jeans and a chambray shirt, picked up the bag that held his uniform and slung his gun belt, with its empty holster, over his shoulder. Finally he was ready to go home.

It had been a long day, made longer by his last arrest. With little more than an hour left on his shift, he had followed one suspected illegal alien into a canyon and found seventeen more waiting there. It had meant staying late to question, photograph and fingerprint them, but now he was finished. Now he could leave.

As he walked down the narrow hall, he heard his boss call his name. Wearily, he stopped in the open door of Jack Melendez's office. "What's up?"

"Close the door and sit down," Melendez invited. He was a big man, dwarfing the small desk he used. He waited patiently until Cody had seated himself; then he said, "The transfer you requested came through. I'm hurt that you want to leave us."

Cody grinned. "You couldn't care less, as long as they send you a replacement. When do I go?"

"Soon. But don't start packing for a move up north," Melendez warned.

The grin faded. The transfer he had requested had been to the border patrol station in Chicago. Born and raised in the desert, he'd had the desire for a long time to live somewhere else. Chicago had seemed like a good choice. Like any place else, the border patrol there was shorthanded, with too many aliens and too few agents. "But you said the transfer went through."

"So I did. The transfer. Not the destination. They're sending you home, Daniels."

He stared at his boss. Home could be any of a number of places, but all in Arizona. As a kid, he'd moved with depressing regularity while his father looked for work, for a better life. They had lived in Tucson, Phoenix, Flagstaff, Yuma and Winslow. The last town he'd lived in in Arizona had been...

"Esperanza, Arizona," Melendez said, leaning back in his chair and folding his hands over his stomach. "Sounds like a pretty little town. Is it?"

The roaring in Cody's ears made it difficult to hear his boss's next words, and the numbness spreading through his mind prevented him from understanding them. He just stared blankly at Jack.

He didn't want to go back to Esperanza. He had sworn the day he'd left over eight years ago that he would never return, and, so far, he had kept his word. They couldn't send him back now. They couldn't!

"Are you okay?"

Despite the dryness in his mouth, Cody managed to swallow. "Yeah," he murmured. "Yeah, I'm okay."

Melendez looked at him strangely, unconvinced, and repeated the last part of the conversation anyway. "They're having some problems over there with a smuggling operation. They know that some local people are involved, and they've got a suspect, but they don't have any proof. That's where you come in."

Concentrate on business, Cody instructed himself. This has nothing to do with her. Nothing at all. "How many people are they bringing in?"

"It varies. Some weeks no more than five, sometimes as many as twenty."

Cody took a deep breath and focused on those numbers. They intrigued him, helping him regain control, because something was wrong with them. Only five to twenty illegals a week hardly constituted smuggling. Not when other operations brought across upwards of three or four hundred a month. "What's so special about these illegals?"

"You've heard of Carta Blanca?"

Cody nodded. He didn't follow the international news closely, but you couldn't pick up a paper these days without reading something about the small Central American country. Like its neighbors, Carta Blanca was in the midst of a civil war. Its government had distinguished itself from the others by being particularly brutal; it was savage and merciless in its dealings with the rebels, the *contras*. No one could estimate how many thousands had died at the government's hands, usually tortured before they were allowed to expire. Thousands more were in prison, and many others had disappeared, picked up by the army, only to be seen no more.

"Well, these illegals are from Carta Blanca—kids whose parents are dead or in prison. There's an underground railroad set up to funnel the kids straight from Carta Blanca to Esperanza. From there they go to homes run by various churches, and they put them in foster homes."

"So they're doing a good deed. Why bother them?"

"The official U.S. policy toward Carta Blanca is neutrality," Melendez said with a frown. The recently elected president had won because of his policy of noninvolvement in foreign affairs. As long as Americans weren't directly threatened, he believed the U.S. should mind its own business. It was a popular stance. "However, the Carta Blancan government is starting to make noises about this. They claim the children are being kidnapped and brought here against their will, and that our government is helping them by allowing it to happen.''

Cody's smile was faintly sarcastic. "I bet they also claim that the children are safe and well cared for at home, even though their parents have been murdered for their politics.''

Jack nodded. "You know it's bull, and so do I, but..." He sighed. "Anyway, you're being assigned to Esperanza to look into it. The U.S. doesn't want to let Carta Blanca make us look bad in the eyes of the world, so orders have come down to find whoever's responsible and stop them.'' He glanced at his watch, then stood up. "Come on, let's get out of here.''

They walked outside into the late spring heat. Cody automatically pulled a pair of aviator-style sunglasses from his pocket and put them on.

"The senior agent in Esperanza is Kyle Parker,'' Jack said, stopping next to his car. "I've worked with him before. He's a good man.''

"When do I leave?'' Cody asked absently. He wasn't looking forward to returning to Arizona. He had too many memories of the state, and of the small border town—too damned many memories.

"The sooner, the better. Let me know when you're ready, and I'll tell Kyle you're on your way.''

Cody nodded, then turned away to his truck. He made the short drive home without conscious thought. Inside the apartment, he dropped into a chair and tilted his head back, letting his eyes close.

Esperanza. The word meant hope, but Cody had found little hope in the town. The nine years he'd lived there hadn't been particularly good ones. He had lost the only people he'd ever cared about there—his father to a better life, his mother to booze and, later, to death, and Mariah...

He hadn't said her name aloud in more years than he cared to remember, at least not consciously. He tried it now. "Mariah.''

He loved the name, just as he had once loved the woman who suited it so beautifully. It was soft, flowing, lyrical. She was soft, too, so soft....

He swore viciously. Mariah had left him. She had hurt him. She had made him wish to God that he'd never been born. She was cold, selfish and heartless. There was nothing soft about her. But she was beautiful, incredibly beautiful, and he had deeply, intensely, hopelessly loved her.

Don't think about her.

The command was easier given than followed. Mariah, with her black hair and black eyes, with her angel's smile and devil's heart, was part of him; she owned him. She had bewitched him, enchanted him—had claimed his heart and his body and even his mind for her own. For weeks after he'd left Esperanza, his grief at losing her had eaten away at him until he could barely function, until he more closely resembled a living, breathing machine than a human being. It had taken him months to get over her, to feel again, to live again.

She had almost destroyed him, and now they were asking him to go back to the town where he had met her, where he had loved her. To the town that was filled with memories of her—sweet, painful, unwelcome memories. How could he do it? God, how could he do it and survive?

Chapter 1

Cody pulled the truck to the side of the road, shifted into neutral and rested his head against the steering wheel. Despite the cold air blowing from the air conditioner, a thin film of sweat made his face glisten. Leaning back in the seat, he closed his eyes. His head ached intolerably, and he could hear and feel his heart pounding hard and fast.

Mariah. It was all her fault. The closer he got to Esperanza, the stronger the memories, the more intense the pain, and it was all Mariah's fault.

Last week he had called a friend who worked in the Phoenix border patrol office. After a little checking, she had called back with the information that Mariah Butler—no, he corrected himself, Mariah Lowell—was still living in Phoenix. Of course she still lived in Phoenix, he thought now, his expression marked with cynicism. That was where her precious job was. That **was** where her precious husband was. She probably never visited her family ranch outside Esperanza; the chances that he would ever see her were minimal.

So why was he finding it so difficult to put the truck in gear and drive into town?

Resolutely checking the road behind him, he pulled into the lane again. Within a minute or two he had reached the speed limit. Ten more miles and he would be in Esperanza. Ten more miles and he would be home.

That was Jack Melendez's word, not Cody's. "They're sending you home, Daniels." Esperanza wasn't home any more than the other towns he'd lived in. It should have been, though. It *would* have been if Mariah hadn't changed her mind. He had planned to spend the rest of his life in Esperanza, working, living with Mariah, raising their kids. But Mariah... She'd had different plans for her life—plans that hadn't included him.

His exhalation was deep and painful. He hated thinking about her. For ten days, since Jack had told him about his transfer, he'd been fighting the thoughts, fighting the memories. He was afraid it was a battle that he would have to keep fighting for a long time.

He concentrated on the road ahead of him, even though he hadn't seen another car in twenty miles or more. He looked at the countryside, which had hardly changed in the last fifty miles, pretending that he'd never seen it before. He thought about the job waiting for him and the one he'd just left. Anything to keep Mariah out of his mind.

When Esperanza first came into sight, it appeared picturesque, quaint. Up close, Cody knew, it looked tired, dusty and worn-out. It wasn't a very prosperous town—never had been and never would be. It served the immediate needs of the local ranches and the border patrol station; anything more extensive than food, drink, gasoline and supplies had to be purchased in Tucson, some seventy miles to the north.

He stopped at the only motel, a dilapidated building on the edge of town. Cracks resembling intricate spiderwebs inched across the stuccoed exterior, and the vacancy sign over the door hung by one rusted hook. The hum of window air conditioners came from several units as he walked past to the office.

The clerk behind the desk was a bored young woman flipping through the pages of a popular gossip magazine.

She was a stranger to Cody, but most people in Esperanza were. In all the years he'd lived there, he had made few friends and had kept in touch with none of them. The woman rented him a room and took his money without any sign of recognition.

His room was at the back, away from the highway. It was clean, but that was the best he could say about it. The furniture was cheap and scarred, the walls needed painting, the linoleum was cracked, and a leaking faucet had left a permanent stain in the bathtub. It was a depressing place, reminding him of some of the shabby little houses he'd lived in as a boy.

He laid his suitcase on the bed, on a spread faded as bluish white as his jeans, and looked around him once more. If he found a place to live today, it couldn't be too soon, he thought grimly. He wouldn't stay in this room any longer than necessary.

Cody left the room, locking the door behind him, and climbed into his truck. His first priority, Melendez had reminded him this morning before he'd left El Paso, was to meet Kyle Parker. A place of his own had to come second.

The border patrol station was located on the southeast side of town. The building was low, with uniformly spaced windows breaking the buff exterior and double doors located exactly in the center. Cody stepped into the coolness inside and asked to see the supervisory agent.

Kyle Parker was a handsome black-haired man in his early forties. He greeted Cody with a firm handshake and invited him into his office. "You're taking some vacation time, is that right?" he asked, glancing over the file he'd pulled from the cabinet.

Cody nodded, settling back in the chair. When he had finally accepted that he was being sent back to Esperanza regardless of his own desires, he'd requested a few days off to get settled in. He needed the time to adjust to being back—to adjust to being in Esperanza without Mariah.

Kyle glanced at the calendar that hung behind his desk. "We sure can use you. For a while, after the latest immigration law went into effect, the crossings really slowed down. Then they decided that feeding their families is worth the risks, and they're coming across in droves. Plus we have this Carta Blanca thing, too. Did Jack tell you about that?"

"Some. Not too much."

Kyle rubbed his jaw in exasperation. "It's a real hassle. It's been going on for months, and nobody ever cared—after all, it's only kids. It hasn't been real high priority stuff for us, not when the *coyotes* are bringing across a hundred or more illegals a week and charging them three to five hundred dollars apiece." He sighed deeply. "But when that lunatic in Carta Blanca started making accusations, everyone from the president right on down jumped. They're demanding an investigation—and, by God, they want results. That's *your* job." He paused for a moment to light a cigarette. "They tell me that you used to live here."

Cody nodded once.

"Long time ago?"

Driving through town, it had all been so familiar that it had seemed like yesterday. "Yeah," Cody said curtly. "A long time ago."

Something in his voice, hard and private, warned the older man not to pursue the subject. "You worked on some of the ranches around here, didn't you?"

Cody wondered if his irritation at this line of questioning showed. It was pretty clear that Parker knew when he had lived in Esperanza and where he had worked. He probably also knew why he had left. Unconsciously, the muscles in his jaw tightened as he replied, "Yeah, I did."

"Our only suspect is named David Green. Do you know him?"

He shook his head.

"He used to live in Tucson, where he was active with one of those groups that brings in illegals from Central America. Refugees, they call them. He was arrested and convicted of smuggling, transporting and harboring illegals, but he only got probation. Lately he's become pretty outspoken against the Carta Blancan government, and since he moved here about six months ago, the estimates of Carta Blancan kids going through here have gone up pretty high."

He paused to somberly study the young man before him, then leaned forward and continued in a quiet voice. "Here's what we want you to do."

Cody walked out of the border patrol station and across the parking lot to his truck. He was unaware of the heat radiating in waves off the pavement. He stood motionless for a moment before pulling his sunglasses from his shirt pocket and sliding them on. The tinted glass eased the sun's glare, but he didn't notice. When he opened the truck door, the chrome handle burned against his fingers, but he didn't notice that, either.

Somehow he made it back to the motel. He found himself lying on his back on the faded blue-white bedspread, staring at the water-stained ceiling, not remembering how he'd gotten there. Not caring.

Kyle Parker's request—his command—was out of the question. He wouldn't do it. He *couldn't* do it.

For almost eight years he had given the border patrol all he had. He had been a damn good agent. He had done everything he'd been told, everything that had been asked. He had even returned to Esperanza when it was the last place on earth he wanted to be. But this...this was more than he could give. More than anyone should be asked to give.

"We're pretty sure that David Green is our man," Kyle Parker had said, "but we've got to prove it. We want you to get a job at the ranch—work with him, watch him, get to know him. Catch him with the kids. Find out who else is involved."

Then he had dropped the bombshell that had left Cody reeling. "You shouldn't have any trouble getting hired on where he's working. I hear the Butler place is looking for help."

Everything inside Cody had screamed "No!" on hearing that name, but aloud he'd said nothing. Somehow he had gotten to his feet without revealing that he was dying inside, and he had returned to the motel.

He rubbed his eyes until they ached. They were asking him—telling him—to get a job at the ranch owned by Mariah's parents. The ranch where he had met her. The ranch where he had fallen in love with her, where he had made love to her and had planned his life with her.

He couldn't face those memories. Loving Mariah had cost him dearly, and he couldn't pay again. He couldn't relive the loving. The loss. The pain.

He rolled over, burying his face in the pillow, muffling his faint groan. "I can't do it. Dear God, I can't...."

Cody stared at himself in the mirror. His jaw was shaved smooth, and his hair was still damp from this morning's shower, but it would dry on the way out to the ranch. His mouth had compressed itself into a narrow line, making his expression grim. His blue eyes were grim, too, as if he were about to face a firing squad.

He felt that way. During the night he had reached a decision: he had to do his job, no matter what it cost him personally. Ever since he'd found out he was being transferred here, he had let his emotions run free, feeling once again all the anger and pain and bitterness. He had learned a lesson from all those months of hurting—that emotions were unreliable, that feelings couldn't be trusted. His job was the one thing in his life that had never let him down. His father, his mother, Mariah—they had all failed him, but his job never had.

The ranch was a place, a piece of land; it couldn't hurt him if he didn't let it. He would simply ignore any memories it conjured up, would push them into the dark, dismal corners of his mind where they belonged, and he would do his job.

He was wearing the uniform of the Southwest: jeans, a faded shirt, sleeves rolled to his elbows and scuffed boots. He only needed a cowboy hat to complete the picture; with a sigh, he leaned down to pick it up. He was ready to face the memories.

His journey took him out of town on a seldom-used blacktop lane that led to only one place: to the Butler ranch.

A makeshift fence paralleled the road. During his time with the border patrol, Cody had seen mile after mile of that fence—broken-down, torn full of holes. A pathetic marker of the border that separated the United States from its poorer neighbor to the south. It also marked the southern border of the Butler ranch.

As he neared the house, the road veered northwest, away from the fence. He pictured the place in his mind before it came into sight ahead of him, shimmering in the afternoon heat. The U-shaped adobe house was more than a hundred years old, but it had aged gracefully. Arched windows and doors softened its blocklike appearance. Slightly rounded red tiles on the sloping roof smoothed the sharp corners where the arms of the U stretched back on either side.

The pale, almost yellow, adobe required endless plastering. The color came from the clay used for the plaster, and it changed slightly with each new coat. Over the years he had seen it in buff, tan and white, but he liked the soft yellow. As he got closer, though, he could see faint changes. The adobe needed repair, and scattered tiles on the roof were cracked or chipped and needed to be replaced. It was the first time he had seen the house in less than perfect condition, and it made him curious.

Signs of neglect were also evident in the other buildings. The barn and the stables looked worn, badly in need of attention. But if the quality of the buildings had gone downhill, that of the livestock certainly hadn't. The horses inside the corral were fine animals.

Cody parked his truck near the corral and got out. If Arcadio Muñoz, the foreman, was around, Cody knew he'd find him somewhere in the small complex of buildings. He was right; behind him, a familiar voice said in faintly accented tones, "I heard you were in town. I wondered if you would come and see me."

Cody turned toward the voice with a welcoming smile. Arcadio had worked for Mariah's parents and her grandparents before them, and he was the one man in the town of Esperanza that Cody could call a friend. He was at least seventy-five years old, although he claimed not to know his exact age. His shoulders were stooped, making him appear several inches shorter than he actually was. His skin, after years of hard work in the harsh climate, was leathery and brown, and his eyes, also brown, were locked in a perpetual squint. His iron-gray hair was heavy and coarse, brushing over the collar of his work shirt. He was a tough-looking man, but that hardness disappeared when he smiled. "Welcome back."

Cody accepted the hand the old man offered, then pulled him closer for an embrace. "How did you know I was back?" he asked, his voice teasing and friendly. "I only got in yesterday, and I haven't seen anybody I know."

Arcadio lifted his bony shoulders in a shrug. "News of strangers travels fast in Esperanza."

Did that news include the fact of his visit to the border patrol station? Cody wondered curiously. "How have you been, Arcadio?"

"I've been all right." The old man moved to the corral to lean against the peeling boards. "We've missed you, Cody."

He accepted the statement with a half smile that hid his pain. Had Mariah missed him? Had she even given him a second thought after he'd left Esperanza? "No one's missed me except maybe you, and then only when you had to do the work that you used to put off on me. Are you still running this place?"

"I do what I can, but I'm an old man."

Cody thought of the crumbling adobe, the cracked tiles, the rotting, peeling boards. Was Arcadio the reason? Was he too old to supervise the ranch—perhaps even a little bit senile? But one good look at him dispelled that thought. His eyes were as sharp and clear as Cody's, and, old as he was, he could probably outlast men half his age. So what was the problem with the ranch? Money?

Even as he discounted that possibility, he also wished it were true. If the ranch was going broke, he couldn't possibly get a job there, and Kyle Parker would have to find another way to carry out his investigation. But Jerry and Helen Butler had more money than they could possibly spend in their lifetimes; besides, the ranch had been in the Butler family for generations. They wouldn't let it go under.

Cody took a deep breath and plunged in. "Maybe you could use a little help."

Arcadio's eyes narrowed even more. He stared at Cody for a long time, so long that Cody began to worry. Maybe the old man's loyalty to the family for whom he had worked all his life was stronger than his friendship with Cody. Maybe he blamed Cody for everything that had happened with Mariah all those years ago.

"I know this is the last place anyone would expect me to ask for work," Cody began uncomfortably, "but...I need a job, Arcadio."

The older man finally looked away, turning his gaze on the horses in the corral. "They're beautiful, aren't they?" Without waiting for an answer, he continued, "If it were up to me, Cody, I'd hire you right now. But...I'll have to clear it through the boss first."

Cody's attempt to smile was a sickly failure. "Jerry Butler never liked me much, but he didn't have any complaints about my work. Besides, he's seventy miles away in Tucson. Why should he care who you hire?"

Arcadio took his hat off and turned it over and over in his hands. He ran his thumb and forefinger over the crease in the brim, then brushed a speck of dust away, before finally facing Cody again. "You've got the wrong Butler. Jerry isn't running the ranch."

"Then who is?" Cody asked in bewilderment. He couldn't imagine the elegant and sophisticated Helen taking any interest in the operation. That left only...

"Mariah."

Suddenly Cody's palms felt clammy, and his head was starting to throb again. He felt the sweat trickling down his spine, and his smile grew sicklier. "Well...hell, Phoenix is even farther away than Tucson," he feebly joked.

The smile disappeared altogether when Arcadio shook his head. "She's living here."

Cody felt as if his feet had been kicked out from under him. He reached out and grasped the top rail of the fence, unmindful of the prick of splinters. He gripped the rail until his knuckles turned white and the pads of his fingers were numb. "I checked before I came here," he said in a voice that was barely more than a whisper. "She's in Phoenix. I checked."

"I'm sorry, Cody." Arcadio cleared his throat, then clamped his hat on his head. "Do you still want that job?"

No. That was more than he could take. He could live in Esperanza. He could even work at her ranch. But, God help him, he could not see her. He couldn't face her and know that she had once been his, that he had lost her.

Arcadio was waiting for an answer. It came from someplace deep inside Cody that his mind couldn't control. "Yes," he said quietly, moving away from the fence. His expression was frozen, his movements wooden. If he relaxed, if he let himself think, he would know that this was insanity, and he would run away. After letting her control him for so long, he would be giving in to her again. She would win again.

"I'll talk to her, but I really don't think she'll hire you, Cody."

Cody's smile was mocking. "Who knows? She might enjoy playing boss—proving her superiority over me one more time," he said bitterly. Bitterness was good; it could keep the pain at bay. He could use it to stop the hurting.

Arcadio's look was sad. "Why don't you go up to the house and say hello to Bonita?" he suggested. "I'll come up as soon as I talk to Mariah."

Cody nodded once, then started across the wide yard that separated the house from the buildings. He concentrated on walking, on putting one foot in front of the other. He tried to forget that Mariah was here, probably back there in the office, only yards from where he'd been standing. He tried not to think about the fact that, in less than two weeks, his perfectly satisfactory life had collapsed around him.

It didn't matter that he hadn't been particularly happy before. It didn't matter that he had been alone, with few friends and only occasional lovers. He had been contented—those few commitments had been the only ones he'd wanted. He hadn't had any longing for a different life, hadn't felt any desire to fill that emptiness inside him left by Mariah. He had been satisfied. Now it was all destroyed.

First they'd sent him back to Esperanza. Next they had told him to get a job at the ranch. Now they expected him to work for Mariah, to live only a few hundred yards from her, to face her on a regular basis. He just couldn't do it.

Was she still beautiful?

The question stole into his mind. He wanted to turn it away, but he couldn't.

Still beautiful? Probably, he admitted. She had been the most beautiful woman he'd ever known. Eight years couldn't change that.

He tried to stop thinking about her. He didn't want to think, didn't want to remember the feelings she had always aroused in him, from the first time he'd laid eyes on her until the last time he'd seen her. Longing. Desire. Need. Love.

Each arm of the U-shaped house had a door. The one on the left opened into the hallway near Mariah's old bedroom. The one on the right entered close to the kitchen. That was the door Cody chose.

Bonita Muñoz was humming softly to herself in the kitchen while she cooked. Enticing aromas filled the air. Cody stopped in the doorway, taking in a deep breath before softly speaking her name.

She gave a little cry of surprise and pleasure at seeing him. Wiping flour-dusted hands on a frilly yellow apron, she hurried across the tile floor and hugged him tightly, kissing first his left cheek, then the other. But as suddenly as the pleasure came, it disappeared. Mariah, Cody thought resentfully. Bonita was worried how his return would affect Mariah.

Damn her! Wasn't it enough that everybody else in the world loved her? Did the only two people he had left have to love her, too? She had her parents, her husband, all her friends. She'd even had *his* love. Couldn't she leave somebody for him?

Bonita took a step back but still held his shoulders. "It's been a long time, Cody."

Silently he agreed.

"When did you get into town?"

"Yesterday." She hadn't known he was back, he thought curiously. Arcadio had known, but he hadn't told his wife. Had Mariah known, or was she, like Bonita, finding out now?

"Have you seen Arcadio?"

"Yes." He pulled away from her and walked to the window. "He told me that she's back, too." He didn't even have to say her name.

"Would you like some coffee? Sit down. I'll get you a cup of coffee and a piece of cherry pie. I just baked it."

"I'm not hungry, Bonita," he said, but she paid him no attention, so he pulled out a chair at the small wooden table.

When she had served him, she sat down across from him. "Will you be staying?"

He shrugged. "It depends." It wasn't a lie. If he couldn't get hired somewhere so he could quietly investigate David Green, maybe he could get that transfer to Chicago after all. He took a bite of warm pie, complimented Bonita on it, then asked quietly, "Why are they here?"

"'They'?"

"Mariah and . . . her husband." He said the phrase reluctantly, bitterly. *He* was supposed to have been her husband; she had promised herself to *him*. But she had married Chadwick Martin Lowell III instead.

He had always known that she would get married someday and that it would be to someone like Chad Lowell, but for months after he'd seen the announcement in the paper, he had gone to bed at night with an ache that he'd thought would never quit. How easily she had forgotten her love for him when someone more suitable had come along, someone who had no doubt met with her parents' approval.

Cody had desperately wanted Jerry and Helen Butler's approval himself, but he'd never gotten it. They had been aghast at the thought of their daughter—the daughter of a prominent attorney and a judge, the only child of one of the most widely respected families in Arizona—married to a ranch hand. It simply wasn't proper. So she had fallen out of love with Cody and in love with Chad Lowell, whose family background was equal, or possibly even superior, to that of the Butlers.

She had pleased her parents, and herself. Had she ever given any thought, he wondered, to how she had hurt *him*?

Bonita was looking at him, her expressive brown eyes wide with surprise. "Didn't Arcadio tell you?"

Cody pulled himself from his dismal thoughts. "Tell me what?"

"Mariah and Chad are divorced."

The office at the back of the stable was small and cramped, intended for use by only one person. Two desks and two chairs left precious little room for anything else. When Arcadio entered the room, he had to sidestep a box of receipts to get to the empty chair. He waited until Mariah finished totaling the column of figures in front of her and looked at him. From the expression on her face, he could see that the numbers didn't add up to good news.

"Where have you been?"

"Talking to an old friend." He didn't question her about the figures. The financial end of the ranch was her business; when she wanted to discuss it with him, she would bring it up. "You still want to hire another hand?"

"No," she replied with a scowl. "But I guess we don't have much choice, do we? You, Antonio, David and Philip—it's not enough. We need help." She dragged her hand through her hair, dislodging it from its loose braid. Reaching behind her, she removed the band that held her hair and shook her head, letting it fall free. "I don't suppose you know someone good, reliable and cheap."

Arcadio heard the faintly hopeful note in her voice. The fact that the answer was yes wouldn't matter, not when he told her who it was. "As a matter of fact, I do. He's experienced, he's a good worker, he's smart and he's dependable. On top of that, he's already familiar with the place."

"He sounds too good to be true. By all means, let's hire him before someone else does." She looked back at the rec-

ords on her desk and sighed. One more employee. They
needed the help badly—they were operating with a minimal
crew as it was—but where was she going to find the money
to pay one more man?

Realizing that Arcadio had remained silent in response to
her approval of the new hand, she looked up at him again.
"Is there something else I should know about this man?"

He nodded. "His name."

Her puzzlement began turning to dread. There was only
one person, only one cowboy, whose name could possibly
matter to her. Using one booted toe, she swiveled her chair
around to face him. "Who . . . who is it?" Her voice trem-
bled.

"Cody Daniels." Arcadio noticed that her hands were
trembling, too. "He's come back."

Mariah stared, her black eyes wide and, for a moment,
empty. Her breathing slowed until it was imperceptible;
then, blinking rapidly, she dragged in a deep breath, praying that she had misunderstood, yet knowing that she
hadn't. "Cody?" she whispered. "Cody's here? In Esperanza?"

"He's up at the house." Arcadio paused before asking,
"Should I send him away?"

"Yes!" Mariah rubbed her hand over her eyes. The last
thing in the world that she wanted or needed was to see
Cody Daniels again. He had brought her nothing but
heartache—enough to last a lifetime—and seeing him again
could only bring more. Still . . . "Wait, Arcadio."

He lowered himself back into the chair at her whispered
command.

"He wants a job?"

"Yes."

"He must be pretty desperate to want to work for me."

"He didn't know that you own the ranch until I told
him."

That figured. He probably wouldn't have set foot in the
county if he'd known she was there. She laced her fingers
tightly together in her lap. "Maybe if I help out more, we
could get by without another hand," she mused.

Arcadio calmly eliminated that argument. "Between keeping the books and taking care of the kids, you don't have time to help out more."

At the mention of the children, her expression grew even more somber. "What about the kids, Arcadio? We can't risk him finding out about them."

"Philip and Antonio don't know about them. There's no reason why Cody should find out."

She looked doubtful. "You really think I should hire him, don't you?"

"Hiring him would be the best move you could make right now, Mariah." He was prepared when she started to protest; stubbornly he insisted, "He needs a job, Mariah, and we need an experienced hand."

"No."

"He knows this place better than you, David and Philip combined."

"No."

"You won't have to work with him."

"No."

"You won't even have to see him."

"But I'll know he's here!" she exploded. Her dark skin was suffused with red—from anger? Shock? Or suddenly remembered pain? Lord, there had been so much pain—pain that had dictated the past eight years of her life. "Arcadio, how can you even suggest hiring him after everything that happened?"

The old man stood up and walked to the door. When he turned back to answer her, it was in a firm, no-nonsense voice. "I can suggest it because we need good, experienced help, or you're going to lose this ranch. I can suggest it because I don't believe in letting emotion stand in the way of good business, and, right now, hiring Cody Daniels is good business."

Mariah's shoulders stiffened. He was hinting that she was behaving like an emotional female, and all good ranchers knew that an emotional female had no place trying to run a ranch. It was an attitude that she had frequently faced in the seven months since her parents had signed the property over to her. No one believed that a woman like her was capable of running a ranch.

Her gaze fell to the papers on her desk. Maybe they were right. The ranch had been losing money steadily for several years; if she was going to hold on to it, she had to turn it around soon and start making money for a change.

Arcadio moved a few steps closer to her. He hated to see her looking so depressed. In a soft, comforting voice, he said, "Mariah, I know that you were hurt when Cody left Esperanza. I know how you loved him. But it happened a long time ago. You can't let it affect your judgment today."

She turned her chair so that her back was to him. He sounded like her parents. "It was a long time ago. It doesn't matter anymore. Forget about it, forget about *him*, and get on with your life." She'd heard that from them with annoying regularity. Was time supposed to make a difference? Was a broken heart supposed to hurt less because it happened "a long time ago"? What was the magical time limit when the pain suddenly stopped and everything was right with your world again? She wished someone could tell her, because after eight long years, even after her marriage to Chad, Cody Daniels still had the power to cause her pain.

"I'm going to send him in here to talk with you," Arcadio said. "You decide what you want to do. If you don't want to hire him because of what happened before, that's your business—it's your ranch. But you'll be the one to tell him so."

When the door closed behind him, Mariah lowered her head to rest in her hands. Her hair fell forward to hide her face. It wasn't fair, she moaned silently. With everything else that had gone wrong in her life, it simply wasn't fair that Cody had returned.

"But not to you," she said aloud with a bitter laugh. "He didn't come back to you." He'd had eight very long years to come back to her, but he had chosen not to. Now that he *had* returned, it was to the town, to the ranch. For a job. Not for her.

She lifted her head, squeezed her eyes shut and sighed. It didn't matter, she told herself firmly, emphatically. She didn't care why he had come back—she didn't even care if he'd forgotten that she existed. He meant nothing to her—nothing but sorrow. He had given her a few brief moments of happiness, and she had paid for them with endless months of grief. She had paid the penalty for loving the wrong man, and now he meant nothing to her.

But with her very next thought, she denied that. How could she give him a job that would mean seeing him every day? How could she live peacefully knowing that he was living in one of the cottages near her house? How could she look at him and not feel the pain? Worse, how could she look at him and not remember the love?

She wiped her hand over her cheeks. She was surprised to find they were damp. If even the thought of Cody could make her teary eyed, what would seeing him do to her?

Her only option was obvious: she would have to send him away. As soon as he came in, she would tell him that she didn't want him on the ranch, and he would leave. He was really good at leaving, she thought caustically. He was even better at leaving her behind.

But what about the ranch? Arcadio knew ranching—he'd been the foreman here for longer than Mariah had been alive—and he wanted to hire Cody. Could she risk letting her emotions make the decision for her? The ranch was all she had left. If she lost it . . .

She walked to the window and looked out over the desert. The ranch had been in the Butler family for over a hundred and fifty years. It was her home, more than the houses in Tucson or Phoenix had ever been. She couldn't bear to lose it, to see strangers take it over. She couldn't face knowing that her children would never be able to visit here, as she had done when she was small, that they would never have a chance to fall in love with the land and the work and the animals, with the *history*.

If hiring Cody Daniels could help in any way—and she conceded the advantages in hiring a known quantity over a stranger drifting into town—didn't she owe it to the ranch, to her father, her grandfather, and all those before, to try? Wasn't preserving her home worth a little heartache?

The tap at the door made her stiffen. Her neck was already starting to ache from holding her head so high, so erect, as she turned from the window to face the door. "Come in."

He hadn't changed at all, she thought mournfully when he stepped inside the room. She wished he had aged. She wished he had missed her, had suffered for the pain he'd caused her, but apparently he hadn't. He was tall, broad shouldered, slender hipped and long legged, with hair the color of dull gold and eyes the same shade as a summer evening sky. He was incredibly, breathtakingly handsome. And he was looking at her as if she were a stranger, no more than a prospective employer.

She laid her hands on her hips to keep from clenching them, and tried valiantly to ignore the sharp stab of pain in her chest. She had expected to feel it, even though it had been "a long time ago" when he'd walked out of her life.

It was okay to hurt, she silently whispered. After all, she had never believed that she would see him again. During all those years, even though she had sometimes hoped he would return, she had never really believed he would. And now he was back. Back and, once again, wanting something from her. Hurting a little wasn't unusual.

Determined to be businesslike and completely unemotional, she gestured to the chair at Arcadio's desk, set at an angle to hers. "Sit down."

When he closed the door and moved toward the chair, she leaned casually against the wall, letting it support her; then, with her face blank, her eyes empty and her voice coolly neutral, she said, "So...Arcadio tells me you're looking for a job."

Chapter 2

Cody pulled the chair into the middle of the tiny room and settled down, crossing one ankle over his knee and balancing the battered brown cowboy hat there. Slowly, lazily, he raised his eyes to hers.

Nothing about her had changed. Her mouth was full, her lips sensuous even when turned down in a frown. Her eyes glittered like black ice underneath a web of long, curling lashes. Her nose was straight, and her hair was silky and long, reaching to her waist, with shorter strands falling across her forehead. She was still beautiful. Achingly so.

Curiously, he considered his response to seeing her again after such a long time. There was longing and desire—but they had always been there and always would be. He had accepted that after long years of countless sleepless nights, lying in bed, achingly hard for her. For no one but her. There was resentment that she had remained so beautiful, that she still had the power to make him feel so much, and bitterness that she was no longer his. But there was no hatred. Cody was relieved by that. It would have saddened him to learn that he was capable of hating the woman he had once loved.

Displeasure at his scrutiny made her move away from the wall to her desk. He had a brief glimpse of slender hips and long legs in tight-fitting jeans, and when she sat down and folded her arms over her chest, the fabric of her red plaid shirt stretched over her breasts. Her body was still beautiful, too, he noticed grimly. To distract himself, he transferred his attention to her clothes. Jeans, shirt, boots—whether she actually worked or not, she dressed the part, he thought with a mocking smile.

"Arcadio is convinced that you can still do the job."

The smile turned cynical. "I can." She made it sound as if he were too old. At thirty-two, there were damned few things he couldn't do. Given a chance, he would show her some of the things he *could*.

"*I* own the ranch now. *I* give the orders."

"No wonder things are looking run-down."

Her face flushed until it was as red as her shirt. She was painfully aware that the house and the buildings needed repairs—her parents pointed it out every time they visited—but she had only so much help and, worse, only so much money. The livestock had to be her first priority. "I don't want you working here," she said bluntly. "I don't want you on my ranch."

Or in her life? Cody wondered. Judging by her hostility, she hadn't forgotten how different things used to be between them. Like the ranch. She had run that into the ground, too. He picked up his hat and got to his feet.

Mariah wet her lips nervously. "I'm not finished."

Cody looked down at her, not bothering to disguise his irritation. "I can get a job at any ranch in Arizona," he said arrogantly. The fact that it wasn't true, that he needed a job at *this* ranch, didn't slow him one bit. "I don't need the hassle of putting up with you, Mrs. Lowell." In truth, he was relieved that she didn't want to hire him. Now he could return to Kyle Parker and tell him that he'd tried his damnedest but had been unable to get hired. Then he could get on his knees and beg the man to send him someplace else—*any place* would be better than here.

Mariah stiffened at the sarcastic emphasis he'd given her name. "My name is Butler," she coolly informed him. After the divorce, it had seemed important to her—a gesture of independence, she supposed—to take back her maiden name. She hadn't taken Chad's money; she didn't want his name. She continued after a moment, making the offer that she knew was only going to cause her trouble. "*I* own the ranch, but Arcadio is still the foreman, and he wants to hire you. He may not be a good judge of character, but he's a damn good rancher. Do you want the job?"

He looked at her, his blue eyes cold, his mouth hard. No, he wanted to say. This was his chance to tell her to go to hell, his chance to walk out and never return. If he had a brain in his head, he would do it.

But all he had was an obligation to do his job. A duty. A responsibility. He had never been one to sidestep an obligation or shirk a responsibility. "Yeah. I want the job."

She wet her lips nervously. "When can you start?"

He still had a few days of vacation left, but he didn't want to spend another night in the motel. "I'll move in today."

She nodded once. "Arcadio will assign you to one of the cottages and introduce you to the others."

He heard the dismissal in her voice and walked to the door. There he paused and smiled an ugly smile. "Welcome back," he said softly, maliciously. "To both of us."

Arcadio introduced him to the other hands. Philip Blake was a young man, maybe twenty-two or so, Cody guessed, with a boyish grin, a crushing handshake and a pleasant nature. David Green was older, in his mid-thirties, and a good deal more serious than Philip. He was an average-looking man, not too tall, thin, with brown hair and brown eyes. Cody decided the instant he shook hands with Green that he didn't like the man. He couldn't name anything in particular that bothered him; it was just a general feeling.

He was also reintroduced to Antonio Chavez, an older man who had worked at the ranch most of his life. Cody remembered both him and his wife Rosalie.

With the introductions out of the way, Arcadio took Cody to the housing complex. There were two rows of houses that faced each other, five in each row. The one nearest the main house was designated the foreman's and was larger. The other nine were identical. "Take your pick," Arcadio said. "Antonio and Rosalie still live across from us. This one is Philip's, and David lives in that one. The other six are empty."

Without hesitation Cody chose the house on the end, farthest from the other occupied houses—farthest from Mariah's house. If questioned, he could offer the excuse of privacy, but Arcadio didn't say a word. "Do you have your things with you?"

"No. I spent last night at the motel. I need to go back and check out."

Arcadio nodded once. As they walked together back to Cody's pickup, the old man asked quietly, "How did the meeting with Mariah go?"

"It must have been all right—she gave me the job, didn't she?" Then he flushed, embarrassed by his flippancy. "It was okay, Arcadio. She didn't want to hire me, but she did. It'll just take some time getting used to each other, I guess." That was an understatement. How could he ever get used to seeing Mariah again? How could he get used to this new, cold, hostile woman in place of the soft, warm, passionate one he'd fallen in love with so long ago?

Perversely, he was grateful that she *was* cold and hostile. As long as she remained that way, he would have less trouble remembering what she'd done to him. He could focus on his own hostility and forget about the love they had shared. That way he would be safe.

"Why don't you get your things and get settled in?" Arcadio suggested. "You can start work tomorrow morning. Will you be back in time for dinner?"

Cody nodded. It would take him only a few minutes to check out of the motel, since he hadn't unpacked; then he'd need a few minutes more to talk to Kyle Parker again.

"We take our meals in the main house now, same time as usual. Since there are so few of us, Bonita cooks for everyone."

So he would be expected to eat with Mariah. That would be a real pleasure, Cody thought cynically even as he nodded once in acknowledgement. "I'll be back by then." He got into his truck, then stuck his hand out the open window. The old man shook it firmly. "Thanks, Arcadio."

"You've already got the job?" Kyle Parker sounded surprised. "You don't waste any time, do you?"

"Have you ever stayed in the motel here in town?" Cody asked dryly, and Kyle laughed.

"It's not a palace," he agreed. "So you'll be living at the ranch."

Cody nodded.

"What did you think about the owner? Did you meet her? She's really pretty, isn't she?"

Instead of answering, Cody asked a question of his own. "Did you know I'd worked for the Butlers before?"

Kyle shook his head. "Not them in particular. They just told me that you'd worked a couple of ranches around here." Settling back in his chair, he explained, "I didn't pick you for this job, Cody. I'm like you—all I do is follow orders. Do you think there will be any problems?"

Not for the investigation, Cody admitted. He wasn't so sure about himself. "No," he said with a taut smile. "No problems."

"If I need to get in touch with you, how do I do it?"

"If it's important, call the ranch. Arcadio will get a message to me. Otherwise, I'll keep in touch with you periodically."

They talked for a few minutes more before Cody left to return to the ranch. He would probably have enough time to unpack before dinner—before dinner in Mariah's house, with Mariah. It was enough to make him lose his appetite.

Bonita and Rosalie Chavez were at his house, sweeping and dusting, when he returned. The bedroom was already finished, and they were in the living room, chatting rapidly in Spanish while they worked.

"It's almost dinnertime," Bonita said from the open bedroom door. "We'll finish here tomorrow. You come on up to the house in a few minutes, all right?"

"All right, I'll be there soon." Cody hung the garment bag he was holding in the closet. Inside it were five sets of dark green uniforms, the trousers and short-sleeved shirts neatly pressed. A second bag held his uniform jackets, and on the floor underneath them, in a box, were his hats—a Smokey the Bear style hat, a cowboy hat, and a couple of baseball caps bearing the border patrol emblem. His ID, gun belt and service revolver were in another box, on the closet shelf. He pushed everything back into the darkest corner, where, with luck, it would stay unnoticed should anyone come around snooping.

Now it was time for dinner. He smiled grimly. Time to see Mariah again.

Luck was with him. Mariah was noticeably absent from dinner—because of him? he wondered. He would bet that she now regretted her decision to break Butler tradition and bring the hands together for meals in the family home. With such a small crew, it must have seemed sensible to her at the time—but that was before she'd hired *him*. She probably dreaded the idea of facing him at dinner so much that she preferred not to eat.

She'd had no appetite that evening, it was true. While Bonita and Rosalie were serving dinner, Mariah had slipped out of the house, saddling her horse and heading out into the desert.

It was quiet in the early evening hours. She sat comfortably astride the horse, the reins gathered loosely in one hand. She usually found a soothing calm here among the cactus and the brush, but tonight there was no peace—only memories. The first time she had seen Cody, she had been riding out here. The first time they'd ever talked, beyond shy, awkward hellos, had been out here. The first time they had made love had been out here.

Why had he come back? Why, when he could have gone to any other ranch, as he'd bragged? He had stayed away for eight years; he could have waited eight—or eighty—more. Why had he come back?

And why did she care?

That question troubled her more than the first. She no longer loved Cody—he meant nothing to her. She didn't even care enough to hate him. So why was she so disturbed by his return?

Maybe it was her instinct for self-preservation. Cody had hurt her. Maybe, deep inside, she knew how easy it would be for him to do it again—to make her need him, want him, love him. Maybe she knew she had to protect herself, to stop him from destroying her all over again.

Could that be his reason for returning? Could he want to destroy her? To punish her for their breakup?

She scoffed at the thought as she turned the horse back toward the house. Cody hadn't loved her enough to marry her; he hadn't loved her enough to compromise, not even when their future was at stake. He had left her and Esperanza without a backward glance. She was foolish to think that he might care enough eight years later to want to punish her for it.

She rode past the adobe cottages where the employees lived, wondering curiously which one Cody had chosen before she saw the dark blue pickup parked next to the last one. He had gotten as far away from her house as he could. As far away from *her* as he could.

It was dark by the time she reached the stables. She took care of the horse, then started for the house, where Bonita had left a light burning in the kitchen—and dinner in the oven, Mariah was sure.

She walked only a few yards, then stopped. Someone was standing in the shadows, watching her, and the tingle that started somewhere in her middle and radiated outward told her who it was. Slowly she turned around to face him. "What are you doing here?" It came out cold, unfriendly. Self-preservation, she reminded herself.

Cody moved out of the shadows to lean against the corral fence. "Am I restricted to the house when I'm not actually working? Or do I get free run of the ranch as long as I keep my distance from you?"

He spoke in a slow, lazy drawl that had once sent shivers down her spine, a drawl that she'd never forgotten, that she still heard in her dreams at night. She vowed she wouldn't let it affect her now. "You can have free run," she replied coolly.

"What about the rest? Do I keep my distance from you? Or would you prefer to have me a little bit closer?" The moonlight showed his mocking smile, but the brim of his hat cast shadows that hid his eyes.

Were they as cold as his voice? she wondered.

When it became apparent that she wasn't going to answer, he moved a step closer to her. He was near enough now to see the elegant lines of her face, and if he concentrated, he could smell her perfume, separating its scent from the competing smells. "What are *you* doing here, Mariah? You don't belong here. You should be in the city, with your friends and your family and your career."

He made the last word sound ugly, like a curse. Mariah clenched her jaw but gave no other response. To the Cody she had loved, a career *was* a curse. He hadn't wanted her to have a career, or friends, or any ties to the city. He had wanted her to give up everything for him, but he hadn't wanted to give up anything in return.

"This is my home," she said quietly.

Her answer angered him. He had asked her once to make her home here with him, but she had refused. She couldn't live in Esperanza, she had declared; there were no jobs, no money. How dare she call it "home" now? "This isn't 'home,'" he said in disgust, with no trace of the sexy drawl. "It's another one of your temporary little flings—like me. Like your career. Like your marriage. Where will you go when you destroy this ranch the way you've destroyed everything else?"

Her gasp echoed in the quiet night, and Cody knew that he had gone too far. Despite her tan, she suddenly looked pale in the moonlight, but she stood tall, holding her head high. "You haven't changed, have you?" she asked quietly, with just the slightest tremor in her voice. "You still take pleasure in hurting me." She turned and started toward the house, and she was swallowed up by the darkness after a few steps.

Involuntarily Cody moved away from the fence, to follow her. To apologize. But before he had gone two feet, he stopped. The way he was feeling—angry, confused, hurt—he knew it was best if he left her alone. He moved again, but not after her. This time he went to the little house that was his. He turned on one dim lamp long enough to undress and find his way to the bed, and then he climbed in, turned his face into the pillow and waited, hoped and prayed for sleep.

Mariah slammed the back door, stomped down the hall, then returned to lock the door. On the kitchen table she found a note from Bonita saying that dinner was in the oven, just as she had expected, but now she felt even less like eating than she had when she had left for her ride.

Damn Cody! He'd had no right to say those things to her! She didn't have "flings"—her career and her marriage had been important to her. Was it her fault that both had failed? The ranch was important to her, too . . . but it was also failing. And Cody—God, *he* had been the most important of them all, and he had been her most miserable failure.

Her anger changed to self-pity as she sank into a chair, hiding her face in her arms on the tabletop. Maybe he was right. Maybe she just naturally destroyed the things—the people—she cared about. Maybe she wasn't meant to have success or happiness. Maybe she wasn't meant to have love.

No, she insisted stubbornly, that wasn't true! Sure, she'd had some failures, but she wasn't the only one to blame. It was true that she'd been dissatisfied with her job as a social worker, but Chad had lost interest in their marriage long before she had, and the ranch had been losing money at an alarming rate even before she took it over. And Cody had destroyed any chances of resolving their problems, of salvaging their love, by leaving the ranch without a word to anyone. Without a word to *her*. She wasn't completely responsible for the problems in her life, and she wouldn't feel guilty because Cody wanted her to. She wouldn't give him that much power over her.

She rose from the chair and went to her room, where she showered and dressed for bed, sliding beneath the covers in the darkness. It was still early, but she didn't mind. She would have to face Cody again tomorrow. She needed the rest.

She managed to avoid him most of the next day by staying inside the small cramped office. She even had lunch—a bag of chips and a cup of coffee—there so she wouldn't have to return to the house. But late that afternoon, as she was leaving the office, he appeared outside the door.

"What do you want?" she asked warily.

He had counted himself lucky at not seeing her all day and had come to the office only to look for Arcadio, not her. But now that he *had* seen her, wearing a pair of faded and fitted blue jeans and a white shirt that closely followed the contours of her body, he ignored the command from his brain to turn and walk away without speaking. "This is a mighty big ranch, Mrs. Lowell," he drawled. "You don't have to confine yourself to such a small part of it to hide from me."

Standing directly in front of her, he removed his hat and ran his fingers through his hair. He looked hot, tired, sweaty and dirty, but still handsome—unfairly so, in Mariah's opinion.

"I haven't been hiding," she disagreed. "I had work to do." She reached behind her to close the door, then pointedly waited for him to move out of her way. When he didn't, she asked, "Don't *you* have some work to do?"

"No, ma'am, Mrs. Lowell, I'm through for the day."

Mariah's face colored. "Don't call me that."

Cody almost smiled. She thought he was taunting her. She didn't know that he did it to remind himself that she had let him down—that, although she had claimed to love *him*, she had married another man. That he couldn't trust her.

She was growing more uneasy with each passing second. If only somebody else were around... She would accept help from anyone to get away from him. But they were alone in the stable. "If you'll excuse me," she said politely, taking a step forward.

He stared at her for a moment, wondering where she'd learned to be so cool and formal and businesslike. From her hotshot lawyer husband, he guessed. She hadn't been like that when he had known her. She had been soft and funny and friendly and warm; falling in love with her had been the easiest, most natural thing in the world for him. He reined in the memories. That was a sure way to get himself into trouble. She had been all those things, but she had also been spoiled, selfish and unreliable. Like his father and his mother, she hadn't been there when he'd needed her. She had been too concerned with her own wants to care about his. She had let him down, and that was one thing he couldn't forgive.

Remembering that helped harden him against the desire that curled through him. Under normal circumstances, he wouldn't object to wanting her—it was natural. She was a beautiful woman and an exceptional lover—after all, he'd taught her himself. It would be okay to want her, as long as it was on a purely physical level. The problem was that the circumstances weren't normal, and his desire for her had *never* been purely physical. From the very first time he'd met her, he'd known that the sensation turning him inside out was more than lust. If he accepted the desire, the rest would come with it—needing, trusting, caring, loving—and those were feelings he couldn't live with. Not for Mariah.

She was beginning to panic when he suddenly moved away and turned toward the door, leaving her free to pass. It took her a moment to send the message to her muscles to move.

His eyes narrowing against the light coming through the open door, he said in a lazy drawl, "It looks like you've got company."

Mariah stopped beside him to watch a slender, blue-eyed blonde enter the stables. The woman's reaction when she saw Mariah was a bright smile. It dimmed when she recognized Cody.

"Hi," she greeted then, pushing her hands into the pockets of her red slacks. She looked curiously from Mariah to Cody.

"Hello, Lissa." Mariah's smile was tentative. She was normally glad to see Lissa Crane, but when her friend showed up unannounced, it generally meant trouble. Something had gone wrong—and why shouldn't it? Everything else was wrong with her life right now. Why shouldn't Lissa dump more trouble in her lap?

"You're...Cody Daniels." Lissa stuck her hand out, and Cody shook it.

"You have a good memory." He had never really known the blonde, and it had been more than eight years since he'd last seen her. He was surprised that she remembered him.

"I never forget a handsome face." She smiled hesitantly, then withdrew her hand and looked away.

She was uncomfortable with him, Cody realized. And Mariah was more uneasy than usual. The polite thing to do would be to remove himself from their presence. That was just what he did. "Excuse me."

As soon as he disappeared through the door, Mariah invited Lissa into her office. "What is he doing here?" the blond woman was asking before she'd even sat down.

"He's working here." Mariah's expression made it clear that she didn't want to discuss it right now. "What are *you* doing here?"

"I went across the border today, and I seemed to be getting a little more attention than usual when I came back, so I thought this would be a good time to visit my dear friend." Lissa shrugged. "Here I am."

"And what did you bring across the border with you?"

Lissa smiled. "Seven of the sweetest kids you ever saw."

"Where are they?"

"In the house with Bonita."

Mariah exhaled slowly, loudly. What else could happen to her? As if the daily struggle of holding on to the ranch wasn't bad enough, the Lord had given her the added burden of Cody Daniels. Now Lissa had brought her seven children—seven of the sweetest kids. Carta Blancan kids. Illegal kids. All she needed next was a visit from the border patrol to make everything just perfect.

She sighed again, chiding herself silently for her uncharitable thoughts. She was the one who had suggested that the ranch could be used for temporary shelter when necessary. It wasn't Lissa's fault that Cody had returned, that there was one more person to hide their activities from.

Lissa had seen the frustration on her friend's face. "I know you weren't expecting us, but I just didn't think it was safe to go on today. If it's going to cause problems for you, though..."

"No, no problem at all," Mariah said hastily. She had three empty bedrooms in the house; space was no problem. Besides, with the problems she already had, what difference could seven sweet little kids make? "We'll just have to make sure that they stay quiet while the hands are eating dinner."

"I'll stay with them," Lissa offered.

Mariah's smile was weary. "No, that's all right. I'll stay with them. It will seem more natural."

Lissa considered that for a moment, then reached the obvious explanation. "Have you been skipping meals since Cody got here?"

She nodded guiltily. "Only three."

"When did he come?"

"Yesterday. So if I don't show up at dinner tonight, he'll think it's because of him." And he would be right. Swiftly, she turned the conversation from him back to the children. "Whose attention did you attract today?"

"Who drives little green trucks and has the instincts of a bloodhound? The border patrol. It wasn't three minutes after I picked up the kids that this agent started following me. He lost interest before we got into town, but then another one started. I know they couldn't have seen the kids, but I couldn't risk getting stopped, so I came here. The guy followed me about halfway, then turned around and headed back to town."

Mariah's brow wrinkled into a frown. She wished Lissa hadn't led the agent out of town on a road that went straight to the ranch and nowhere else—the last thing she wanted was to draw the border patrol's attention here. Then she corrected herself. The last thing she wanted was for the children to get deported back to their homeland. "Let's go up to the house. You can introduce us."

The seven children waiting in one of the guest rooms looked frightened, tired and hungry. Mariah knew the risk she was taking in letting them stay. If the border patrol agent who had followed them got curious and came back with a warrant, he could arrest all of them—the children, Mariah and Lissa, David, Arcadio and Bonita. Then she wouldn't have to worry about the ranch anymore, because the government would confiscate it. Anyone caught harboring illegal aliens stood a damn good chance of losing their property.

Worrying didn't come easily to Mariah, but then, she thought with an impish grin, neither did breaking the law. Good Lord, her parents were both lawyers—her mother now a judge and her father one of Tucson's top prosecutors—and she had married a lawyer. She had been raised to respect the law, to have faith in the judicial system. Before becoming involved in the movement to bring Carta Blancan orphans to the United States, she had never done anything the slightest bit illegal—she'd never even gotten a parking ticket. Now she was committing felonies on a weekly basis. It had been a difficult decision to make, but, in the end, her moral and ethical obligation to help these children had won out over her respect for the immigration laws.

Now she realized that the children were looking at her, seven grim little faces. Smiling gently, she knelt to put herself on their level and spoke softly. *"Hola. Me llamo* Mariah."

Cody was the last to come to dinner. He slid into the seat across from David Green. They sat in the same seats from habit: Arcadio at one end of the table, with Antonio, Rosalie and David on his left, and Bonita, Philip and Cody on his right. The chair at the head of the table, occupied tonight by Lissa Crane, had been empty during the previous meals. He assumed it was Mariah's.

Would she exile herself from the dining room the entire time he was there? he wondered with a dark scowl. Did his presence disturb her so much that she couldn't bear to sit at the table with him? He knew he should be grateful; the less time he had to spend with her, the easier his job would be. But he couldn't help feeling resentful.

No one asked about her. Had they already heard her excuse for missing dinner again? Or did they know that she was avoiding *him*?

The hands had shown little curiosity in him. Antonio, who had worked at the ranch almost as long as Arcadio had, hadn't seemed to see anything unusual about his return. And Philip Blake and David Green had asked only a few questions—where he was from, if he was married, where else he had worked. If they knew anything of his past involvement with the lady boss, as Philip teasingly referred to her, they kept it well hidden.

While the others were engaged in a loud and lively conversation, he turned to Lissa and quietly asked, "Where is she?"

Just as quietly, she answered, "She had a headache. She was planning to go to bed early."

He cursed. "If she has a headache, it's from lack of food. Is she afraid to face me?" He expected a rapid and completely unbelievable denial, but Lissa surprised him.

"Maybe she is." She pursed her lips thoughtfully. "After the way you treated her."

"The way *I* treated *her*?" He started to protest the absurdity of that remark, but a question from David Green stopped him.

"Philip and I are going into town tonight. Why don't you go with us?"

"It's Friday night," Philip said when it looked as if Cody would refuse.

Friday night. A good time to party when you were young, like Philip, or in the mood for some entertainment, like David. The only thing Cody was in the mood for was Mariah, any way he could get her.

That made it an invitation he couldn't refuse. If he didn't go, he would hang around the ranch thinking about Mariah—something that he already did entirely too much of. Besides, his real job here was to keep an eye on David Green, to get to know him. He couldn't turn down an opportunity to do that. "Yeah," he said, forcing a smile, "I'd like to."

"It's safe to come out now. Everyone's gone."

Mariah rose from her position on the floor. The children had eaten all the food Bonita had brought them; now they were sleeping soundly, sprawled across the room's two beds. "I tried to put some of them in the next room, but they wanted to stay together," she said, stretching her arms over her head.

Lissa nodded. "They tend to cling to each other. I guess it's natural—they've lost all the important adults in their lives. Did you eat anything?"

"Not yet. I'm starving."

"That's what you get for trying to avoid Cody. Come on, we'll see if anything's left from dinner." Lissa led the way down the tiled hall, and Mariah followed her. The house was silent except for their footsteps.

Lissa waited until they were seated at the small kitchen table, the remains of the roast beef and vegetables and half an apple pie between them, to speak again. "Cody's gone into town."

Mariah lifted her shoulders in a shrug. "It's Friday night. His time is his own."

"That doesn't bother you at all? That he's gone out with David and Philip, probably to get drunk and pick up some women?"

"Cody doesn't drink," she said with certainty. "His mother was an alcoholic. After seeing what it did to her and to his dad, he swore he would never drink."

"What about women? Did he swear off them, too?" Lissa asked sarcastically.

The roast beef, tender, juicy and hot from the microwave, suddenly tasted like cardboard.

Yes, the idea of Cody with another woman bothered her. She wasn't even sure why. She didn't want him for herself. All she wanted from Cody was to be left alone; she wanted him out of her life once and for all.

"Did you ever quit loving him?" Lissa asked softly.

"Of course I did." Mariah's answer was quick, automatic and too forceful.

"Chad never thought so." Lissa didn't flinch under Mariah's dark glare. "He always believed that you couldn't love him completely because you never stopped loving Cody." When her friend started to protest, Lissa interrupted. "Mariah, you know darn good and well that was one of the biggest problems in your marriage."

There were drawbacks to confiding your secrets to your best friend, Mariah thought with a frown. She could throw them back in your face when it came in handy.

That *had* been one of the problems in her marriage. Chad had always believed that she still loved Cody, still wanted him. He had felt that she was comparing him to Cody and finding him lacking. She had denied it then—had denied it so often that it had become second nature—but now she wondered if, just maybe, Chad had been right. Had even a tiny bit of her love for Cody survived his leaving? That would explain why seeing him again after so many years was so upsetting—and so damn painful.

No. She didn't love Cody. Seeing him was painful because of the memories, not because of any lingering love. It was painful because he had once been the most important person in her life, and now they couldn't even talk to each other. It was painful because he had once loved her, and now he couldn't stand her. But she didn't still love him. She *couldn't*.

"My marriage is over, okay?" she said sharply. "I don't think we need to discuss it anymore."

Lissa had been Mariah's best friend too long to take offense at the harshness of her voice. "Okay," she agreed. "Want a piece of pie?"

"Antonio tells me that you used to work for the Butlers."

Cody leaned back in his chair, casually crossing his ankles, and fixed a cool blue stare on David Green. "Yeah."

"He says Mariah was living here then, too."

"Part of the time." Green had been talkative tonight; since arriving at the tavern, Cody had learned the man's life history without asking a single question.

Green had grown up on a ranch in central Arizona, a small place that had since been sold out of the family. He had then moved to Tucson, where he'd gotten married; the marriage had ended a few years earlier, as so many do, in divorce, with no children. He had worked for a shipping company in the city and became involved with the refugee movement through a friend at work. When he was convicted of smuggling Central Americans into the country, the company had let him go, and Mariah had offered him a job at her ranch. He had been tired of the city and was more than willing to return to ranching.

Reserved by nature, Cody found it difficult to trust a man who talked as freely about himself as Green did, and he wondered about the few things Green had left out of his monologue. Was he still involved in smuggling? And how had he met Mariah? Her friends in the city had been people like herself and Lissa—wealthy, privileged, upper-class. Friendship with a mere ranch hand and shipping clerk hardly fit the image.

Unless Mariah had changed more than he'd expected. Maybe when she'd given up life as Mrs. Chadwick Martin Lowell III, he mused, she'd given up a lot of other things, too. He considered the idea, then discarded it. He didn't want to think of her as an average person. It was easier if he kept her on a pedestal, surrounded by the people, the values and the money that had taken her from him.

"Are you sure you don't want a beer?" David asked.

"I'm sure." Cody hadn't bothered to explain to the other man that he didn't drink; it was no one's business but his own.

"How well did you know Mariah back then?" David asked with what sounded like only mild curiosity.

Cody's jaw clenched in anger. That was another subject that was no one's business but his own. He answered with a careless shrug.

"She's a looker, isn't she?"

"She's pretty," Cody agreed, then asked the question that nagged at him. "How did you meet her?"

For the first time, David looked wary. "Mutual friends in Tucson," he replied. He could tell what Cody was thinking—that David Green was an unlikely choice of friend for Mariah Butler Lowell—but he couldn't explain without divulging her involvement with the orphans, so he left it at that vaguely unsatisfying answer.

Mutual friends. Cody couldn't imagine any circumstance that would allow Mariah to become friends with Green. Unless . . . could she have friends involved in the refugee movement? In Phoenix she had worked as a social worker. It was conceivable that she'd had contact with the refugee workers in that city, who could have introduced her to their partners in Tucson, including Green. Was it possible that she knew Green was smuggling the kids and had offered him the job so he'd be closer to the border? After all, the southern border of her ranch was also the border between the United States and Mexico.

Then came another, more disturbing question. Could she be directly involved herself?

The idea was so impossible that it was laughable. Mariah was as straitlaced and law-abiding as anyone he'd ever met, probably more so. Her mother was a hard-line judge, the twentieth-century version of a hanging judge, and her father had convicted enough criminals to singlehandedly fill the state's prisons. Even her precious husband had been a lawyer. She was probably constitutionally incapable of breaking a law.

"Have you ever been out with her?" David asked curiously.

Cody was quickly getting tired of questions about Mariah. His eyes hardened as he stared at David. What was the point? Was Green interested in Mariah himself and suspicious of any possible competition? Or was he testing Cody? Had someone told him all about Cody and Mariah's affair and was he asking questions now to see if Cody would tell the truth? "Anything that ever happened between Mariah and me," Cody said slowly, in a quiet, cold voice, "was just that—*between Mariah and me*. Understand?"

Getting to his feet, David nodded. "Yeah, I understand. Look, I see a friend over at the bar. Don't hang around here because of me. I'll get a lift home later."

Philip had said the same thing only minutes after they'd arrived. Glancing around, Cody saw that the younger man was nowhere in sight. Neither was the redhead he'd been dancing with. He waited long enough to see the dark-haired woman Green approached, then rose from the table and left the bar.

It must be nice to be so certain of your welcome, he thought more than a little wistfully as he drove away. There was no one to welcome him, no one who would be glad to see him. Mariah certainly wasn't. She hid from him, sneaking around her own property to avoid him. What would it take to make her welcome him?

He swore viciously. He didn't want Mariah, and she sure as hell didn't want him. He was a fool for thinking that she might give a damn about him. Whatever she had felt for him had died long ago, before she had married Chad Lowell. Before *he* had left Esperanza. She had stopped caring about him, and he had stopped caring, period. For weeks, even months, he hadn't cared whether he lived or died. His life had centered around the hurt and the grief until, mercifully, he'd become unable to feel anything at all.

For a time it had scared him—he'd been afraid that he would never feel anything again. Then his life had slowly returned to normal. Once again he'd been able to feel, to live. But now, for one brief instant, he remembered that numbness with longing, because the pain—along with need, anger, resentment and about a dozen other emotions that he couldn't name—was tearing him up inside.

It was Mariah. The pain had come back because *she* had come back. *She* was the hurt that was killing him.

Chapter 3

Mariah rose from her bed slowly. She didn't like getting up early in the morning—ideally she would sleep until noon—but conditions on the ranch were far from ideal. Besides, she and Bonita had an agreement: breakfast could be served late on Sunday mornings if Mariah cooked it. That way Bonita was free to attend church services in Esperanza, and everyone else got a little extra sleep.

Dressed in a white cotton skirt that reached nearly to her ankles and a bright red tank top, she went barefoot down the hall to the kitchen. She wasn't much of a cook, but she could fry bacon, bake refrigerated biscuits and cook waffles in the electric waffle iron, and she made a good pot of coffee.

David was the first one in. He poured himself a cup of coffee and sat down at the table. Mariah knew from past experience that Arcadio had already eaten and Rosalie had fixed breakfast for herself and Antonio before they'd left for church. Because that left only the two single hands—three, she corrected herself, adding Cody—to cook for, breakfast was served at the small kitchen table.

She hadn't seen Cody since Friday evening, a fact for which she was most assuredly grateful. Saturday she had remained inside the house with Lissa and the children until they had left shortly before lunch. After snacking on the cookies Bonita had made for the children, it had been easy enough to skip lunch, and she had stayed away from the office that afternoon.

Skipping dinner had been unnecessary, since Cody, David and Philip had gone into town together to eat and do whatever else it was single men did on a Saturday night—drink, dance, party and find willing bed partners? Had Cody found someone to share his bed?

The thought made her frown, and it brought a curious question from David. "Is something bothering you?"

"Hmm." But she had no intentions of discussing it with David or anyone else right now. Besides, it was none of her business. Cody could have affairs with every single woman in Esperanza, and it wouldn't bother her in the least. She had to keep telling herself that. More importantly, she had to make herself believe it.

She looked at David and smiled. "You're going to have to give in and marry Suzanne, David. These late nights are starting to show."

He smiled, too. "I'd marry her if she'd have me...and if she weren't the sheriff's daughter. He's not too thrilled about the idea of having a convicted felon for a son-in-law."

His smile became tinged with sadness, but there was nothing Mariah could say. Although she risked arrest on every run she made from the border to Tucson, she couldn't really understand what it was like for David, to be branded a criminal for the rest of his life because he believed those kids deserved a chance to live. She said a silent prayer that she would never have to find out.

"Maybe it'll work out," she said softly, laying her hand on his shoulder.

The clump of boots on tiles made Mariah look up to see Cody and Philip standing in the doorway. Cody was staring at her, his eyes narrowed and cold as ice. Self-consciously, she removed her hand from David's shoulder and turned to the stove. She set platters of food on the table, then poured two cups of coffee and set them in front of the two men before she sat down next to Philip.

"Good morning, Mariah," Philip said so cheerfully that she couldn't help but smile. He reminded her of a huge, playful puppy. He was over six feet tall, with shoulders as broad as a door, an engaging grin, blond hair and green eyes, and a reputation as a real lady's man. She knew that he'd already collected more than his share of young hearts— and bodies—but she thought he needed about ten years' more maturity. If some lucky woman hadn't caught him by then, he would be a serious heartbreaker.

Like Cody. Her smile grew subdued as she murmured a quiet "Good morning" to both of them.

There was silence around the small table while the men filled their plates. Mariah concentrated on buttering a biscuit and ignoring the discomfort Cody had brought into the room with him.

"We didn't see much of you yesterday," David said, directing the remark to her.

She shrugged. "I spent the morning with Lissa and—" She stopped herself before saying "the children," covering her slip by taking a drink of coffee. "And I had a few things to take care of in the afternoon."

Cody was watching her, the look in his eyes chilling. It was almost as if he knew she was leaving something out, she thought, flushing under his intense gaze. She didn't try to stare him down; she just turned to look out the window.

She remained silent through the rest of the meal, impatiently waiting for the men to finish and leave her alone again. Sunday was a free day, and the men usually spent it away from the ranch. Philip would visit his family in Nogales, and David usually managed a few private hours with Suzanne Fox, or visited with friends in Tucson. That left only Cody—the one she most wanted to get rid of. He had no family or, as far as she knew, friends. Unless he had a Suzanne of his own tucked away somewhere.

It was logical, even likely, but she didn't like the idea. It was natural to be jealous of a man she had loved eight years ago, wasn't it? It didn't mean anything—just that her emotions then had been strong. Old habits were hard to break. But she could do it. It would take a lot of work and a lot of concentration, but she would get Cody Daniels out of her system . . . or die trying.

"I'm heading over to Mom and Dad's," Philip said. "See you in the morning, boss."

David was the next to leave. He had been sitting back in his chair, looking curiously from Cody to Mariah. It had been so obvious that he was trying to decide if it was all right to leave her alone with Cody that she'd almost smiled. "Are you meeting Suzanne?" she asked as a signal that he could go.

"Yeah. We're going into Tucson." He hesitated. "You're welcome to come along if you want."

"No, thanks. Be careful on the highway."

After he left, she began gathering dishes from the table. Cody sipped his coffee and watched her work. "Don't you have any plans?" he asked as she filled the sink with water.

"Sure. I'm going to wash the dishes, then I'll probably wash my hair. As long as I'm being so industrious, I might as well wash some clothes, too."

He carried the remaining dishes to the counter, then leaned against it and watched her while he finished his coffee. "Why didn't Lissa stay for the weekend?"

"She had to get back yesterday."

"Why?"

Mariah plunged her hands into the hot, soapy water. "I don't know. I didn't ask her."

"Is she married?"

"She was. They're divorced now."

"Your little circle seems to have bad luck in the marriage department. David, Lissa . . . you." What had happened to her marriage? he wondered. She had chosen Lowell over him because of his money, his power and his background, but that hadn't been enough to make their marriage work. It hadn't been enough to keep her happy. What had she wanted that Lowell hadn't been able to give?

She finished the last cup and placed a stack of dirty plates in the water. "What about you? Did you ever marry?"

The question was out before she could stop it. For what seemed like the hundredth time already this morning, she told herself that she didn't care. The women in his life meant absolutely nothing to her. Nothing!

"No. I came close once…twice, counting you." His smile was unpleasant. "Then again, I really didn't come that close with you, did I? All we had was an agreement that we would be married on the eighteenth of June. But agreements are so easy to break."

Her hands stilled in the water, and she turned her head to look at him. "Easy? Do you think anything about that time was easy?" Every argument had been filled with pain, every day filled with the fear that it would be the day when he told her he no longer wanted her. In the end that fear had come true, only he hadn't told her—he had simply disappeared from her life, leaving her with no goodbyes and no chance to change his mind. No chance to tell him that she loved him and would do whatever he wanted.

It had taken her so long to get over him. It had been months before she had been able to even think about another man, years before she had been able to think about Cody without renewing the ache. And he had the gall to say it had been easy for her.

Cody lifted his shoulders in a graceful, lazy shrug. "You got what you wanted." *And it wasn't me.* God help him, but it still hurt that she hadn't chosen him.

"You never knew what I wanted, Cody," she said, scrubbing the dishes with a vengeance. "You never listened to me when I tried to tell you. You were too concerned with proving that *you* were the man, that *you* held the power."

"Power?" he scoffed. What a joke. The only power he'd ever held over Mariah had been in bed, while *she* had held the power to make his life hell—and she'd done it. "I tried to hold you to your word, and you make it sound like some sort of macho power struggle."

"You wanted to make me come back—"

"*Make* you? You *promised* to come back and marry me—
or have you forgotten that? I only asked you to do what
you'd promised."

"You didn't 'ask' anything—you demanded. You gave
orders. You issued ultimatums."

"Call it what you want," he said angrily as he crossed the
room. At the door, he looked back at her. "But you can't
change what really happened that summer. You can't
change the truth."

Mariah stared at the empty doorway long after he'd gone.
The truth? The truth was that he had forced her to return to
college to finish her last year, when all she'd wanted was to
marry him. The truth was that he had commanded her to
return to Esperanza after graduation, where she couldn't
find a job, where he could barely make enough to support
him and his mother, to say nothing of Mariah and the children she'd hoped to have. The truth was that he had given
her an ultimatum; then, without giving her time to accept or
reject it, he had left town without a backward glance.

Turning back to the sink, she finished the dishes and
wiped the counters. Truth was a funny thing, she thought.
You believed it was inflexible and unchanging, but it depended on the way you looked at it. Cody's truth about the
past was apparently greatly different from hers. It didn't
necessarily mean that one of them was wrong, just that they
saw the same event from different perspectives.

They had been so different that their friends and Mariah's family had wondered—often and aloud—what they
saw in each other. But the biggest difference between them
hadn't been the contrasts in their personalities, or the dis-
parities in their bank balances, or the dissimilarities in their
upbringing. It had been in their maturity. At twenty-one,
Mariah could now admit, she had still been a child in many
ways, while Cody, at twenty-four, had been a man. Her
parents had always taken care of her, looked out for her and
protected her. Cody, on the other hand, had been responsible, hardworking, reliable, trustworthy—everything a man
should be. He had, at a young age, reached a level of maturity that had taken Mariah years longer to attain.

Maybe he hadn't been trying to prove anything when he'd demanded that she come back to him. They'd had an agreement: she would finish college, then return to the ranch, and they would be married. That had been their plan, but Mariah hadn't been able to follow through with it. After getting the degree that had meant so much to Cody, she had wanted to use it, and jobs for social workers were nonexistent in Esperanza. Maybe he'd been wrong in insisting that she come back; maybe she'd been wrong to insist that he leave the ranch and live with her in Tucson. But there was no question, no doubt in her mind, that he *had* been wrong to leave that way. He had been so wrong.

Mariah sighed deeply as she left the kitchen to start a load of laundry in the room next door. Why think about it now? It was years in the past; who was right and who was wrong didn't matter now. All that mattered now was surviving the present.

Bonita insisted on cooking a big dinner when she and Arcadio returned from church, in spite of the fact that there would only be four of them there to enjoy it. Mariah helped fix it, following the older woman's instructions. She swore Bonita would make a cook of her yet, given enough time.

The meal hadn't been too bad, Mariah reflected as she and Bonita removed the dishes. The food was delicious, and Cody had done nothing to make her feel uncomfortable. Of course, it helped that they ate in the dining room, at the big carved table, rather than at the smaller, more cramped kitchen table.

The ring of the phone disturbed their dessert. Bonita started to rise, but Mariah was on her feet first. "I'll get it." She took the call in the living room, talking only a few minutes before returning to the table.

"That was my mother," she said slowly. "She and Dad are on their way here for the afternoon."

Slowly three pairs of eyes turned to Cody. He managed a sardonic smile. "I guess that's my cue to get lost for the rest of the day." He looked at Mariah and saw the almost imperceptible movement of her head. He half wished she would tell him to stay. He wished that she didn't feel it necessary to hide him, that she was willing to stand up to her parents where it concerned him. But she hadn't been willing to do it in the past, and she wasn't willing now. Would she ever grow up enough to do it? he wondered cynically as he pushed his chair back.

He shouldn't be complaining. For his own sake he didn't need to see Jerry and Helen Butler. The old man despised him, and Cody wouldn't put it past him to use his contacts with the Tucson Police Department to run a background check on him. The last thing Cody needed was for Jerry to find out that he worked for the border patrol, that he had lied to Mariah about his reasons for being here.

"When can I come back?" he asked when he reached the door.

"They plan to stay for supper. They'll probably be gone by eight o'clock." Mariah was too ashamed to meet his gaze. He probably thought that she was a coward for not wanting her parents to know that he was back, but he didn't understand. If they knew that she'd given him a job, they would expend so much energy trying to convince her to get rid of him that they would drive her crazy. She had enough problems without adding that to the list.

"Then I guess I'll see you folks tomorrow." He quietly walked away, closing the back door with a soft click.

He covered the ground between the main house and his smaller house, where his truck was parked, with long strides. He wasn't angry—no, annoyed was a better word to describe his mood. Mariah had all but asked him to leave her house and stay discreetly out of sight during her parents' visit. It reminded him of the past, when she had refused to tell her parents about their engagement until several months later; the few times that they had visited the ranch with her, Cody had been forced to sneak around to see her. It had been a distinctly unpleasant feeling.

He drove aimlessly after leaving the house. He had no place to go, nothing to do, no one to see. He could drive to Tucson and spend the rest of the afternoon there, but he had no desire to do that. He ended up wandering around the border town of Nogales, bored, restless and itching to go home.

At home, Mariah was restless, too. Supper had ended an hour earlier, and she was impatiently waiting for Jerry and Helen to leave. But they wouldn't, she knew, until they had brought up two subjects: the ranch, and Chad. No visit was complete until those two topics, distasteful as Mariah found them, had been discussed.

They sat in the living room, Helen sitting near her daughter on the sofa. Jerry was stretched out comfortably in a recliner nearby. Soon, Mariah thought, looking from one to the other. Soon they would get to the subjects she dreaded. While she waited, she looked at them, studying them.

They were a handsome couple. Jerry was in his mid-fifties, but there was little evidence of age in the smooth lines of his face, and there were only a few strands of gray in his hair. Even on a relaxing Sunday visiting his daughter, he wore a tailored three-piece suit of summer white. He looked elegant, dignified, refined.

So did Helen. When she'd been younger, Mariah had always envied her mother's beauty without realizing how closely she resembled her. Helen was tall and slender. Her complexion was darker than Mariah's, but her eyes and hair were black, and when they stood side by side, they looked like before and after pictures. Youth and maturity. Or, Mariah thought, only partially joking, flawed and flawless. She wanted to be her mother when she grew up.

"All right," she said at last. "I've been waiting ever since you got here, but you haven't said a word. Shall we discuss it now?"

Jerry smiled fondly. "You've grown to expect it, haven't you?"

Mariah's nod was somewhat weary. "A visit from you wouldn't be the same without a lecture about the ranch."

Since she had raised the topic herself, Jerry felt no qualms about launching into it. "You're still losing money, aren't you? The house needs to be plastered again, the barn and the stables need painting and repairs, and you can't afford to have it done.''

"But my herd, small as it is, is prime. And we haven't lost nearly as much money in the last six months as you did in the previous six months," she pointed out. "Dad, ranching is an expensive business. It's hard work, and there aren't any guarantees, but you do the best you can.''

"And sometimes the best isn't enough. You could still lose this place.''

"We'll pull through.''

Jerry shook his head in dismay. Mariah was beginning to think that a good deal of his dismay was an act—he seemed to enjoy knowing that she was going to refuse his next suggestion. "If you're as smart as I think you are, you'll get rid of this place—sell it before you lose it. You might even be able to make a small profit.''

To her parents, the ranch was "this place," nothing more than a piece of real estate. To her, it was her heritage. She could no more sell it than she could sell *them*. "And if things keep going the way they have been," she said with a smile, in spite of the finality of her voice, "we may even make a profit *without* selling it." After a brief pause, she turned to her mother. "Your turn."

"Are we really that predictable?" Helen asked.

"You really are." Mariah's voice was only faintly strained.

"Oh, well . . ." She wouldn't let that stop her. "We saw Chad last week. He said to give you his best. He also said that he would like to see you sometime."

Why? Mariah wondered. Chad couldn't possibly want to get back together with her. He enjoyed being a bachelor again too much to bother with her. Surely he was just being polite, to please her mother. She stifled a grin. Chad Lowell's politeness shouldn't be underestimated. Sometimes she thought he had proposed to her because it had meant so much to their parents; it would have been impolite to disappoint them. And sometimes she thought that she had accepted for the same reasons.

Helen waited a long moment, trying to assess the meaning behind her daughter's silence, before gently asking, "Are you absolutely certain that you two can't work things out, Mariah? You were so happy together that first year."

"And not so happy the other three years. I'm certain, Mom." She laced her fingers together in her lap, hiding them in the fabric of her skirt. "The divorce was final a long time ago. Chad has a new life now, and so do I. We couldn't make things work then, and I don't want to try again."

"But you were so well suited to each other."

She tilted her head to one side. "Well suited? Chad and I had nothing in common except that our parents were friends. That's a fine basis for a friendship, or even an affair, but it doesn't do much for a marriage."

"But you loved him," Helen reminded her.

Mariah smiled tautly. "Maybe I did. I don't know anymore." Cody had her so confused that she wasn't certain of *anything*.

"Is there someone else?" Helen asked softly.

She felt their eyes drilling into her. There was, but not in the sense her mother meant. "No. I haven't had a single date since the divorce—and I like it that way. Now, I hate to be rude, Mom, Dad, but you've got a long drive home ahead of you, and it's a quarter of eight. Hadn't you better be going soon?"

Helen looked at the gold and diamond wristwatch that she wore. "Yes, we'd better. I have to be in court early tomorrow morning. When are you going to come and visit us?"

"I don't know, Mom. Sometime soon." She walked them to their car, where she received hugs and kisses from both of them.

"Be sure you do come soon," Jerry said, holding her tight. "We love you."

"I love you, too." As she watched them drive away, she repeated the words softly. *I love you, too.* It had been such a long time since she'd said those words to anyone. They were simple, tiny little words that could be trite, overused or meaningless, but she missed the warm feeling saying them had always given her. She missed the even warmer feeling that hearing them could bring.

The night was cool, and the sleeveless lavender sweater she wore offered little protection against the chill. She stood there motionless for several long minutes; then, folding her arms across her chest for warmth, she set off across the yard.

She was going to Cody's house. She didn't look for reasons, for excuses or explanations. She knew he probably wasn't home yet, but she wanted to see him, so she could wait. She was in no hurry.

Lights were on in the first three houses she passed, but the remaining seven were dark. When she reached the last one, the truck was still gone, and the door was locked. She sat down on the top step, spread her full skirt around her, leaned back and looked out over the desert while she waited.

The sun had set, and stars were beginning to light the sky. The rising moon shone on the cactus, on the gentle hills and shallow valleys, casting a luminous glow that created eerie shadows. It was quiet and peaceful, with only the desert noises to break the stillness.

She loved it here. She had been a fool not to return when Cody had asked her to. If fate had known that she would end up here anyway, why hadn't it brought her back then, when he was waiting for her? And why had it brought him back now, when he no longer wanted her?

The sound of the truck's engine interrupted her thoughts. Cody parked between the two houses; then he got out and came toward the steps. He was at the bottom step before he saw her.

He said nothing.

She had expected anger at being asked to leave so her parents wouldn't see him, but his face was expressionless in the moonlight. For a long time they looked at each other; then she slowly stood up. Her skirt fell in folds around her calves with a soft whisper of sound.

He hadn't expected to find her waiting for him. He didn't know what to say. All the sarcastic, sardonic, mocking remarks that he could have fallen back on fled his mind. He could think of nothing... except how he wanted her.

"How was your visit with your parents?" he asked, his voice huskier than normal.

"I'm sorry about that. Mom and Dad want me to sell the ranch and try to patch things up with Chad, and..." She raised her hands in a helpless gesture. "I couldn't give them something else to use against me."

Cody moved up one step. "Are you going to?"

"Sell the ranch? How could I? It's my home."

He shook his head. "Try to patch things up with Chad."

She moved her head back and forth slowly. "No," she whispered. "I can't."

He moved up another step, then turned his head away from her. He was searching for control, and he would never find it while looking at her. She was too beautiful, too soft.... But he found no help in the desert, either. He could still feel her presence, hear her breathing, smell her perfume. He still knew that she was standing only an arm's length away, that he could so easily pull her to him and hold her, kiss her, touch her. He could so easily love her.

He looked back at her and moved one more step. She recognized the smoky change in his eyes and caught her breath. Years had passed since she'd seen that look, but her response was the same—swift, intense, hot. It left her weak and breathless, awaiting his next move.

Now they were on almost the same level, only inches apart. He reached out to catch a handful of her hair, to finger its silky length. He touched each strand, let it fall through his fingers to form a fragile web across her breast. When the last strand had fallen, he reached around her and filled both hands with more.

His arms rested on her shoulders, and his chest, broad and strong under a cream-colored shirt, filled her vision. She forgot that she had been cool only minutes before, because the heat radiating from him warmed her all the way down to her toes.

He slowly withdrew his hands from her hair and laid them on her shoulders. He neither drew her to him nor held her away. He simply touched her, sliding his hands beneath the narrow strips of fabric that crossed her shoulders. Her skin was smooth and soft, warm against his callused palms. She was like that all over—her back, her breasts, her belly, her thighs. . . . Smooth and soft and perfect.

He had few needs that he couldn't fill himself, and in his lifetime he had found only one person who could fulfill them. He was holding her now, and he needed her now. Mariah.

He closed his eyes, shutting out the sight of her. He *couldn't* need her. If he needed her, she would destroy him. Lust—that was all he could feel for her. Only lust.

With his hands, he guided her to him, until their bodies were touching, intimately together, and with his arms around her, he held her there. Her breasts were flattened against his chest, and his hardness was cushioned against her belly.

Could this be lust, this feeling of rightness? This feeling that he couldn't get close enough to her to satisfy the ache in him? This feeling that he would never, ever get enough of her?

He shook his head. It couldn't be something that simple, that base. But that was all he could allow himself, and so that was what he would call it. Lust.

He lowered his head, and she instinctively raised hers, lifting her mouth to his. He took just a brief taste, to see if he could stand the torture of kissing her and doing nothing else.

The kiss had a pain all its own—overwhelming, stunning in its intensity. Dear God, he marveled, when he made love to her, he would probably die from the pure, intense pleasure of it.

He lowered his head and kissed her again, heating her blood, stirring her senses, feeding her need until it threatened to consume her. Her hands came up to grasp his shoulders. She needed his strength to support her. She needed . . . anything. Everything. Him.

Cody ended the kiss and pressed her head against him, her face hidden in his shirt. His breath was a ragged sigh that brushed across the top of her head. He felt more than heard her whisper his name, and slowly, calling on every ounce of strength he possessed, he raised her head so he could see her face. "You are so damn beautiful," he said, his voice rough with raw emotion.

The compliment sounded as if it had been dragged unwillingly from the depths of his soul. He didn't want to think she was beautiful, and that saddened her.

His fingers brushed along her jaw, over her mouth, down her throat, and he swallowed hard. He wanted to kiss her again—he *needed* to kiss her again—and for that reason he wouldn't. He had liked kissing her—had liked it so much that he might never again be able to live without it.

Without her.

Lust, he reminded himself. Lust was all that he could feel. He pushed her away, then released his hold on her. "Good night, Mariah," he said brusquely and turned toward the door.

"Cody?" she whispered, confused that he was sending her away after the kisses they had shared.

He somehow managed, when he looked at her, to appear unaffected by her. "What?"

How could he speak so casually when he had just aroused every single nerve in her body? How could he be so unmoved when she was trembling and weak with desire?

He pulled his keys from his pocket, then unlocked the door and swung it inward, before looking back at her. "I'm really tired, Mariah, and your apology was more than adequate. Can I go now?"

"But..."

"Look, I hired on to work the ranch—*not* to keep you satisfied," he said harshly. Then he grinned. "But, if it means that much to you, I suppose we can work something out."

For a long moment she couldn't breathe because of the ache around her heart. Finally she succeeded at filling her lungs, and she even got her lips to curve upward in a semblance of a smile. "No, I don't think we can. I hope you sleep well."

Like hell you do. He watched her walk away before he went inside and locked the door behind him. He wouldn't get any sleep until the ache in his belly went away, and experience told him that was going to take a very long time.

Mariah made it to the house and the privacy of her bedroom before she let the first tear fall. It was hot and salty, and quickly followed by more. She couldn't remember the last time she had cried, but tonight she made up for all those dry-eyed months, sobbing herself to sleep in the solitary warmth of her bed.

Chapter 4

Cody was in the long central aisle of the barn, saddling a horse, after a long, sleepless night, when he heard Mariah's voice. Turning, he saw her standing at the office door, talking to Arcadio. Apparently she wasn't planning to work like the rest of the world today, he thought sourly. Her usual boots, jeans and work shirt had been replaced by a pair of white shorts that fitted smoothly over her slim hips and left most of her long legs bare, and a white cotton blouse that ended just below her ribs. Her hair was pulled back, braided and fastened with bright red bands. She looked lovely and cool despite the rising temperatures outside.

Despite the rising temperatures *inside*, he corrected himself running a finger along his shirt collar.

She liked to wear white, he remembered, because it emphasized her black hair and tanned skin. It made her look angelic and innocent. Untouchable. But she hadn't been untouchable last night. She had wanted him in the most basic, most intimate way possible. He had been wrong to send her away.

But he would have been insane to let her stay.

"What time do you think you'll be back?" Arcadio asked.

They were coming in his direction, but Cody made no effort to move away, to avoid her. It wasn't necessary, because she was completely ignoring him.

"I don't know," she replied with a shrug. "Probably late this afternoon."

When she started to walk past him, Cody stepped around the horse and right into her path. "Good morning," he drawled.

She looked at him the way he remembered her mother looking at him almost nine years ago when Mariah had announced that they were going to be married. Despite being almost six inches shorter than Cody, Helen Butler had somehow managed to look down her nose at him with an air of superiority and smiled condescendingly. "We'll see about that," she had said in her elegant, cultured voice.

"Good morning," Mariah said, as coolly as if greeting a stranger—or an employee. She stepped around him and turned back to Arcadio. "Is there anything you need me to get while I'm gone?"

"No," the foreman replied, watching Cody lead the horse outside. The young man's back was straight, his head held high. Arcadio knew that Cody was angry at the snub; she spoke to the animals with more warmth and friendliness than she'd offered him.

"We'll let you know if we're going to be late." Mariah walked away, then returned. "In case... in case anything happens, take care of things for me, will you?" Then she left again, walking quickly back to the house.

David was waiting for her in the kitchen. He smiled, wrongly interpreting the tension that knotted her hands into tight fists. "Hey, there's no reason to worry about this," he said in an effort to make her smile. "I've done it dozens of times."

Mariah *did* smile. "And you got caught, too, remember? I have no desire to be the first Butler in history to rot away in jail."

"Don't be so melodramatic. You're not going to go to jail," he chided her. Then he grinned again. "You would probably just get a suspended sentence and probation, like me."

She didn't find much comfort in that. Whether the punishment was prison or probation, it would still be a felony conviction, and it would still cost her the respect of the people she loved.

She chose an apple from a bowl on the counter and forced a cheerier smile. She didn't have as much at risk as David and some of the others; having already been convicted once, another arrest would almost surely mean prison for them. It came down to which was stronger—her concern and love for the children, or her fear of arrest. She could live with a prison record. She couldn't live knowing that some of the children might die because she was too concerned with her own welfare to care about theirs. "Are you ready to go?"

When David nodded, they walked out to the car that Arcadio had parked near the house and left.

They drove in silence—into Esperanza, over the border and into the small dusty town of San Benito, twenty miles farther south. The house they went to was on the edge of town, no different from its neighbors. The man who answered the door greeted them with a somber smile.

"*¿Están listos?*" David asked.

The man nodded, inviting them inside. "There are four of them today," Efraín said, gesturing to the children sitting on the floor. "Pedro, Sylvia, Ruben and Esperanza."

At the mention of her name, a young girl about six looked up. "*Me llamo Esperanza,*" she said, smiling shyly at Mariah.

While David and Efraín talked, Mariah knelt next to the girl. "The town where I live is named Esperanza, too," she explained to them in lilting Spanish. The name hadn't brought much hope to the town, but maybe it would be different for this child, she thought, brushing her hand over the girl's silky black hair.

"We'd better go, Mariah," David said. To Efraín, he confirmed their usual plans. "Give us about a ten-minute head start. We'll meet you there in forty-five minutes, okay?''

"All right. Be careful.''

Mariah drove as they headed back toward the border. The dusty station wagon was used mainly for ranch business, but it came in handy on her trips to San Benito. Unfortunately it was old, and the air conditioner had long ago stopped working. While the car was moving, it wasn't so bad, she thought, but sitting in line at the border crossing, there wasn't even a whisper of a breeze to cool them. She wiped a trickle of sweat from her throat, then leaned forward to peel the soaked back of her shirt from the seat. "Lord, it's hot.''

David said nothing. There was no sense in agreeing, and he certainly wasn't going to argue.

"Why haven't we gotten the air conditioner in this junk heap fixed?''

"Because it *is* a junk heap, and it isn't worth the money the repairs would cost.'' He grinned at her cross mood, not caring when she glared at him.

She eased her foot off the brake, and the car moved forward, stopping only inches from the bumper of the pickup ahead. "I hate the waiting.'' With every minute that passed, the chances of something going wrong increased, and they couldn't afford to get caught.

"Tell me, did you wake up on the wrong side of bed this morning?'' he asked good-naturedly.

Not the wrong side—the wrong *bed*. She had wanted to spend the night in another bed. She scowled fiercely. She was being so incredibly foolish—she, who had so calmly dealt with the divorce that had ended her marriage; she, who had so levelheadedly made the decision to take part in the smuggling. She was behaving like a first-class fool. Only Cody could do that to her. Only Cody could reduce her to tears because he had refused to take advantage of her.

"Do you know anything about these kids?''

Mariah eased the car forward a few more feet. "Only what Father Espinoza told me. It's the same as usual. Their parents were dissidents, or teachers, or doctors, or lay workers.'' Anyone who provided aid to the people of Carta

Blanca risked his life. She continued in a toneless voice. "Their mothers and older sisters were raped and murdered. Their fathers and older brothers were tortured to death, or disappeared."

"Los desaparecidos." David said the phrase softly. "The disappeared ones" were people whom the government considered a threat. They were taken prisoner by the military or police and were never seen again.

Finally it was their turn. She slowed to a stop next to the customs officer, who greeted her with a nod. "You have anything to declare?" the man asked in a bored voice.

"Not today."

The agent wiped his hand over his forehead, and it came away wet. He hated standing out here in the midday heat asking the same questions of every driver crossing the border. "What was the purpose of your visit?"

"We were visiting friends in San Benito." It wasn't a lie, Mariah thought defensively. Efraín *was* a friend.

Bending, the man glanced into the back of the station wagon, saw nothing of interest, straightened again and waved them on.

Mariah's muscles tensed as she pressed the accelerator down. Getting across the border was the easy part—after all, they'd done nothing wrong...yet. Now the hard part would start.

In town, they passed a light green truck belonging to the border patrol. Kyle Parker was behind the wheel. Mariah recognized him and returned his friendly wave.

"You still worried about getting caught?" David asked.

Mariah smiled faintly. What would her friend think if she told him that what was worrying her today wasn't this run with the kids, but was instead Cody Daniels? She wasn't sure she wanted to find out yet. "I guess I always worry a bit."

"It probably wouldn't be so bad for you, because of your mom and dad."

"You think the judge would be lenient because of them?" She shook her head. "I always thought the punishment would be a little harsher because of them—because I haven't followed the fine example they've set for me."

"It was spooky, being in that courtroom. The day I was sentenced was probably the most frightening day of my life. I'd never even gotten so much as a speeding ticket before, and there I was being sentenced for eight felony convictions. I was sure the judge would lock me up for the rest of my life."

"And that's exactly what he will do if you get caught again," she reminded him.

David's only response was a shrug.

Mariah drove east out of town, slowing when the paved road gave way to dirt. Their plan was simple: they had chosen a suitable place for sneaking across the border, and Efraín would meet them there with the four children. All they had to do was drive to that spot, pick up the kids and head for Tucson, praying all the way that they wouldn't get stopped.

Up ahead, on the other side of the border, she saw the ancient green truck that belonged to Efraín, and she slowed to a stop. David jumped out and ran to the fence to gather the four children while she waited with the engine running.

"Ready?" she asked as the car doors slammed.

The answer came from David as he settled into his seat again. "Ready."

She waved to Efraín, then drove away, turning in a large circle and heading back toward town. Now they had to make it to Tucson.

The children were silent as David tried to explain to them about *la migra*, a term that applied to the border patrol as well as to Immigration and Naturalization. They were too young to understand, so he stated it plainly: if he yelled, *"la migra,"* they would lie down in the back seat or crouch on the floor.

"They think it's a game," he murmured to Mariah.

"They're only children." They must be frightened, she thought, watching them from time to time in the rearview mirror. Their families were dead, and they were in a strange country fifteen hundred miles from home, where the language was different and they knew no one. She wondered how they found the courage to survive.

They were only a few miles north of Esperanza when they spotted the first border patrol truck. Mariah was grateful for the distinctive pale green and white colors that made it so easy to pick out the trucks from a distance. The children, coached by David, disappeared from view long before the truck passed them.

Mariah drove carefully, observing the speed limit, nervously checking the rearview mirror every few minutes. No matter how many times she made these trips from San Benito to Tucson, she never quite got used to the nervousness. All it would take was being stopped for one infraction—something as minor as a broken taillight—and she and her passengers would be given a free ride to the nearest federal holding facility.

Their destination was a small church on the outskirts of Tucson. Mariah pulled around to the back, where the car was shielded on three sides by buildings and on the fourth by a tall fence. There a dark, slender man, several inches shorter than she was, was waiting. "Any problems?" he asked softly, looking past her to the four children.

She shook her head. "None at all. How are you, Father Espinoza?"

He smiled then, showing even white teeth. "Better, now that you're here." In Spanish, he greeted the children, politely asking each his name and introducing himself. He instructed them to follow him into the church. Mariah and David brought up the rear.

"Hey, long time, no see," Lissa said to Mariah as she swung Esperanza into her arms.

Mariah smiled. "All of two days. Did you make it back okay Saturday?"

Lissa nodded. "How is it that I've come close to getting caught several times driving a van that no one can see into, and you use a station wagon, where anyone with eyes can see, and no one ever pays attention to you?"

"Easy. I've met most of the border patrol agents in town, and none of them would ever suspect that the daughter of

Judge Helen Butler and Prosecutor Jeremiah Butler—not to mention the granddaughter of Eli Butler—would ever do anything the least bit illegal, so they don't even bother to look."

"We'd better get going, Mariah," David suggested after glancing at his watch. The less time they spent at the church or with Father Espinoza, the harder it would be for anyone to connect them to each other.

"The next time you come, plan on having lunch with me, will you?" Lissa asked.

"Sure." Mariah brushed her hand over Esperanza's cheek. *"Buena suerte, Esperanza."* Good luck.

"Let's talk about something interesting," David suggested when they had left Tucson behind.

Mariah glanced at him. "All right. There are an awful lot of things in life that I find interesting. Where do you want to start?"

"With Cody Daniels."

She turned her eyes back to the road. That was definitely an interesting subject, but she wasn't sure she could discuss it right now. She was still feeling the sting of rejection, and she didn't want to do anything to make it stronger.

"How well did you know him when he was here before?" David knew he was snooping, but he also knew that if she didn't want to discuss it, she would tell him so.

"What makes you think I knew him at all?"

"'What makes you think I knew him at all?'" he mimicked in a prissy little voice that made her smile in spite of herself. "Well, there's the fact that you've been taking your meals alone ever since he arrived, except for Sunday. There's also the fact that the atmosphere actually sizzles when you two are together. There's the fact that, when I asked him about you, he got all defensive and refused to talk." He paused for a moment, then gently added, "And there's the fact that I saw you two together on his porch last night."

She blushed hotly. So they'd had a witness to their embarrassing little scene. Cody's rejection hadn't been as private as she'd thought. She concentrated on her driving for a few minutes, then said flatly, "Cody and I were going to be married eight years ago."

"What happened?"

"Things went wrong. He made demands." After a moment, she reluctantly admitted, "And so did I. We both held out for what we wanted, and . . . we both lost."

David knew how deeply affected she was by the lack of emotion in her voice. "Eight years is a long time ago."

She laughed sharply. There it was again: a long time ago. When her parents said it, it implied criticism. *It was a long time ago. Why can't you let it go and get on with your life?* When David said it, though, it sounded thoughtful, questioning. *It was a long time ago. If it still matters, then you must still care.*

"If seeing him hurts you so much, why did you hire him?"

"Because Arcadio asked me to. It was important to him." She turned onto the highway that would take them south to Esperanza. "He's a good worker, and he knows the ranch. We needed another hand."

"But you knew you would have to face him."

She shrugged, trying for nonchalance. "I'm learning to deal with him. In a way, it's good that he's come back. Things were never really settled between us. We had a couple of arguments, then suddenly he was gone. Now we have a chance to settle the past and put it to rest." Then maybe the turbulent emotions inside her would ease and, for the first time in eight years, give her peace.

It was midafternoon when they arrived back at the ranch. Mariah traded her shorts and sandals for jeans and boots while David saddled two horses; then they rode out to find Arcadio and the others, who, according to Bonita, were replacing a section of fence.

Even though the men were far away when they spotted them, Mariah had no trouble identifying each of them. Antonio was the smallest of four, short and lean, and Arcadio's white straw hat marked him. Philip was the biggest, his height and broad shoulders making them all look smaller, and Cody... She smiled. She would recognize Cody in the black of night, simply from the responses of her body. He was working some distance from the other three, with his shirt discarded on the ground.

She studied him as she drew closer. His shoulders weren't as broad as Philip's, but they were strong. His skin was darkly tanned, and it rippled with the flexing of his muscles as he worked. His hair, damp with perspiration, gleamed like gold underneath the sun, and the thick strands formed wet curls of darker gold on his neck beneath his hat.

He was handsome, she thought with a smile. Just the sight of him could make her remember his kisses last night. It could make her want him again. But it also made her remember his words. *I hired on to work the ranch—not to keep you satisfied. But, if it means that much to you, I suppose we could work something out.* Last night she had told him that he was wrong, that they *couldn't* work something out. Now she wondered. If that was the only way to get his kisses, his caresses, his lovemaking, would it be so bad? Could she bear knowing that he looked on making love to her as just another of his duties around the ranch?

Just then he turned around and looked at her. The expression in his blue eyes, in spite of the hundred-degree temperature, was as cold as ice, and the curl of his lip was derisive.

No, she thought sadly. She couldn't bear that. After the tender relationship they had shared in the past, she couldn't settle for anything less. She couldn't accept his coldness, his disdain, his complete dislike of her, not even for the indescribable pleasure of his lovemaking.

She reined in the horse a few feet away and studied him for a moment. The lines of his face were hard and unyielding. His bare chest, smooth and finely muscled, glistened with sweat that trickled down to the faded jeans he wore low on his slender hips.

"Where did you and your little friend disappear to?" he asked in a low, nasty voice that only she could hear.

How could he make a phrase as innocent as "little friend" sound so vulgar? she wondered, still watching him with narrowed eyes. "We had business to take care of," she replied.

She was using that voice again, the one she'd greeted him with that morning, and it made every muscle in his body taut. In one brief, simple sentence, she had made it clear that he had no right to question her. She had reminded him that he was nothing more than an employee, with no reason to care how she spent her time.

Last night he had sent her away by suggesting that he would be willing to have sex with her as part of a business arrangement. Now, for just a moment, jealousy forced him to wonder if she already had a similar arrangement with David Green. Arcadio had hedged when Cody had asked him where Mariah and Green were, and Philip had told him that they frequently went off together during the week. The younger man didn't know what their "business" was, nor did he care. He did his job, and he got paid for it; that was his only interest in "business."

"What kind of business?" he practically snarled.

If she'd had any reason at all to think that Cody gave a damn about her, she would have thought he was jealous. But since she knew he didn't care, she decided he was just bad tempered. She leaned closer to him and answered with two words. "*Private* business," she whispered. Straightening in the saddle, she urged the horse over to Arcadio, leaving Cody silently, furiously cursing.

Mariah showed up in the dining room for every meal the rest of the week. Her seat was at the head of the table and Cody's was on her left, but they never spoke to each other. Each quietly pretended that the other didn't exist. Those were the only times she saw him. He avoided her office during the day and stayed away from the barn when she was around.

It wasn't comfortable, but it was bearable. It was something Mariah tried to convince herself that she could live with. So he didn't want to be friends—or lovers or anything else. So she was the last woman on earth he wanted a relationship with. She could handle that; she was doing a very good job of handling it.

Until Friday evening came, and Cody left for another night in town with David and Philip.

They left shortly after dinner. From the privacy of her bedroom, Mariah watched them drive away. As soon as Cody's midnight-blue truck was out of sight, she sank down on the bed with a weary sigh.

Who was she kidding? She couldn't handle this cold, just barely businesslike attitude of his. She dreaded every day, from the time she got up in the morning until bedtime. She dreaded seeing him at meals and pretending that nothing was wrong, and she dreaded *not* seeing him at other times, never having a chance to establish some kind of truce.

She berated herself for wanting more from him than he could give. He had hurt her. He had left her, and in eight years, he had never cared enough to call her, to see if she was all right. He had never cared about the pain he had caused her. And now she was practically begging him to do it again. Thank God he had the sense this time to push her away. To protect her from herself, she thought with a wry grin.

There was just one problem, she lamented as the grin faded, leaving her sad and lonely. She didn't want to be protected—not from herself, and certainly not from Cody.

She couldn't lie to herself anymore. She couldn't look at Cody and feel the emotions that lived so deep inside her and tell herself that she had stopped loving him. No matter what had happened, she had always loved him—probably always would.

Always. God, that was such a long time. A long time to argue, to be alone, to be empty. Or a long time to love and be happy. Which would it be for them?

Cody sat at the largest table in the bar, a nearly full glass of beer in front of him. Crowded around him were Philip and his red-haired girlfriend, David and the dark-haired Suzanne, and half a dozen of their friends from other ranches. The men were loudly discussing everything from ranching to rodeos to women, and the women were talking quietly together, their voices too low for the others to hear. Cody was talking to no one.

If this was a sample of nightlife in Esperanza, he could do without it. His eyes were burning, and his head ached a little more with each new song on the jukebox. He squinted to see his watch in the nearly dark room and stifled a groan. It was almost eleven o'clock, and he was dead tired. His lungs craved a breath of fresh air, and his body craved sleep. He wanted to go home, to his quiet house, with no music, no cigarette smoke and no noisy friends, with only the sounds of the desert, the light from the moon...and Mariah by his side.

He tilted his head back and closed his eyes. He missed her. He had seen her three times a day every day this week, but he still missed her. She had been so cold every time he'd seen her, so damned superior and patronizing. So damn beautiful.

He had been wrong to deliberately hurt her Sunday night, and the fact that he'd simply been trying to stop himself from taking her to bed couldn't make it all right. He'd spent most of the week trying to convince himself that he wasn't to blame—*she* had come to *him*; *she* had been the one who wanted to stay. But he couldn't deny that he had wanted her to stay—had wanted it so badly that it had scared him. His reasons for sending her away had been good, but his methods had been cruel, and nothing could change that.

But an apology was a place to start.

He leaned close to the man beside him and spoke in a voice loud enough to be heard over the music. "Do you mind if I leave now?"

David looked at him for a moment. He had wondered how long Cody would be able to stay at the bar when Mariah was alone at home. "Go ahead," he said quietly. "Philip and I will find a ride home."

By the time Cody got home, he was wide-awake. He parked his truck and started toward the main house, determined to find Mariah, to apologize to her. When he was almost there, he came to a sudden stop in the moonlight and stared.

She was leaning against a small stone fountain in the patch of desert that served as a backyard. Eli Butler, her grandfather, had installed the fountain for his wife, Cody recalled, but it was empty now. Water was too precious a commodity in the desert to waste on a pretty little fountain.

She hadn't realized yet that she was no longer alone. The fountain stood as high as her waist; she had laid her arms on its wide rim and bent forward gracefully over the empty bowl. Her hair was loose, trailing strands lifting lightly in the evening breeze, and her face was raised to the sky, to the clear, bright, twinkling stars.

He could have stood there all night, simply looking at her in the clear moonlight. Dear Lord, she was beautiful! So beautiful... The guilt inside him twisted into an ache that yearned for relief.

"Mariah..."

He didn't know he'd spoken aloud until she turned her face toward him and found him in the moon's glow. He waited, half-afraid that she would go inside, close the door on him and leave him alone. Unbearably alone.

She looked at him for a long moment, then lifted her eyes to the sky again. She was wearing a faint half smile. She had come outside to indulge in a childhood fancy, wishing on the stars. She had wished for Cody, and here he was, in the flesh. If only the stars could grant the rest of her wishes so easily.

When she didn't go, Cody slowly moved closer. He didn't stop until he stood on the opposite side of the fountain. Only two feet of stone and concrete separated them.

She spoke at last, her voice low, husky, mesmerizing. "Did you have a good time in town tonight?"

He had to swallow hard to get his reply out. "Not particularly."

"Apparently not. It's not even midnight yet." His answer pleased her. For reasons she preferred to ignore right now, she didn't want him to have a good time, not with anyone except her.

"Do you always check up on your employees, Mariah?" He rested his palms flat on the fountain's rim. The stone still held the day's heat, warm against his skin. It was an erotic contrast to the cool night air.

Just the hint of a smile played about her lips. "Is that all you are? An employee?"

His heart began pounding relentlessly, leaving him short of breath and with an achingly tight feeling in his chest. "I don't know," he almost whispered. "You tell me."

She was silent for a long time before finally admitting, "I don't know, either."

He moved his hands on the stone closer to hers, and she watched, fascinated by them. They were strong, his fingers long and slender and his palms callused from years of hard work. They were capable of inflicting great pain. They could also tenderly, gently soothe. And they could bring intense pleasure.

She smiled faintly. "Why are you back so soon? Couldn't you find a woman in Esperanza worthy of your company?"

Now his hands were only millimeters from hers. His mouth was dry, and his heart was beating a million times a minute. It was amazing—he hadn't even touched her yet, but his entire body was tingling, aching, swelling. "I found one."

For an instant she looked stunned, then terribly hurt. Then she smiled again, trying to pretend that it didn't matter. "Then why did you come back?"

Just the tips of his fingers made contact with the tips of hers, but it was a shock that spread like wildfire through his entire system. Cody remained motionless, breathless, thoughtless for a moment; then he said in a sexy, low intimate drawl, "Because this is where I found her."

She looked stunned again, even a little bit frightened. She pulled her hands away and clutched them together in front of her. "No, Cody," she whispered.

"You wanted me to make love to you the other night. Have you changed your mind?"

"You didn't want me," she painfully reminded him.

He smiled, his blue eyes chiding her. "Do you really believe that, Mariah? Do you think the day will ever come when I don't want you?"

"It came eight years ago, and it took me a long time to get over it." She looked up at him, her eyes gleaming with tears. "You hurt me."

She spoke with a simple honesty that made him long to hold her, to soothe away the pain. To heal her. But he didn't touch her, fearful that, once he did, he would never be able to let her go again.

His hands slowly knotted into white-knuckled fists. "And you think I wasn't hurt then, too?" He smiled. It made him look curiously sad, she thought. "Leaving here without you was the hardest thing I've ever done. I still wanted you. I still loved you. But I couldn't stay here without you."

Mariah reached out, unfolding his hands, smoothing them flat on the stone, then twined her fingers with his. "You never gave me a chance to choose. You issued an ultimatum, and then you left."

Her fingers were delicately shaped but strong. They were cool against the warmth of his hands, soft against the roughness. Cody remembered how they felt on his face, his chest, everywhere else, and shuddered. If they weren't going to make love tonight—and he was sure that they weren't— he couldn't bear her touch another second longer. Gently he pulled his hands free and walked away, toward a nearby bench.

"We moved to Esperanza when I was fifteen," he said softly. "My father thought life in a small town might be better for my mother."

Mariah remained where she was, listening intently. She remembered Laura Daniels, a pretty, blond-haired woman who was usually too drunk to care how she looked or what she did, or if she even lived. She had been a sad woman and a less than adequate mother; instead of taking care of her son, her son had taken care of her. But Cody had loved her fiercely, and he had always been so gentle with her, treating her as if she were a fragile object that might shatter. And in a way, Mariah supposed, that was what had happened to her.

"When she continued drinking, he reached the point where he'd had enough. A year after we moved here, he left her." Cody stared past her, seeing visions from the past that she couldn't share. It wasn't easy, talking to her like this. In the year they'd been together, his father was the one subject they had never touched on. He'd never told anyone much about Bill Daniels. "He wanted me to go, too. He wanted a normal life for both of us."

But Cody hadn't gone. Mariah wasn't surprised. Instead, he had remained behind, had accepted the responsibilities of a man at the age of sixteen, and had supported, cared for and loved his mother until her death.

"She got worse after he left, and she eventually drank herself to death eight years later. Eight years ago." At last he turned his head to meet her gaze. "She needed him. He was her husband, and she *needed* him...but he wasn't there. He cared more for himself and his own comfort than he did about the wife he'd sworn he loved."

There was no accusation in his voice, but Mariah felt the corresponding guilt. Was that how he saw her? As a woman who cared more for herself than for the man she had sworn to love? Did he feel she had let him down when he needed her by refusing to return to the ranch?

"She spent all those years alone," Cody continued, "waiting for him to come back. She always thought he would come back because he'd said he loved her. When she died... all I could see was me...us. Dad loved her, but not enough to stay with her. You loved me, but not enough to come back here. He wasn't willing to give any more of himself to her, and you weren't willing to give any more of yourself to me. She died waiting for him to come back. I couldn't do that. I couldn't wait any longer."

Mariah walked to the bench and sat down at the opposite end. She sighed softly as she folded her hands in her lap. "So you left town without so much as a goodbye. And you never came back. You never called. You never tried to see me. You never gave me a chance to give you my answer."

"Like I said, leaving was the hardest thing I'd ever done. I couldn't come back. It wouldn't have mattered, anyway. It wouldn't have made a difference, would it?" He was challenging her with his words, his eyes, the tone of his voice—challenging her to admit that he was right. He *had* to be right!

She glanced at him before lowering her eyes to her hands. She felt closer to him than she had since his return—and more distant, too. There was a part of her that wanted to ignore his question, to let him continue believing what he had believed for eight years. But that would be too easy—too cowardly. If they were going to set aside the hurts and sorrows of the past, she had to answer him honestly.

"You know how I found out that you were gone? I called here to talk to you. Arcadio told me about Laura's death. He said her funeral had been two days earlier. I knew then that you had changed your mind about us. If you had loved me—if you had truly loved me—you would have called me when Laura died. You would have turned to me instead of going through it alone." She remembered her sorrow on hearing that Laura was dead, and her pain when she had realized what that meant. It had been inconceivable to her that a man who loved her wouldn't turn to her for comfort when he lost the only other person he loved. The conclusion that he hadn't truly loved her, after all, had been inescapable.

They sat in silence for a few minutes, neither looking at the other. The only sound was the faint beep of Cody's watch. It was midnight.

"Do you want to know why I called you that day?"

He shook his head. He didn't want to hear her say it. After eight years, could it really matter? Would telling him accomplish anything besides shifting the blame from her, where he had placed it so long ago, to himself, where it belonged? But he retracted the silent answer with a hoarse, "Yes. I want to know."

"I was ready to come home. To the ranch. To you. I had decided that living here with you, without a job or any money, had to be better than living anywhere else without you. But you were gone. Arcadio said you'd left the day before.'' She stood up and faced him, her fingers laced tightly together so she wouldn't reach out to him. "So you see, Cody, it would have made a difference—if you had come back, or called, or written. If you had done a single thing to let me know that you still cared. It would have made all the difference in the world.''

He rose to his feet, too. He was close to her, their bodies separated only by inches of cool night air. Raising his hand, he brushed his fingers across her cheek, then over her hair. He followed the silky black length to her waist and let his arm settle there, holding her gently. With his other hand, he tilted her chin up, cupping it while he lowered his mouth to hers.

The kiss was sweet and infinitely tender, but it was also unsatisfyingly brief. Mariah had barely been given a chance to respond before he was ending it. "I still cared,'' he whispered. "I cared so damn much.''

Once again, he bent to kiss her, this time just a feathery touch of his lips. "Good night, Mariah.'' He left her standing alone in the moonlight.

Mariah watched him go, then turned toward the house. The tingling he had started inside her was slowly fading. Once again he could have seduced her, and once again he had decided against it. But this time there was no pain. This time she was smiling when she entered her bedroom.

Cody hadn't left because he'd stopped loving her. He had loved her, had missed her, had ached for her—the way she had ached for him. He had chosen not to make love to her tonight, but she didn't mind. The time would come when he wouldn't walk away, when he wouldn't even think the word "no.'' The time would come when they would be lovers again—she knew it in her soul. Because of that, she could be patient. She could wait.

Chapter 5

Cody sat on the porch steps, his legs stretched out in front of him. His feet were bare, and he wore no shirt. It was early—cool, still and quiet. There was a curious soft pastel glow on the desert as the sun began its journey. Soon the sky would be bright, with everything clearly, sharply defined, but now it was hazy, dusky.

Mariah was probably still asleep, he thought idly. She liked to sleep late, liked to awaken slowly, by degrees. How many times had he watched her do just that?

Sadness crossed his face. Too many. Not enough.

He had slept restlessly last night, still seeing her, touching her, smelling her, feeling her. For the first time in years he had dreamed of her and awakened with an ache that couldn't be assuaged. The only relief for it was Mariah. If he could have gone to her, if he could have buried himself in the sweet, silken warmth of her body...

He could have.

That knowledge had made his night even harder to bear. He could have gone to her and made love with her all night long. He could have awakened in bed next to her this morning. But he had chosen instead to return to his empty house. He had needed time—time to understand what she had told him.

She had wanted to come back. Even now, after hours of repeating it to himself, the words brought a joyous smile to his lips. She had loved him enough to let him win their argument. She had loved him enough to marry him.

He stood up and went inside to finish dressing, then fixed breakfast in the tiny kitchen at the back of the house. Cold cereal, toast and instant coffee didn't begin to compare to Bonita's breakfasts, but after his restless, erotic-dream-filled night, he didn't want to see Mariah in the company of others. When he was ready to see her again, it would be alone.

Was it possible, he wondered, suddenly somber, that he still loved her? Everything in him rebelled at the thought. He had spent too many years resenting and blaming her, too many years hurting because of her. Now, because she had said a few pretty words in the moonlight—words that she had known he wanted to hear—was he really willing to forget all the anger and all the hurt and rekindle his love?

Maybe.

He sat quietly at the rickety dining table, a cup of coffee in front of him, and let the memories, all the feelings of the last eight years, drift through his mind. If asked, he would have said that his life had been all right—not particularly happy, but not particularly sad—but now he knew that wasn't true. There had been an emptiness, a place that no one could fill. It had been there even with Andrea, the woman he had thought about marrying. Was it because of Mariah that he'd been unable to love Andrea?

He didn't want to believe it—God, it could destroy his soul if he believed it—but the evidence was damning: all those long nights he had lain in bed, wanting her so desperately that he'd been unable to even think of other women; the relentless pain that had haunted him for weeks after he'd read about her marriage to Lowell; the inability to make a commitment to any other woman; the bitterness that she hadn't loved him enough which had been his defense, his protection, against her memory; the growing satisfaction of being back in Esperanza. Because it was where he had loved Mariah. Because she was here.

Was it possible to love someone for so long when you didn't see her or talk to her, when you weren't a part of her life? Their love had been very special, but that was years ago. She had grown into a woman he didn't even really know.

But she couldn't have changed that much. She was still Mariah. The woman he had fallen in love with. The woman who had brought happiness and warmth into his life. The woman he had wanted to marry.

He would be crazy to let himself love her again, he thought as he rinsed his dishes. Hadn't he lived with enough pain after their affair had ended to last a lifetime? Was he really foolish enough to ask for more?

But hadn't the pleasure of their love been worth the pain?

He was thirty-two years old—old enough to want to get married, to want to love someone, to want a family. If he was old enough to enjoy the benefits of love and marriage, then he was old enough to take the risks.

But did he want to take those risks with Mariah? Did he want to marry her, to love her again, to give her once more the power to make his life unbearable?

Feeling as if he were facing a battle that he'd already lost, he sighed deeply. He was going to have to be damn careful to come out of this with his heart in one piece.

Mariah stayed in the office until midafternoon, although her mind wasn't on her work. She found herself daydreaming, remembering her talk with Cody last night—remembering his kisses. She had awakened this morning feeling better and happier than she had in months, certain that the late-night conversation had meant the start of a new relationship for them. But when she'd gone into the dining room and found his chair empty, the doubts had set in. She had hurried through breakfast and gone to the stables, hoping she might find him there, but one of the horses was already gone. There had been no sign of him at lunch, either.

He was avoiding her. She'd had too much practice at evasion not to recognize the signs. Why? Had he regretted explaining his actions in the past? Or had he lied?

She pushed her chair away from the desk and stood up. The room was too small to pace, so she had to be contented with staring out the back window.

Had he lied? she wondered, biting her lower lip. Everything in her insisted that he couldn't have—he *wouldn't* have. But everything in her wanted him to want her. She wanted him to care. She wanted him to love her. Was she twisting reality to make it fit her dreams?

"Are you busy?"

She was unable to stop the smile that suddenly lit her face as she turned around. Cody was standing in the door, his white shirt stained with sweat and dirt, his jeans dusty. He had never looked more handsome. "No," she replied honestly. "Whenever I get depressed, I stare out the window. The view isn't great, but it's mine."

He glanced out the window over her shoulder, then at the pile of papers scattered over her desk. Why was she depressed? Because of the ranch? Or him? Uncomfortably, he removed his hat and slapped it against his leg. Little puffs of dust reflected in a shaft of sunlight, then dissipated.

Mariah gestured to the chair at Arcadio's desk. "Have a seat."

He pulled the chair out and sat down, stretching his legs straight out in front of him. He tossed his hat onto the desk, folded his arms over his chest and looked at her.

"You've been working hard today."

He nodded.

"Too hard to take the time to eat?"

"I needed to think more than I needed to eat." He had completed his work with little conscious awareness of what he was doing; his thoughts had centered on Mariah. "Problems?"

With a shrug, she walked to her own desk and sat down. "Always. It's nothing new."

Cody was hesitant to question her further. The ranch's financial difficulties were none of his business. He wouldn't even be keeping the salary that she paid him; the money would be turned over to Kyle Parker and would eventually end up in some government fund. But still, he offered her the chance to talk. If she refused, he wouldn't push it. "The ranch is in trouble, isn't it?" he asked quietly.

Mariah smiled sadly. "Yes." She wouldn't admit that to her parents, but she trusted that Cody wouldn't use it against her as Jerry and Helen would.

"What happened?"

"Beef prices dropped. The market was pretty bad for a long time." She began gathering the papers on her desk, sorting them into neat stacks.

"And your parents aren't helping."

"They were going to sell the ranch outright. I convinced them to give it to me—sort of an early inheritance. They did so with the agreement that, if I couldn't keep it solvent, I wouldn't ask them for money." She had put every penny she had into it; so far, she was just barely holding on. "This place has lost money pretty steadily for the last five years or so. In the last six months, it's gotten better, but . . . it's still a tough business. Maybe that's one of the problems."

Cody lifted one brow curiously. "What is?"

"To Dad, this is a business. As long as it's profitable, you stay in it. When it begins to lose money, you get out. He didn't see any reason to keep putting money into it when he wasn't getting any returns—sort of throwing good money after bad. That's not a sound business judgment," she explained with a faint smile.

"But no business is going to succeed without ample capital, especially a ranch." Cody turned to the picture of Mariah's grandfather on the wall. "It's too bad your father isn't more like old Eli."

She nodded in agreement. Eli Butler had had ranching in his blood. He would have given his life to save this place from financial ruin. But Eli had wanted more for his only son. He had encouraged him to learn books instead of cattle, to go to college instead of gaining the experience and the love needed to take over the ranch. Jerry had gone on to law school and had quickly established a reputation as an ambitious and tough attorney, one who cared little about his father's land. "It's too bad I wasn't a boy," she remarked with a sigh. "Then I would have been taught everything I needed to know as I was growing up, instead of trying to learn it now."

Cody was grinning broadly. "Well, I, for one, am damn grateful that you weren't a boy," he teased, but his next question was serious. "You said that business had gotten better in the last six months. How long have you been in charge?"

"I've been here seven months," she admitted. "But I'm not really in charge. Arcadio lets me pretend to be, but he's still running everything behind the scenes. He and Bonita and Antonio have been here all their lives. They can't risk losing their homes because I want to play rancher."

The shaky little note in her voice reminded Cody of the insult he'd thrown at her his first night back about her "flings." He cleared his throat. "I'm sorry about that, Mariah. I was wrong."

She nodded once. "Yes. You were."

The quietly confident way she spoke made him study her thoughtfully. She had grown up. He had always wondered when, or if, it would happen, and finally it had. The woman sitting in front of him was far more mature than the girl he had left behind.

What had made him so serious? Mariah wondered. Whatever it was, it had been more important to him than eating.

Whatever it was. She was fairly certain, without conceit, that he'd been thinking about them, about her. She was also fairly certain that he hadn't reached any decisions yet, judging by the hesitant way he'd approached her here in the office.

Well, she had made enough decisions for both of them. She had decided—decided? or finally admitted?—that too much of her love for Cody still existed to ignore it. With a little nurturing, it could once again be a full-blown, red-hot, passionate force—a force that, like it or not, he would have to reckon with. Maybe they still had a chance at happily-ever-after. Maybe they didn't. But she had to find out for herself.

"Will you have dinner with me tonight?"

Cody looked blankly at her. Of all the things she could possibly have asked him, that was the most unexpected. She could have asked him to take her to bed and he wouldn't have been as surprised.

She smiled, gently teasing. "You know—dinner? In a restaurant? You and me?"

He opened his mouth to tell her no, that he had other plans, but the refusal wouldn't come out. For another of those gentle little smiles, he would probably agree to anything she wanted. "All right. Where do you want to go?"

She chose Tucson. There were two decent restaurants in Esperanza, but she didn't consider them. The time factor made Tucson a better choice. Dinner in Esperanza would take less than two hours, including the drive in and back. The trip to the city and back again would in itself take longer than that. "I'll pick you up...." Her voice trailed away at the sudden narrowing of his eyes. She might have asked him out, but he would take over from there. She smiled in deference to his male ego.

"*I'll* pick *you* up at six-thirty," he said sharply.

When he reached the door, she replied in a soft voice that was filled with promise, "I'll be ready."

He was certain she would be. He just hoped that *he* was, too.

Mariah dressed for the evening with care, wanting everything to be perfect. Tonight would be an important step in their fragile relationship—but would it be a step forward or back? she wondered as she brushed her hair. Would Cody decide that it was all right to trust his feelings? Or would he hold on to the anger that had protected him for so long?

She knew what she wanted. Little had changed since they'd become lovers nine years ago. She had wanted him then—all of him—and she wanted him now. There were some differences, of course. Then she had been an immature girl who had expected eternal bliss as her due. Now she knew that she would have to work to build a relationship with Cody. She would have to give as well as take. She would have to learn to compromise. And she would have to convince Cody to trust her again. She would have to convince him to love her. Tonight she would start.

One last glance in the mirror assured her that she looked nice. Turning off the light, she hurried down the hall to the living room, where Cody had been waiting for the last five minutes.

He was standing at one of the windows, staring out. When he heard her footsteps, he turned toward the door. Motionless, he simply stared.

She wore a sleeveless white blouse that left her arms bare. It had a deep V-neckline and fastened with a row of tiny, closely spaced buttons that pulled it snug from shoulders to waist, following the curves and lines of her upper body. In contrast, the matching skirt was soft and full, falling to her calves and swirling around her bare legs as she walked toward him. Her hair was pulled back at the top of her head and held together with a large oval clamp of beaten silver; then it fell down her back in a narrow, long stream. The silver was repeated in a delicately fashioned concha belt that she wore around her narrow waist. White leather sandals completed her outfit.

Cody cleared his throat and murmured, "You're lovely, Mariah." Too lovely. Did she really expect him to drive all the way to Tucson, sit across the table from her at dinner and drive all the way back without stopping in the first reasonably private place and ravishing her?

He knew the answer was no. She was planning to seduce him. What he hadn't given willingly, she was going to take, by touching him, kissing him, arousing him, until he couldn't say no, until he was ready to die for her. He cursed her silently, viciously. He was having enough trouble with the treacherous part of himself that wanted her so intensely; how could he hold out against her now, when she had decided she would have him?

She was still smiling when she picked up her handbag. "You look very nice. I don't think I've ever seen you in anything but jeans." Or nothing at all.

He looked down at his clothes. Wearing a suit had been out of the question, since the only one he owned was packed away and wasn't appropriate for the summer heat. He had chosen, instead, a pair of khaki trousers with an emerald-green knit shirt. "Are you ready?" he asked brusquely.

"Yes."

The silence in the truck was strangely comfortable for Mariah. Cody had never been particularly talkative. His usual calm quiet was one more sign of the responsibilities he'd had to accept at such a young age.

But the silence grated on *his* nerves. When she'd been quiet, she had generally been planning something. He had to find a way to protect himself tonight, before she could plan something else. "Where do you want to eat?" he asked abruptly.

"I don't care. You can choose a place." Although she had lived in Tucson most of her life, she knew that Cody was also familiar with the city. She would trust his choice in restaurants. She reached across to turn on the radio, switching stations until she found a song that she liked. Leaning back again, she looked out the window and softly hummed along.

When she had moved, the air conditioner had picked up the airy, floral scent of her perfume, carrying it to Cody. He inhaled deeply, then squeezed his eyes shut for an instant. She used the same scent in her bath oil, powder and lotion, so her entire body smelled of it. Sweet. Erotic.

She shifted to face him as much as the seat belt would allow. "Tell me about the woman you almost married, Cody. What was her name?"

His hands tightened around the steering wheel. "Andrea." His voice sounded harsh and hoarse.

"Andrea." Mariah gave no sign of the pain that filled her with the simple speaking of the name. Had he loved her? Had he wanted her? Had he made love to her the way he had made love to Mariah—exquisitely, tenderly, lovingly? "Was she pretty?"

He didn't know. He could barely remember her face, and what he could see was shadowed by black hair, black eyes, tanned skin. "I—I guess so."

He hadn't been looking for beauty when he'd found Andrea. He had wanted...softness. Affection. Protection. He had spent too many nights alone in his bed, too many nights disturbed by dark, loving dreams. Andrea had been a way to keep the dreams at bay. She had been sweet and nice and caring, willing to give, willing to accept what little he could offer. She had been...a substitute.

"Did she love you?" Of course she had loved him. What woman could know Cody and not love him?

"I guess so."

"And when you left her? Did she still love you?"

He smiled finally, a sardonic twist of his lips. "I didn't leave her. *She* left *me*." She had known that whatever it was he needed to be happy, she couldn't provide. She had encouraged him to find the woman he loved and be happy with her. At the time, Cody had pretended that she meant he should find a woman he could love and be happy. Now he knew that she had said exactly what she'd meant. She had believed that he still loved Mariah and couldn't be truly, genuinely happy with *her* because of that love.

Mariah looked out the window at the road ahead of them. She had driven it so many times that she could drive it with a blindfold. Without a landmark to speak of, just miles of desert on either side of the highway, she knew exactly where they were. "You were hurt when she left."

Cody glanced at her. It was no longer lighthearted questioning on her part. His answers disturbed her. "Yes. Andrea was there when I needed her. I depended on her. When it was time for her to move on, she did. But I hated to let her go."

She felt the accusations in every softly spoken word. She felt the guilt. *Andrea* had been there for him. Mariah hadn't. He had been able to depend on *Andrea*. Mariah had let him down. She blinked back the tears that stung her eyes. "You didn't love her," she said softly, certainty ringing in her voice, "but you wanted to."

He didn't even need to nod. Everything about him gave the answer. Mariah turned in the seat again and looked out the side window. She envied Andrea, whoever she was. Maybe Cody had still loved Mariah, but it had been unwillingly. He hadn't wanted to care about her. He hadn't wanted to need her. She smiled sadly. She would rather have no more than lust, willingly given, than love, taken by force.

Cody wanted to say something, to wipe away the glimmer of unhappiness he'd seen in her eyes, but he couldn't find the right words to cheer her without causing more damage to himself. At last he settled on a subject more likely to bring an argument than cheer her. But arguing was better than crying. He could stand up to an angry Mariah; a tearful one was likely to lead him right into bed and God knew where else.

"What happened to your great career?"

She knew what he was doing. He didn't want to see her cry. That was something she would keep in mind for the future. "My career?" she echoed.

"Yeah. The one you couldn't have in Esperanza. The one that meant so damn much to you."

"I enjoyed my work. Since I speak Spanish, I worked with mostly Hispanic and Mexican families. It was very rewarding. But..." She sighed in remembrance. "It was depressing, too, to see people who were trying so hard to make it, and they just had so many problems."

"And they were turning for help to a woman who knew nothing about problems, about poverty or hunger or abuse or any of a thousand other difficulties a family can have. What did you do? Hand out Daddy's money to them? After all, that's how you handled your own problems."

"Don't be ridiculous." She folded her hands primly in her lap. "I used Chad's money."

The laugh came from somewhere deep inside him and was out before he could stop it. Mariah smiled smugly. Even if they spent the rest of the evening bitterly arguing, she would have this small bit of progress to comfort her: she had made Cody laugh about money.

He chose a family-run restaurant that served the best Mexican food in the city, he claimed. It was small but too crowded and too brightly lit to be considered at all intimate—probably the real reason that he had chosen it, Mariah thought. She didn't mind, though. They still had the long drive home ahead of them, and he couldn't avoid her then.

After they'd given their orders to a pretty girl of about sixteen, Mariah began a new conversation. She sat comfortably in her chair, her fingers laced together and resting on the red cotton tablecloth. "What did you do for eight years to stay away from Esperanza?"

Cody shrugged. "I worked."

"Doing what?"

"Whatever jobs I could find."

It was clear that he didn't want to discuss the past anymore, but Mariah ignored that. "What kind of jobs?"

This was it, he thought grimly. The first cold, deliberate lie he would tell her. He had no doubt that there would be more in the future. "Construction, farming, ranching—anything."

"Where?"

Cody knew the rules of lying: keep it simple, stick as close to the truth as possible. "California and Texas, mostly."

"Were you happy?"

He stared at her for a long, long time before turning his head away. Pretending interest in the diners around them, he shrugged. "Do you know anyone who's really happy?"

"My mother and father, Arcadio and Bonita, Rosalie and Antonio." She ticked each name off on a slender finger, then smiled triumphantly. "That's six, and I didn't even have to think about it."

"What about you?"

She leaned closer to him. "I'm sorry. I didn't hear that."

He looked at her, then away again. She'd heard, all right. She just wanted him to repeat it. "It wasn't important," he said crossly.

"I believe your question had something to do with me. Pardon my ego, but I think I'm pretty darned important."

She had been the most important thing in his life for far too long. He couldn't let her have that position again just because she wanted it—not until he was certain that he could deal with it.

When he didn't repeat the question, Mariah fell silent, too. Apparently she wasn't as important in Cody's eyes as she would like to be.

The silence held through their meal and until they were leaving Tucson. At first Cody had been glad that she had finally shut up, but it didn't take him long to miss the soft, husky sound of her voice. He searched for some safe topic of conversation—something that would neither anger nor hurt nor sadden—but he could find nothing. Everything in their lives had been so intense—their relationship, their separation, their reunion.

Finally, he settled on the city disappearing in the desert behind them as an acceptable subject. "Do you miss living in Tucson or Phoenix?"

Mariah looked surprised—not by his question, but because he had bothered to speak to her at all. She glanced at him across the cab, lit by the silvery glow of moonlight, and smiled. "No." It was a simple answer, with no qualifiers. There was absolutely nothing about the city that she missed—not her friends, her parents, the shopping or the cultural events.

"You don't regret giving up your life in the big city and moving to Esperanza?" he asked mockingly.

She looked at him again, but this time there was no smile. She was very serious. "I regret a lot of things in my life, Cody, but that's not one of them."

She knew he would ask the obvious question. He tried very hard not to, to think of something else, but after a few minutes, he gave in to the need to know. "What things do you regret, Mariah?"

For a moment she didn't respond. The answer she was going to give was simple and honest, but it would give him the perfect chance to hurt her. But, her voice low, she gave it anyway. "You. I regret not marrying you. If I could go back and do it again, I would forget about school and a career and all those other unimportant things. I would marry you, and I would never, ever let you go.''

The impact her response had on him was stunning. He admired the courage it took to make such a statement—courage that he himself lacked—but more than admiration, he felt desire. He wanted her more at that moment than ever before in his life. His heart pounded and echoed in his ears, pumping heated blood through his veins until he felt feverish. His muscles were taut, knotted with the effort it took to stop from reaching for her.

He tried for a teasing tone to cover the intensity of his reaction. Instead he sounded gruff. ''You take your chances—making a statement like that when I'm driving down the road at sixty miles an hour.''

''Life is full of chances, isn't it? If you don't take a few, it can be awfully boring.''

''And if you do take them?''

''Maybe you'll be very happy.''

''And maybe you'll be miserable.''

''Is that what you were with me, Cody? 'Miserable'?''

It had been nine years since he'd first met her. One summer had been very, very good, and one summer had been very, very bad. The rest of that first year had been good despite some serious arguments from Mariah about finishing school, but the remaining eight years had been awful. Miserable.

He let the silence be his answer.

Tears stung her eyes, and pain sliced through her heart. ''Since I made your life so miserable, I'm surprised that you can bear to be in the same state with me,'' she said sarcastically.

''You'll notice that I lived in California and Texas for those eight years.'' he reminded her softly.

''Then why did you come back now? After eight years, why come back?''

''Maybe I needed to suffer some more.''

''You didn't know I was here when you came back.''

He looked at her in the moonlight. His gaze was measuring, calculating. He decided to tell her the truth. ''I asked a friend of mine in Phoenix about you. She told me that you were still living there. That was when I decided that it was okay to come back home. How is it that she didn't find out about your divorce?''

Mariah shrugged, unsure whether to be hurt or pleased that he'd tried to find out about her. It wasn't very flattering to know that he wouldn't come back until he had been told that she wasn't there. Still, she could borrow some of David's reasoning: if the idea of living near her had bothered him that much, then maybe he cared more than he was letting on. ''The divorce was very quiet. One of Chad's partners handled it for us.''

''And nobody's noticed that you two haven't shown up in public together for seven months?''

She shrugged again. ''We haven't shown up in public together for a lot longer than that. It's a good thing that your friend isn't a cop. She's obviously not very good at investigating people.''

Cody stiffened slightly. If Mariah had any idea that Karen was a federal agent, she would probably choke on that last remark. Still, he had to admit that she was right. No matter how quiet the divorce, Karen should have found out about it with a few calls.

''So why did you come back now?'' she asked again. ''Did you run out of work in Texas?''

''How do you know I was in Texas before I came here?''

''Because those are Texas plates on this truck,'' she said in a voice that asked how dumb could he be. ''It's a mighty big state. Surely you could have found something there to keep you away from Arizona.''

''My reasons for coming back here are none of your business.''

''Oh? Why not tell me anyway and let me decide?'' She didn't know why she was pushing him for an answer. Maybe she wanted him to say that he had come back because of her—that eight years had been long enough to hold a grudge, that he was now ready to settle it. That would make her happy. Happy? Try ecstatic, she thought wryly. Because she was convinced that there was only one way to set-tle their past. Together. With each other. To make a future.

"Let's put it this way," he said, his voice sharp with irri-tation. "They have nothing to do with you. I didn't sud-denly start missing you, or get the urge to see you or hear your voice." No, those things had been with him all along—he had *always* missed her and wanted to see her, to talk to her. "I was ready to move on, and this place seemed con-venient. Don't flatter yourself, Mariah. I lived in Esper-anza for nine years. I knew you for one of them. I have a lot of memories of this town that have absolutely nothing to do with you."

It was a bald lie, but she didn't know it; she didn't know much about his life in Esperanza before her. She remained quiet for a long time, studying her hands in her lap. She knew without looking up when he turned off the highway onto the narrow road that led to the ranch. She even knew the exact moment when the headlights would catch the house in their beams, illuminating the soft yellow adobe. She looked up then, her gaze moving lovingly over the house. It didn't look so bad in the weak, artificial light; the places that needed repair were shadowed and less notice-able.

Cody stopped in front of her house, but he didn't turn off the engine, hoping she would take it as an unsubtle hint to get out. She didn't. Removing her seat belt, she turned sideways, leaning back against the door and looking at him. "You're right. Whatever reasons you had for coming back to the ranch, they're none of my business. They don't mat-ter anyway."

His eyes narrowed suspiciously. It wasn't like her to give in without getting the information she wanted.

"All that matters," she continued in that friendly, warm, casual voice, "is that you're here. And so am I."

Before he understood her hidden warning, she had moved across the seat to him. She turned his face toward her with the gentle pressure of her fingers. While her fingers ca-ressed the smooth line of his jaw, then moved to his cheek, she simply looked at him. Solemnly. Longingly. Hungrily.

Cody dragged in a brief, shallow breath. It wasn't enough air, but his lungs refused to accept any more. He swallowed once, twice, then dropped his gaze downward. He couldn't look into her eyes and see the need that was reflected in his own. He couldn't let her see how much he wanted her, how easily she could have him.

But in another moment his eyes were drawn back to hers. He couldn't turn away.

She leaned forward to kiss him, bringing her lips into intimate contact with his. She moved very slowly, the tip of her tongue sliding between his lips to meet the obstacle of his teeth. Without thought, he opened his mouth to her, giving her momentary refuge in the dark, moist warmth.

The moment he had seen her in that white outfit, he'd known that she had planned his seduction. With the heat, the feel, the scent, the taste, of her filling his senses, he knew that he couldn't tell her no. He should walk away—hell, he should run as fast as he could!—but he was going to stay. He was going to give in to what she wanted—what *he* wanted. What he needed.

"Oh, Mariah," he groaned, the words little more than sounds of need. He reached for her, closing his hands around the cool, satin skin of her arms and lifting her toward him.

But she didn't come willingly, as he had expected. Twisting, she pulled free of him and slid across the seat to the door. He was so surprised that he let her go.

She looked at him as she opened the door and smiled gently. "Thank you for dinner," she said softly. "I had a very nice time."

"But . . ."

She leaned over, kissed his cheek and climbed out of the truck. "Good night, Cody."

Chapter 6

Cody slowly opened one eye and looked at the bedside clock, then rolled away. It hadn't worked. He had been sure that if he closed his eyes and pretended to sleep, time would pass at its usual pace, instead of crawling, every minute lasting an hour, as it had done all night. He felt as if he had lain in bed for a lifetime, when really it had been less than six hours.

Muttering a weary curse, he got out of bed and went into the small bathroom, then turned the shower on. The cold water made him shiver, but it didn't clear the cobwebs from his mind. He could blame those on Mariah. He had spent the night tossing from one side of the bed to the other, unable to sleep for wanting her and unable to fully awaken for fear of going to her. If he had appeared at her house in the middle of the night, aroused and hard and needing to make love to her, he knew that she would have welcomed him, but he wasn't ready to take advantage of that welcome . . . yet.

It was almost seven o'clock when he got dressed and left his house. He couldn't face breakfast with Mariah and the others, so he'd decided to drive into town to eat. While he was there, he could get in touch with Kyle Parker and let him know what was happening.

Which was absolutely nothing, Cody admitted with a scowl as he went down the steps to his truck. He had learned next to nothing about David Green, because he had been concentrating all his energies on Mariah. Lovely as she was, she wasn't his job.

As he circled the truck, he became aware of the horse and rider moving slowly toward him. He cursed again. He could get in his truck and drive off. She was far enough away that he could pretend that he hadn't seen her. But he remained where he was, motionless, watching as she rode in from the desert.

Mariah slowed to a stop a few yards from him. She saw the keys dangling from his hand and knew that he had planned to avoid breakfast with her. The knowledge brought her a small smile. "Good morning."

Cody shook his head in dismay. She looked rested, fresh, beautiful. *She* had had no problem sleeping last night. "What are you doing out here?" he asked harshly.

His accusing tone made his meaning clear. She was supposed to sleep late, as usual, so he could make his escape from the ranch without seeing her. Mariah smiled again. "I wanted to take a ride before it got too hot for me to enjoy it." She looked once more at his keys. "Are you going somewhere?"

"Yes."

"Will you be back in time for dinner?"

"I don't know."

"Supper?"

"I don't know."

She calmly accepted the dark, hostile tone of his answers. It didn't bother her at all, Cody realized, that he was angry, resisting, because she knew that eventually she would win. She would get what she wanted from him.

And what was that? Did she want a lover? Did she want to prove that she could win him back? Or did she, just possibly, want *him*, the way he wanted her? Forever.

Cody backed away from the thought. An affair with her was one thing; he might be able to handle that. But forever? The only way he could handle *that* was if he still loved her, and he didn't. It had been eight years. He *couldn't* still love her... could he?

"I had a nice time last night," Mariah said softly, drawing his attention back to her. "I enjoyed being with you. Thank you."

He simply stared at her.

When she spoke again, there was a brisk efficiency to her voice. "Today's your day off. I won't hold you up any longer. Have fun."

Cody watched until she was out of sight; then he climbed into his truck. He felt off balance, confused. It was because of the lack of sleep, he decided. Not Mariah. He wouldn't give Mariah the power to disturb him that way.

He reached Esperanza and stopped at the first café he came to that was open for breakfast. From the pay phone just inside the door, he placed a call to Kyle Parker. They arranged to meet at the border patrol station in an hour.

He ate breakfast and drank several cups of strong coffee, hoping the caffeine would offer enough stimulation to put his mind back on track. He needed to be clearheaded when he met Kyle.

Cody was early for their appointment, but so was the other man. In the privacy of his office, he gave Cody a large brown envelope. "Here's the full report on David Green," he said, leaning back in his chair, a cup of coffee in his hands. "We got it in this week."

Cody skimmed over the material. It supplied the details to support the general information Green had given him last week. He had been born and raised near Wickenburg, where the Green family had owned a small ranch until ten years ago. After the ranch had been sold, David had moved to Tucson, where he had married Gayla McArthur. The marriage had ended in divorce three and a half years later; there had been no children. After the divorce, the new passion in his life had been the Central American refugees whom he smuggled into the country. He had taken a vocal political stand on their behalf, which had focused government attention on him and led to his arrest and conviction. He was still attending occasional rallies in Tucson and Phoenix to speak out against the government of Carta Blanca—a direct violation of his probation. No action would be taken on that, Cody guessed, until they had proof that he was also still smuggling aliens into the U.S.

"Anything helpful there?"

Cody shrugged. "Not really. He told me most of this last weekend." He smiled wryly. "Green's not ashamed of his record. He believes in what they were doing."

"Do you think he believes in it enough to still be doing it?"

"I don't know. His biggest concern right now seems to be Suzanne."

Kyle grinned. "Suzanne Fox is the sheriff's only daughter. She's been seeing David since he moved here. Believe me, her dad is none too pleased. He's spent all his life locking up the bad guys, and by God, no daughter of his is going to marry one of them." He laughed good-naturedly. "Of course, he hasn't yet realized that his daughter is twenty-six years old and can do whatever she wants." He paused to refill his cup from the pot behind his desk. "So Green hasn't done anything suspicious?"

Cody considered the day David and Mariah had been gone from the ranch. Suspicious? Probably only to him, and probably only because of Mariah. She had claimed that it was business, and she wasn't the kind of person who would lie. He shook his head in response to Kyle's remark.

"Too bad you can't just walk in on him with half a dozen kids." Kyle sighed. "Do you need anything? Any further information?"

Cody shook his head. "Nothing I can think of right now. I'll keep in touch." He shook Parker's hand, left the office and stood for a moment in the sunshine. It was only a little after nine o'clock. What the hell was he going to do for the rest of the day? Wander around, as he'd done last Sunday while Mariah had entertained her parents? Or go home, where he could see her, think about her, want her?

For the first time in years he wished for a friend. Someone to confide in. Someone to just spend time with. Someone to make him feel less alone.

Mariah had been his friend. As much as he had loved her, as much as he had desired her, she had also been his friend. Today he missed that part of their relationship more than he missed the lovemaking. He would have liked to be able to spend an afternoon with her, without censoring what he said and did.

He sighed. He couldn't handle another day wasted as he had wasted last Sunday. He got into his truck and headed home. Maybe, with any luck, he could sleep the day away and make up for last night's restlessness.

The small house was stifling. With the shades drawn and the curtains closed in his bedroom, the room was dark and the heat hung heavy in the air. The air conditioner did little to lower the temperature, while its steady hum did a lot to keep Cody awake. Finally, frustration and uneasiness forced him out of the bed. He pulled on his shirt as he left the house and headed toward Mariah.

She was folding towels in the laundry room, right next to the kitchen, when he entered through the back door. He leaned his shoulder against the door frame and crossed his arms over his chest, fixing a stony glare on her. "Want to do something?" he all but snarled.

She looked at him while she added a towel to the neat stack on the table in front of her. Reaching down, she pulled another from the dryer, shook it and began folding it, too. "What did you have in mind?"

She looked so calm and cool and peaceful that simply looking at her fueled Cody's anger. He jerked the towel out of her hands, tossed it on the table and pulled her hard against him. "Why don't we go to bed and put an end to this?"

She didn't struggle at all. She merely leaned back against the arm that held her so tight, pushing the lower part of her body into contact with his, and smiled faintly. "Put an end to what?"

"This . . . thing between us." It was such an inadequate phrase, but he couldn't think of anything better. "You want to sleep with me—you've made that clear. So let's do it now."

"I don't 'sleep with' men."

"But you'll sleep with me." He leaned against the washer and fitted her tightly between his legs so that she could feel nothing but his desire.

Mariah smiled again. "You think you're something special, don't you?"

"I know I am." His frustration and anger, his desire and need, made him reckless. He was so positive that she wanted him that he didn't consider the possibility that she might say no.

She rested her hands against his chest for support, feeling his heart beating there. After a long moment of silence she said, "So do I, Cody. That's why I'm not going to 'sleep with' you. You're too special—*we're* too special—to settle for sex when we can have so much more." When we can have love, she finished silently, afraid to say the word out loud when he was in this mood.

The emotions churning inside him grew even stronger, need and desire competing with his anger for control. The latter won. He pulled one of her hands from his chest and forced it between their bodies, twisting it so that it cradled his hardness. "This is all I'm offering you, sweetheart," he drawled sarcastically. "Sex. I don't want anything else from you."

Mariah stared at him for a moment while she moved her fingers into a closer, more intimate fit. She recognized the shock that darkened his eyes, heard the faint groan that he bit off, saw the blood drain from his face. "Sex, Cody?" she whispered. "You want me this much, and you try to call it sex?" She raised her other hand, slipping her fingers into the thick gold of his hair, and leaned forward to touch her lips to his. She kissed him so lightly that he hardly felt it, while lower, she touched him so gently that he would never forget it.

He groaned, low and desperate, and brought his hands up to cup her face while he kissed her hungrily, bursting with need. His kisses were hard and demanding, bordering on brutal. He was searching for satisfaction, but he succeeded only in feeding his passion, in swelling his desire, in tormenting his soul. He wanted her—dear God, he *needed* her!—but he couldn't take her like this. He couldn't satisfy himself at the risk of hurting her—and, if he took her in lust, for sex, without love, she *would* be hurt.

Groaning again, he pushed her away, then turned his back to her to lean against the washing machine. Mariah stood motionless, stunned by the intensity of his kisses and by the depth of her own need. She raised her hands to him, reaching out for more, before she realized that he was putting a stop to their seduction.

"Damn you," he whispered in a taut, tortured voice.

She sank onto a bench against the wall, drew her knees to her chin and hugged herself tightly. She willingly accepted his soft curse.

"You have no right to do that to me." He looked at her over his shoulder, his eyes a stormy blue, his mouth a thin white line. "I've gotten along without you for eight years. I don't need you. I don't want you. I don't love you."

But I love you, she thought sadly. God help me, I love you.

She smiled a bit, but it didn't touch her black eyes. They were bleak and weary. "You still feel something for me," she argued quietly. "I felt it."

"I've gotten hard with a lot of women," he said harshly. "And I didn't love any of them."

"Except me. You loved me."

"Loved—past tense. That was a long time ago. It doesn't exist anymore."

That phrase was going to make her scream out her frustration. Cody had joined the ranks—Jerry, Helen, Arcadio and David—who believed that time could heal all wounds, destroy all feelings, or somehow make a difference. They were wrong. Mariah could feel it in her heart.

Cody dragged his fingers through his hair. "It's just sex, Mariah. Why can't you be satisfied with that? Why do you have to make it something more?"

She unfolded her legs and stood up, leaning down to get an armful of clothes from the dryer. When she moved to the table, Cody walked across the room to the safety of the door. "Because it *isn't* just sex." She spoke in a calm, un-emotional voice, belied by the trembling of her hands as she worked. "Sex is what you have with some woman you pick up in a bar, some woman you'll never see again. Sex is brief, selfish and basic. It involves your body. It has nothing to do with your mind or your heart."

He couldn't argue with her. As angry as he was, he couldn't call her a liar; he couldn't claim that he wanted only sex and none of the emotional pleasures of making love. "You're complicating everything," he said darkly. His life, his job, his needs—nothing was simple anymore because of her.

She smiled. In spite of the pain she felt inside, her smile was almost serene. "If you want sex—just simple sex, with no emotions to complicate it—go into town. You'll find a lot of women there who are more than willing to accept that. But when you've had enough of women who don't care about you, of women you don't care about, I'll be waiting."

Cody was furious again. Anger had driven him to suggest that they go to bed in the first place; now he stormed out of the house without another word, before it prompted him to do something he would regret later.

She was the most manipulative bitch he'd ever known, he raged as he saddled one of the horses. She knew damn well that he would be back, and there wouldn't be any other women in the meantime, either. She knew that he had lied to her—that he wasn't interested in just sex, that he wanted *her*, that he needed her. Damn her to hell, she probably knew that he loved her.

He swore so viciously that the horse warily stepped away. He *did not* love her! That his love was gone, that it no longer existed, was probably the only truthful thing he'd told her today. The only thing he could allow himself to feel was lust. Nothing but lust.

And Lord, he thought, settling carefully into the saddle, he was doing a damn fine job of feeling that.

Mariah folded the rest of the clothes, loaded them into a basket and put them in their proper places. When she was finished with that task, she went into her bedroom, locked the door, sat down on the bed and buried her head in her hands. She was torn between joy and sorrow.

Cody wanted her. No matter how hard he tried to deny it, no matter what excuses he thought up, he wanted *her*.

And he hated wanting her, she acknowledged sadly. He hated her.

How was it possible that the man who had taught her everything she knew about living and loving could now hate her? Maybe she was wrong to try to make him care for her again. Maybe she should stay out of his way until he gave some sign that he wanted her friendship. Of course by that time she would be gray haired, bent with age and unable to remember the joy of his lovemaking.

She fell back on the bed, letting her head hang over the side. The ends of her hair rubbed back and forth over the gleaming rusty-red tiles. She needed patience—that was all.

A world of patience.

Cody was wary around Mariah the next few days, his blue eyes narrowing every time she came near. Finally, Tuesday evening, she stopped him as he was leaving the house after dinner. "Can I talk to you?"

He looked at her hand where it rested against his bare forearm. There was such distaste in his expression that she rapidly pulled it back.

"What do you want?" he asked bluntly.

"I just wanted to tell you that you don't have to act so skittish, like I'm going to attack you without warning." Her face was flushed a deep red, and she was twisting her hands together. "I won't come to your house. I won't ask you out.

I won't kiss you or touch you or even talk to you, if that's what you want."

If that's what you want. Cody closed his eyes briefly to hide the sadness in her face. What did he want? The same thing he'd wanted nine years ago, when he had first seen the boss's daughter standing outside the stables. He wanted to make her his. He wanted to be her friend, her lover, her husband. He wanted to be the most important person in her life. He wanted to be the only person who could make her life complete.

But he didn't want to be hurt again. He didn't want to fall in love, only to have it end too soon, too painfully. He didn't want to neglect the obligations he had to his job. He didn't want to deceive Mariah and Arcadio and the others.

He opened his eyes again and spoke gently. "I don't want you to feel like you have to constantly avoid me, but...I don't want to make love to you." He pretended not to see the flash of pain in her eyes.

"Maybe...maybe we could be friends," she suggested, just a hint of desperation in her voice. Anything would be better than nothing.

"I've been alone so long that I'm not sure I know how to be friends. I'm not sure I have anything to offer a friend." He was trying to warn her that friendship would solve none of their problems. He wasn't certain it was even possible, considering their past—and present—emotional involvement for them to be friends and nothing else.

Mariah accepted his answer as a flat refusal. She smiled a tight little smile and stepped back. "All right." Turning on her heel, she disappeared inside the house and down the hall.

Cody looked up at the darkening sky and gave a deep sigh. He was tired. He might have been strong enough to fight himself, but he couldn't fight both himself and Mariah. He couldn't stand up to a united front much longer. Sooner or later, she was going to get what she wanted—what *he* wanted. He hoped they both survived it intact.

* * *

Wednesday morning was hot. Every summer day in the desert was hot, Mariah knew, but there was something especially oppressive about this day's heat. By eight o'clock it had sapped her energy and left her feeling slow and sluggish. Now, two hours later, she was wrung out. She wished she was sitting in her air-conditioned office, or in the house with its thick walls and cool tile floors. Anyplace would be better than Efraín's tiny, ovenlike house.

Windows and doors stood open wide, and boxy electric fans droned, stirring hot air and dust. Mariah sat on the linoleum floor, her legs crossed, a tiny girl folded in her arms. For Raquel's sake, Mariah wished she had brought her own car instead of the station wagon. The Grand Am, with its air conditioning and smooth ride, would have provided Raquel with a more comfortable trip to Tucson, where Father Espinoza and Lissa awaited her and the others.

A thin film of perspiration lined the sleeping baby's face. Occasionally Mariah used a dishrag given her by Efraín's wife to wipe it away. How could she sleep so restfully, so peacefully? Couldn't she feel the discomfort of the heat, the tension that kept the other three children solemnly silent?

"Isn't she lovely?" Katy, Efraín's wife, knelt beside Mariah, offering her a glass of iced water.

Mariah nodded, looking from the girl to the woman. Katy was American. She had met Efraín eight years ago during her first visit to Mexico. She had married him and moved with him to the poor village of San Benito and, she swore, had never been happier.

"She could pass as your daughter," Katy said softly, reaching out to brush a lock of fine black hair from the baby's forehead. "With you being so dark and speaking Spanish so fluently, you could fool just about anyone into believing that you're Mexican, too."

Mariah stared down at Raquel again. No daughter of hers would ever have to face the horror that this baby had already lived through in less than a year. Three months ago Raquel had been the treasured baby girl of a doctor and a schoolteacher, with four healthy, happy brothers and sisters. Then the soldiers had come, spraying their house over and over with machine-gun fire. The men had been in too much of a hurry to check their victims, and so they had missed the terrified, screaming baby hidden under the body of her dead mother. Neighbors had found her later and turned her over to refugee workers in the next town. Eventually, she had been entrusted to the care of guides who brought the children across Guatemala, Honduras and Mexico, and she had found her way north.

Soon she would reach the church-sponsored home that Father Espinoza and the others had chosen. She would be classified for legal purposes as abandoned, and she would then be placed in a home, with a new family to love and treasure her. She would have no memory of her mother and father, her two sisters and her two brothers, who had been massacred for no earthly reason.

David entered the house, followed by Efraín. "As soon as I wash up, we're ready to go."

Mariah nodded once, handing Raquel to Katy. They should have left half an hour ago, but the left rear tire on the station wagon had developed a leak. Better to fix it now, David had decided, instead of risking a flat, or worse, with the children in the car.

"Take care," Katy said, cradling the baby close to her breast.

"We will." Mariah went outside to the car to wait. David was driving this time; she didn't have the energy to expend on the task. She opened the door and gingerly slid inside the car. The vinyl seat crackled as it burned the exposed portion of her legs.

"One of these days you'll remember to wear jeans or bring a towel to sit on," David said with a grin as he climbed behind the wheel.

"One of these days," she said with a matching grin, "we'll junk this car and buy something halfway decent—with air conditioning."

David chatted idly as they drove back across the border and to their prearranged meeting place. While he met the children and Efraín, Mariah dragged a battered, second-hand baby seat from the back and set it in the middle of the front seat. Maybe if anybody noticed them, she thought as she tugged the seat belt through the unfamiliar device, they would think they were just a normal family—father, mother and four children. As Katy had pointed out, Mariah was dark, and most people wouldn't look closely enough to detect the differences between her and the children.

"You take care of her," David said, handing the baby carefully over the back seat, "and I'll get these three settled. Then we'll get out of here and be on our way."

Raquel had awakened during the rough cross-country ride in Efraín's truck. Now she stared at Mariah with wide, dark eyes. There were no tears, no crying, just that long, solemn stare. "What do you suppose she's thinking?" Mariah wondered as she buckled Raquel into the infant seat.

"Probably that she's hot, hungry and needs a clean diaper." David finished with the third child and took his seat behind the steering wheel. "You ready?"

"Not quite. Do you know how to work one of these things?" She held the ends of the various belts in her hands. When David gave her a chiding look, she threaded the ends through various loops before finally snapping them together. "That looks about right. Let's go."

It was a long, uneventful trip. The three children in the back seat were quiet—abnormally so, in Mariah's opinion. Raquel was beginning to whimper when they reached the Tucson city limits, but her tears didn't start in earnest until they were pulling into the church parking lot. She quieted as soon as Mariah freed her from the tangle of belts and picked her up.

"Isn't she lovely?" Lissa asked, meeting them just inside the door.

Mariah nodded in agreement as she reluctantly handed the baby to her friend. She cared about all the children who passed through her life, but Raquel was the first one whom she hated to let go. It was only because she was a baby, Mariah thought, and she had wanted a baby so badly herself; Cody's return had made her remember that so clearly.

"Are we still on for lunch?" Lissa asked.

Mariah grimaced. She had forgotten her promise to have lunch with her friend on her next trip into town. "Do you mind if we do it some other time?" She just didn't feel like answering the questions that Lissa was sure to ask.

"Sure, no problem." Lissa studied her for a moment, then asked in concern, "Are you okay?"

Mariah nodded again. "I'm fine," she replied, but she knew she didn't sound convincing.

"You want to talk about it?"

She didn't pretend ignorance. "No. There's not much to say."

"How is he?"

"He's okay."

"He's okay, you're okay, the whole world's okay—and you look miserable." Lissa shifted Raquel and gave Mariah a hug with her free arm. "If you decide you want to talk, you know where to reach me."

She smiled. "Thanks. I'll remember that."

David suggested that they eat lunch before going home, and Mariah listlessly agreed. As soon as they had completed a meal of fast-food burgers and fries, they headed back to the ranch.

It was after two o'clock when they arrived. Mariah didn't bother to change clothes; she went straight to her office in the stables and began sorting through the mail piled on her desk. The sharp rap at the door a few minutes later startled her. None of the men ever knocked; they just came right in.

It was Cody, and he had knocked because he felt the urge to hit something. The solid wood door had seemed as good a choice as anything. When she called out, he opened the door, went inside and let it slam behind him. "Where have you been?"

Mariah stared at him. "What business is it of yours?"

"I'm making it my business. Where did you go this morning?" he demanded crossly. He wasn't in the mood to make a stab at friendliness. It was too damn hot, and he'd been too damn worried ever since he'd seen her drive away hours earlier with David Green.

Mariah eyed him warily as she slit open an envelope containing one more bill that she couldn't afford. She glanced at the amount, stifled a groan and replied, "To Tucson."

"Why did Green go with you?"

"Because I asked him to."

"Why?"

"I wanted his company. It's a long drive."

"What did you do there?"

"I had to take care of some personal business." That was an honest enough answer, she decided. Her smuggling was a very personal business. "Would you like to sit down?"

Cody wavered. As the room's air conditioner cooled his body, the anger that had brought him storming in was also starting to cool. He hesitated, then pulled the chair from Arcadio's desk and dropped into it. When he spoke again, his voice was cooler, too. "If all you wanted was company, why didn't you ask me to go?"

Mariah's face darkened into a frown. "I wanted *friendly* company." She dropped the bill into a pile with the rest of them and picked up another envelope. "Cody, just last night you said you didn't want to be friends with me."

"No, I didn't." He stared at the sole of one boot, his brows drawn together in a scowl. "I also said I didn't want to make love to you," he muttered. "And you know I was lying." Before she could respond to that, he looked up, his eyes dark blue and accusing. "Damn it, Mariah, what are you doing, going off with Green all the time? Where do you go? What do you do?"

"We go to a seedy little motel in the city and make mad, passionate love," she replied flippantly. She scooped up a pile of empty envelopes, dropped them into the waste can next to her desk and pushed the mail aside so she could lean her elbows on the desk. "Don't be foolish, Cody. If David and I wanted to have an affair, we wouldn't have to leave this ranch to do it."

Cody stared down again. He was jealous—pure and simple. Only there wasn't anything pure about such an ugly emotion, and nothing simple about the complexity of it. Just last night she had offered to leave him alone—and that was the only way he was going to avoid an affair with her—and here he was, seeking out her company. All because she'd spent a few hours with another man.

"Any other questions?" she asked gently. She couldn't be angry with him. She understood jealousy far too well to blame him for his behavior. She got jealous every time she even thought of another woman with Cody; seeing him with one, believing that that woman meant something to him, would be more than she could bear.

"Why him? Where did you meet him? Why did you hire him? How well do you know him?" It occurred to him as he asked the questions that this was information that Cody Daniels the border patrol agent would be interested in, but that was incidental. There was no doubt in his mind that Cody Daniels the man was asking.

"I met David about a year ago. He was associated with a group of people, mostly church workers, who brought refugees from Central America into the United States. They smuggled them in, provided them with places to live, with jobs, and helped them avoid detection by Immigration." Mariah leaned back in her chair, crossing one long tanned leg over the other. "I was working in Phoenix for a church-sponsored social services agency. We dealt a lot with immigrants, legal and illegal. So did David's group. When refugees were picked up by INS or the border patrol, he and his friends tried to arrange bond while they awaited deportation hearings. They helped them apply for political asylum, provided them with legal counsel, made certain that their rights weren't violated."

Cody bristled at the suggestion that he and his fellow border patrol agents would violate anyone's rights—after all, David Green and his outlaw friends weren't the only people around familiar with immigration law—but he kept his mouth shut.

"Anyway," she continued with a sigh, "that's how we met."

"So you worked with illegals."

She frowned at the term. "Illegal aliens" sounded bad enough—like creatures from some other planet—but she detested the shortened "illegals." She asked him a question that people in movements such as hers frequently asked—and to which they never received an acceptable reply. "How can any human being be 'illegal'?"

Cody had heard the question before, too. He shrugged impatiently. "You know what I mean, Mariah. You provided assistance to people who were living here illegally."

"I suppose I did. It was my job to help people who needed help. When a man came in and said he needed a place for his family to spend the night, I didn't ask to see his immigration papers. When a woman told me that her children were hungry, I didn't ask her if they had permission from INS to starve on this side of the border. Law enforcement wasn't part of my job."

The mention of law enforcement made him distinctly uncomfortable. He tried to put it out of his mind and concentrate on his questions. "So you met Green through your job. Why did you hire him after he lost his last job? Why hire a convicted felon?"

"Why not?" she challenged softly.

He gave no response.

"He's a good cowhand. And a good friend. I wanted to help him."

At last the agent in him surfaced. Carefully, trying to appear casual, he asked, "Is he still smuggling?"

Mariah prayed the tension that suddenly knotted her muscles didn't show. She took a few deep breaths, laced her fingers together lightly and smiled. "I try not to snoop into my employee's private lives. All I ask is that they work hard and earn the salary I pay them. You, of course, are an exception to that rule." The smile faded. "That's natural, I suppose, since you never were *just* an employee."

She had neatly avoided answering his question, Cody noticed. Because Green was no longer involved with the smuggling ring? Or because he *was*? How much did she know? "Is Green 'just an employee'?"

"David is an employee and a friend." She put gentle emphasis on the last word, reminding him that she had offered to be *his* friend. "I don't sleep with friends, Cody."

He couldn't question her further. Deceiving her was bad enough; interrogating her to gain information to use against Green was too much. "So how was Tucson?"

"Not as interesting as it was Saturday night." She grinned at the obvious discomfort the memory brought him. Which part made him uneasy—the talk on the way there? The brief conversation at the restaurant? Or the events when they got back? "Maybe we can go back sometime."

"Maybe." Cody stood up and tidily pushed the chair back in place, out of the way. At the door, he put his hat on and tipped it back on his forehead. "Maybe soon."

He went back to work, grimly enduring the blazing heat. He had worked outside in the sun most of his life, and it showed—in the even brown tint of his skin and the tiny lines at the corners of his eyes. Heat like this was aging, he thought, wiping his shirtsleeve across his brow. It wasn't like this in Chicago. If he'd gotten that transfer to the border patrol detachment at O'Hare, he wouldn't be roasting in the sun nine months a year and baking at a slightly lower temperature the other three.

And he wouldn't have seen Mariah again. Somehow, tolerating the heat seemed a fair price for seeing her.

"Daniels."

The silly grin he was wearing disappeared when he recognized David Green's voice. He turned around to look at him.

"I heard you talking to Mariah in the office. If you have any questions about me, why don't you try asking me?" David was quiet, serious.

Cody fixed a narrow blue stare on him. "What you heard had nothing to do with you."

"I heard my name—"

"The conversation *wasn't* about you." The steeliness of his voice dared David to argue with him.

David nodded in understanding. The conversation had been about Mariah and a man. This time it happened to be him, but it could have been any man who stirred Cody's jealousy. "Mariah's a special woman," he said quietly. "She's beautiful, intelligent, compassionate, kindhearted and sexy as hell.'' He saw Cody's gaze narrow even more with suspicion. "She's also loyal, to her parents, her friends, her land . . . and to her man.''

Cody had never considered it that way before, but he supposed it was logical: if Mariah was his woman, then he must be her man. It was an odd sounding phrase, with an oddly satisfying ring to it.

"Can I ask you something?'' David paused. When Cody gave no response one way or the other, he ventured the question, "Does it bother you that I have a criminal record?''

"No. Why should it?''

"You asked Mariah why she hired a convicted felon. It sounded to me like you have something against crooks and criminals. A lot of people do.''

He was talking about Suzanne's father, Cody guessed. Too bad David hadn't met her before he'd gotten caught smuggling. If he truly loved her, she probably could have talked him into quitting. "Considering what you were charged with,'' he said slowly, "no, it doesn't particularly bother me. If the crime was different, something violent...'' He hesitated for one long moment. "I wouldn't let you get within a mile of her.''

David gave a quiet sigh of relief. "You know, it wouldn't hurt to tell *her* that you care about her.''

Cody squinted and looked up at the sky. It was almost white from horizon to horizon. Then he looked back at David. "Hell,'' he drawled lazily, "*she's* the one who told *me*.''

Chapter 7

Hey, boss lady, want to go into town with us?'' Philip called as he unsaddled his horse. "Suzanne's having a party at her house tonight, and everyone's invited. What do you say? Want to go?''

Mariah was leaning one shoulder against the door frame. Philip was in front of her, David off to one side, and Cody behind him. At the invitation, Cody looked up, his eyes meeting hers. He seemed to be saying something, but she didn't know what. Was he going? Did he want her to go? Did he want her to stay? Or didn't he care one way or the other?

She dropped her eyes to her feet, watching the scuffed leather of her roundtoed boots ripple as she wiggled her toes inside. "Um...thanks, Philip, but...I'm kind of tired...." She could feel her face turning red with the awkwardly told lie. It wasn't easy, trying to give Philip one message and Cody another with the same brief answer.

"What about you, Cody?'' Philip looked at the other man. "Saturday nights are for partying. There will be a lot of people there—some that you probably remember from before.''

Cody shook his head. "I may drop by later," he remarked nonchalantly, "but right now I'm not interested in anything more than a shower and a nap before dinner."

"Hey, it'll be fun," the younger man persisted. "All the single women in town are going to be there—and some of the married ones, too. It'll beat all hell out of spending the evening alone." His grin was engaging. He reminded Cody of an overgrown kid trying to wheedle his pals into doing what *he* wanted.

Cody glanced surreptitiously at Mariah. She was staring uncomfortably at her narrow, booted feet, refusing to look at any of them. She wasn't going to leave him to spend the evening alone—he was counting on it. "I like being alone occasionally, Philip," he said with an indulgent smile. "It's a part of growing old. You learn to appreciate your own company."

"Not me," Philip swore. "I'll never prefer my own company to that of a woman."

And neither would he, Cody silently agreed. Not to *this* woman's. He could think of nothing he preferred to her.

"Come on, Philip," David said. "Let's clean up and get going."

"Have fun," Mariah said as the two men left.

David paused for a moment, looking from Cody to Mariah. He smiled a little. "You too."

After their departure, the silence seemed deafening. Philip could chatter like no one Mariah had ever met, and sometimes it drove her crazy, but right now she wouldn't have minded a little of his gift for gab.

"Well?"

She looked up at Cody. He still stood across the big room from her. Afraid to come closer? she wondered. Their meetings had been easier since Wednesday's talk about David, but he hadn't been particularly encouraging. Still, he hadn't been *dis*couraging, either.

She cleared her throat a bit nervously. "You might want to change your mind and accept their invitation. Bonita and Arcadio have gone to spend the night in Sonoita with her sister, and Antonio and Rosalie are staying in Nogales tonight—it's her mother's birthday. The only dinner you'll get here will be turkey sandwiches, and the only company will be mine."

What more could he ask? "Well, if I get too bored or develop indigestion, I can always go to Suzanne's party later."

His teasing drawl, to say nothing of the light in his eyes, made her uneasy. She had been pursuing this man since his return. Unless her intuition was totally wrong, he had finally stopped running, and she didn't know why. Now *she* wanted to run.

He *had* stopped. He couldn't outrace his memories, his need, his emotions. He had known the night he kissed her on his porch that he would make love to her—at some time, some place. It had been inevitable, unavoidable. Yet he had been trying to avoid it with every ounce of strength he had. Now his strength had run out. His fear had run out. Now, tonight, nothing was holding him back.

"I—I'm going to the house. When you're ready for dinner, come on up." She pushed herself away from the wood that had supported her and left the building. She had to fight the urge to run, to find a place to hide herself away. Clenching her hands into fists, she forced herself to walk slowly, calmly. There she would follow Cody's lead, she decided. She would take a shower and a nap, and maybe in her sleep she would find the courage to deal with him.

The house was cool, dark and quiet. She undressed in her bathroom, throwing her dirty clothes into a tall wooden hamper that stood in the corner. Pushing the clear curtain back, she stepped into the bathtub and turned on the shower.

For sore muscles, she took hot baths, but her showers were refreshingly cool. She stood there under the water for what seemed like hours, until the sweat and grime disappeared under the flow. She shampooed her hair until it squeaked, shaved her legs so they were like satin, washed her body with her favorite scented soap. At last she shut off the taps, wrung the water from her hair, stepped out onto a soft tan mat and reached for a towel.

* * *

Cody sat down in a hand-carved wooden chair in the corner and looked around. He had never been in the master bedroom before. When Mariah had visited in the past, she had always slept in the room at the end of the hall. It was farthest from her parents and closest to the door that led outside. That had been his door. That had been the way she had sneaked him past her parents when they, too, were visiting.

The walls were white stucco, the floor rust-colored tiles. There were four windows, two on the side, facing east, two in the front, facing south. They were wide and deeply set. The outer adobe walls were about thirty inches thick, providing wide ledges for each window. *Sombrajes*, shutters made of wood frames crossed with long, thin branches, were open to allow natural light to illuminate the room.

The furniture had been kept to a minimum: a double bed, two nightstands, a tall armoire-style cabinet and the chair where he sat. Each piece was made of solid ponderosa pine—heavy, golden brown, elaborately carved. Though not old, the furniture was valuable for its exacting workmanship and detail.

Cody's gaze was drawn back to the bed. It was neatly made, covered with a plump, quilted comforter. The fabric bespoke the Southwest craze in everything from architecture to furnishings to art to food. The background was a deep coppery red, with diamonds, triangles and stripes in black, brown, tan and turquoise. It must provide a vivid contrast to her smooth tan skin and straight black hair, he thought.

He swallowed hard and glanced at the door that led to the bathroom. The water had stopped ten minutes ago, and there hadn't been another sound. What was she doing?

Then the door opened.

He hadn't touched a thing in the room, hadn't moved, hadn't spoken. Still, Mariah felt his presence before she saw him. She stopped in the bathroom door, and her hands stilled in the process of wrapping a thick turquoise towel around her damp hair.

He was sprawled in the chair as if it were comfortable, when she knew for a fact it wasn't. He looked relaxed and at ease. At home.

Cody stared at her. It wasn't a situation in which most women would feel comfortable—just out of the shower, hair dripping water, wearing a robe and nothing else—no make-up, no jewelry, nothing to hide behind. But Mariah looked beautiful, heartachingly beautiful, and only slightly surprised.

She took a step into the room. Instead of wrapping the towel turban-style around her head, she rubbed its softness back and forth over her hair, soaking up the worst of the water.

"Do you want me to leave?"

She shook her head. She couldn't speak.

He rose fluidly from the chair and approached her. "Have I told you since I came back that you're beautiful?"

She nodded. He had told her at his house that Sunday night, and he had hated saying it, had hated thinking it. But this time there was no anger in his voice, no dismay—only low, hoarse desire.

"You are. When I was gone, I compared every woman I saw to you, but none of them were as beautiful...not one." He swallowed over the thickness in his throat. Knowing it would quicken the spread of the heat that was taking him over, he let his gaze move slowly, caressingly, over her.

She was wearing a short satin kimono in her favorite white. It was belted at her waist, emphasizing her slenderness. It ended at midthigh, revealing her long, tanned, muscled legs, and underneath it, she was naked. Through the rich fabric, he could see her nipples, hard with excitement. She wanted him.

That could almost be enough, he thought with a touch of wistfulness—to be wanted like this. If for some reason she couldn't love him, he could probably settle for being wanted until the love came.

He had promised himself only lust. Some lust. Here he was facing the woman of his dreams—she was wearing nothing but a flimsy little robe; his body was responding violently to the mere sight and scent of her; she was waiting for him to take her—and all he could think about was being loved.

Mariah held herself motionless. She was throbbing for Cody's touch, to become one with him once again, but she didn't move. He had to be the one to initiate their lovemaking. If he changed his mind later, she didn't want him to demean what they were about to share by claiming that she had seduced him. Keeping herself under taut control, she raised her chin to look at him while she waited.

He had showered, too. His hair was slightly damp, lying in dark gold waves, and he smelled of soap and water and sunshine. His shirt was sky blue, a few shades lighter than his eyes, and his jeans were crisp indigo, unbearably snug fitting. He was so handsome.

He whispered her name, and it seemed to echo in the silence of the house. He was as nervous as he'd been the very first time they had made love, when he had been faced with a sweet, young, eager virgin who had wanted nothing more than to be his lover. She had become his love . . . his life.

"I . . . I'm not prepared for this," he said hoarsely.

Her brow wrinkled; then she smiled. "That's all right."

All right how? Was she on the pill? Was it the wrong time for her to conceive? Or was it all right to risk pregnancy? He had to know. "Are you . . . ?"

She nodded once. "*I'm* prepared."

Cody wondered at the disappointment that flashed through him. The vision of Mariah pregnant with his child was arousing enough to wring a groan from him. He had wanted children—he had planned for them. Someday he would have them.

He raised his hand to touch her hair. As he gathered the silken strands in his fingers, the towel slid from her nerveless fingers to the floor, landing in a turquoise puddle at their feet. His feet were sockless in worn leather sneakers. Hers were bare—long, narrow, oddly elegant.

The satin of her robe was cool beneath his callused hands. Her skin was heated. He brushed the fabric back to reveal one shoulder, smooth and hollowed.

She closed her eyes as his fingers slid along her skin, following the fabric as it plunged in a deep V. When he reached the hollow between her small, aching breasts, she caught her breath, waiting for him to touch them, to stroke so exquisitely over her nipples.

Instead he drew his hand back. She opened her eyes, ready to plead with him not to leave her this time, but he wasn't leaving. His blue eyes locked with her black ones, and he began undoing his shirt, each snap pulling slowly apart with a pop. He tugged the shirt free of his jeans and slid it off his shoulders, letting it fall to the floor.

Like the rest of him, his chest was perfection. It was smooth, tanned, with small, pebble-hard nipples, baby-soft skin and steely muscles. Mariah's fingers ached to touch him, but she resisted. *Not until he asks you to.*

He shifted his weight to one foot while he removed a shoe. Shifting again, he dropped the other shoe to the floor with a thump. His belt came undone with one easy movement, and the button on his jeans slid free with a twist of his wrist. He tugged the zipper to its end and began sliding the denim over his hips.

Mariah gave up his mesmerizing stare to watch him undress. He stood before her, strong, muscular, bronzed, handsome and fully aroused. Incredibly aroused. For just an instant, she, too, remembered their first time together. She had never seen a naked man before, and for a moment she had been afraid that he was too large, or she was too small. But they had fitted together perfectly, then and every other time. Today would be no different.

With his clothes out of the way, Cody turned back to Mariah. He laid his hands on her shoulders, closing his fingers gently around her delicately shaped bones, and drew her to him. The cool satin robe touched his body and immediately turned to fire.

Wrapping his arms around her, he laid his cheek against her hair and simply held her for a long moment. He could smell the fragrance of her hair, could feel the softness of her body pressed against his, from head to toe. There was a comfort in holding her that he had forced himself to forget;

now the memory returned slowly from the dark corners of his mind. It made him feel safe, strong; nothing could ever go wrong as long as she was in his arms. She was his refuge.

He tilted her head back, holding his palms gently against her cheeks, and lowered his mouth to hers. He tasted her with tentative kisses, nipping her full lower lip, tugging it gently between his teeth. When finally his tongue dipped inside the warmth of her mouth, she was ready, eagerly opening to him. His mouth was hard, pressing against the soft flesh of her lips, but she didn't feel the discomfort. She felt nothing but Cody.

Without stopping the heated assault of his kisses, he slid his hands slowly from her face. His thumbs traced along the slender line of her throat until he reached the satin that covered her. He liked the feel of the fabric—so rich and elegant, like Mariah herself. At last he reached her breasts, and his hands cupped them. They were small, but delicately perfect in shape and absolutely beautiful.

Mariah made a soft sound of pleasure as he rubbed back and forth over her nipples, which were already hard and aching for his attention. She raised her hands to her belt, fumbling with the knot she had tied earlier. When she finally freed it, her robe fell open.

Cody pushed the satin over her shoulders and slowly drew it down her arms, tantalizing her with soft, cool, erotic caresses before he let it fall. Taking her hands, he guided her to the bed, gently laying her down on the vivid colors and patterns of the comforter. He had been right earlier: her smooth tan skin and her black hair, fanned out around her, enhanced the brilliance of the cover.

Slowly he lowered himself to her, fitting himself snugly into the cradle of her hips. He was only millimeters from being a part of her, one with her. Supporting himself on his arms, he stared down at her. "Mariah . . . are you sure?"

Reaching up, she twined her arms around his neck and kissed him with a hunger as intense, as violent, as his own. "I'm sure," she whispered with a dazed smile. Sliding her hands down his spine, she reached the enticing curve of his buttocks and pulled him to her.

His entry was slow, smooth and sure. When he had filled her and his hips were pressed closely, intimately, against hers, Cody smiled. In his lifetime, he had never met another woman who matched him as perfectly as this one did, he marveled. He had never felt so complete as he did with her...as he did now.

His smile, Mariah thought, was one of pure male satisfaction. His eyes were half-closed, and the bit of blue that was visible was lazy, slumberous. Did he feel, as she did, that he had come home? That *this* was where he belonged?

He remained perfectly still inside her while he kissed her, while his hands teased and tormented her breasts. When he lowered his head to take one small, taut nipple into his mouth, she gave a cry, arching her back against the solid strength of his body. She slid her fingers into the soft gold of his hair, intending to push him away, but he brought his hands up to pin her arms firmly but gently against the mattress and continued to suckle, first one sensitive nipple, then the other.

Mariah was breathing heavily, unable to stand the sensations rushing through her any longer. She cried his name, her voice commanding, insisting, then imploring, pleading. Cody shared her need as her shivering, quaking body, cloaking him like a glove, worked its own torture on him.

He moved slowly, inch by inch, stroking, caressing, loving every part of her. His mouth was gentle, his hands tormenting, his hardness demanding. And Mariah responded, matching his ardor, meeting every stroke, every demand, making demands of her own. When she strained against him, her muscles flexed to the point of pain, and cried out with the sheer joy of release, it was all Cody needed. He didn't even try to stifle the groan that was torn from his throat.

The shadows slowly receded from his mind, and he opened his eyes. His forehead was resting on Mariah's, so close that he could barely focus on the sweet beauty of her face. Her breath, soft and warm, mingled with his, and her body twinged beneath his with occasional shudders. "Sweetheart, you are..." He paused, trying to find an appropriate word to describe her. Every word he tried seemed too ordinary. He settled on the best one he could think of. "Exquisite."

Although every ounce of energy she possessed had drained out of her, she managed to smile drowsily. "Exquisite, huh?" she murmured. "By myself, I'm nothing. Together, Cody, *we're* exquisite."

Suddenly somber, Cody closed his eyes again, shutting her out. She was right. With Andrea and the other women he had infrequently made love to, he was merely a satisfactory lover, not exciting or breathtaking or toe curling—certainly not exquisite. Only with Mariah. The implications of that were frightening.

He *didn't* love her. He *couldn't* love her. Hell, he couldn't even trust her...could he? But if he didn't trust her, what was he doing in bed with her, still buried in her heated softness? What was he doing making love to her like this—not having sex, but making love? Why had he just given her the power to destroy him—again—unless he was trusting her not to use it?

Mariah reluctantly opened her eyes. There was such tension in Cody's body, tension that should have been relieved by the explosive tremors that had shaken him. Was he regretting their lovemaking so soon? Was he remembering the joy of their love and the pain of its loss and wondering if it would happen again? "Cody?" she whispered. "Don't be sorry...not yet...please."

She felt his uneasiness, he realized. Carefully pulling away from her, he rolled onto his side and gathered her close, stroking her hair lightly. "I'm not sorry," he assured her in a quietly sincere voice. "I swear, honey, I'm not sorry." After a few minutes, he transferred his caresses from her hair to her body, his palm following an unseen trail along her side to her hip.

"It's funny," she said, her voice distorted by a yawn.

"What is?"

"A few minutes ago, the touch of your hand was like torture." She yawned again. Another few minutes, Cody figured, and she would be sound asleep. She liked to sleep after making love.

"Now," Mariah continued, her voice faint and breathy, "it's so soothing...so relaxing...."

He chuckled softly. "Go to sleep, sweetheart."

"You won't leave?"

"No." His eyes darkened with emotion. "I won't leave." Not tonight. Maybe not ever.

She was cold. Unwilling to give up the security of sleep, Mariah reached out a groping hand to find the covers, but she found instead the hard warmth of a body stretched out beside her. Instantly awake, she sat up in bed. Cody was asleep, and she was cold because the sun had set, and she was lying naked on top of the covers. She turned on the lamp on the nightstand, then found her robe on the floor where Cody had let it fall. Nearby were his clothes and the bright turquoise towel she had dropped.

She picked up the robe, but the satin was cool. It wouldn't offer much in the way of warmth. Tossing it across the foot of the bed, she decided to get dressed before she woke Cody for dinner.

A few minutes later, wearing a long loose dress in powder-blue cotton, she sat down on the edge of the mattress, reaching out one gentle hand to shake his shoulder. "Cody...come on, wake up."

He rolled onto his back and opened one eye, then grinned sleepily. "I thought I dreamed..." Raising a long finger, he touched her chin, and his smile widened. "But it wasn't a dream, was it?"

"That depends on your point of view. It was as perfect as a dream...for me, at least."

He pulled her head to his chest, holding it there with the gentle pressure of his hand. "For me, too." A moment later he released her, sat up, yawned and asked, "What time is it?"

"Almost nine o'clock. Are you hungry?"

He considered the question for a moment. There was no question that he was hungry, but for what—Mariah or food? He was about to choose Mariah when the hollowness in his stomach protested. "Yeah," he said with a grin. "I'm hungry. Hand me my jeans, and I'll help you fix something."

She retrieved his jeans from the floor, handed them over, then watched with interest as he stood up and stepped into them.

"Didn't the very proper Judge Butler teach you that it's impolite to stare at naked men when they're getting dressed?" he teased, zipping his jeans with caution.

She stepped up to him, boldly wrapping her arms around him. "My mother taught me to appreciate beauty," she acknowledged in a husky voice. "And I appreciate you. You're so beautiful." She kissed him softly, gently.

Cody tried to swallow over the lump in his throat. "You've got it backward," he said, trying to disguise the effect of her kiss with humor. "*You're* beautiful. *I'm* handsome."

Shaking her head, she glided her fingers over his bare chest, avoiding his small, erect nipples. "I've seen handsome women and beautiful men. Everything about you is damn near perfect, Cody."

Her words had the effect of a blow. He was deceiving her, lying to her, using her to trap Green. Were those the actions of a "damn near perfect" man? A damn near perfect *bastard* was more like it.

Catching hold of her shoulders, he turned her toward the door, pushing her ahead of him. "I'm nowhere near perfect, sweetheart," he said grimly. "Remember that."

They loaded a tray with turkey sandwiches, glasses of iced tea, chips, pickles and slices of Bonita's cherry pie. Cody carried it into the living room, where Mariah cleared a place for it on the coffee table. Then she sat on the couch while he settled on the floor, leaning back against the recliner for support.

While they ate, they talked—about the weather, the ranch, the employees. About Phoenix and Tucson and tiny, unchanging Esperanza. Their conversation was casual and lazy, nothing important, nothing that needed their full attention, because neither of them could give it much attention. They were too busy looking at each other, feeling, remembering.

Cody's eyes moved over her like a gentle caress while he listened to the soothing tones of her voice. He could remember the first time he had ever heard that voice, the first time he had ever seen her, nine years ago. He had been dazed by her beauty, dazzled by her smile, flattered by her interest. The meeting had been brief, lasting less than ten minutes, but, when he had walked away, he had known that he was destined to love her. Later, he had supposed that he had also been destined to lose her. Now he wasn't so sure.

Mariah knew his mind was wandering. If he heard her words at all, he didn't understand them. That was all right. As long as he was thinking about her—and the smoky look in his eyes assured her that he was—she didn't mind if he didn't listen to her.

Cody realized that she had been silent for quite a while when he leaned forward to set his dessert plate on the tray. He pulled a pillow from the chair, pushed it behind his back and leaned comfortably against it. "Talk to me some more," he commanded, when what he really meant was, stop me from thinking about making love to you again. Stop me from thinking about loving you again.

Mariah smiled indulgently. "All right. About what?"

"Your marriage."

The topic surprised him as much as her, but it would certainly have the effect he wanted. How could he think about making love to her when she was talking about the man she had married, the man who had claimed her as his wife, the man who had shared her bed for four years?

Mariah pursed her lips. It was a fair question, she supposed. She had asked him about Andrea; if he had an ex-wife out there somewhere, she would want to know about her, too. "What do you want to know?"

"What happened? What went wrong?"

Sighing, she leaned forward to set her plate on the tray, cupped her hands around her glass and began speaking. "According to Mom and Dad, it was going to be the perfect marriage. They were friends with Chad's parents, our backgrounds were very similar, Chad had a good career ahead of him—he was even a lawyer. They couldn't have chosen a better husband for me themselves."

Cody scowled. He wasn't surprised that Jerry and Helen had been so strongly in favor of the marriage. At the time they had probably thought that anyone was better than Cody. "So you had everything going for you." He sounded gruff. "What happened? Why did you divorce him?"

His automatic assumption that she had left Chad made her curious. "What makes you think *I* was the one who wanted the divorce?"

He answered with cold, harsh honesty. "Because no man in his right mind would leave you."

"*You* did," she softly reminded him.

But he hadn't been in his right mind. He had been heartbroken. "I didn't think you wanted me."

"I didn't know how to live *without* you."

Her sad, haunted look affected Cody all the way through to his soul. He wanted to take her into his arms, to cheer her up, to kiss away her sadness and make her smile again. God, he wanted to love her.

Feeling the natural, swift response of his body to the idea of loving her—the very response that he had hoped to delay with this conversation—he quickly distracted himself by returning to the subject. "Did you leave him?"

"It was a mutual decision, I guess. By the time I moved out of his house, we were living separate lives anyway. We didn't have any interests in common—not even friends. When I told him I wanted a divorce, he was relieved. He wanted it, too. He just hadn't known how to tell me."

She sighed softly. There had been so many things wrong with their marriage. They had married for the wrong reasons, because it would please their parents; they'd had no common interests; Chad hadn't approved of her work. He had wanted things she couldn't give, and she had wanted him to be something—someone, she corrected herself—that he wasn't.

"Did you love him?"

She stared at Cody. Her first, protective response was that he had no right to ask her that. But he did, her heart whispered. He, of all the people in the world, had that right.

"Did you love him?" he repeated insistently. He knew she didn't want to answer—knew he didn't want to hear her answer—but he had to. He had to know just how completely he had lost her.

She looked around the room for a moment, as if searching for some excuse to avoid answering. She found nothing. "It's not that easy, Cody. I thought I did. I told myself I did. I truly was fond of him—he's a nice man. If I could have loved him, our marriage would have been as perfect as my parents wanted it to be. So I tried. I pretended. There was just one problem."

Cody's heart was pounding in her chest. He was barely able to make his voice work. "What was that?"

"He wasn't you."

He sat still for a long moment, hearing her answer, feeling it in his heart. *He wasn't you.* She had still wanted him. Even when she had been Mrs. Chadwick Martin Lowell III, she had still loved *him*.

He rose to his feet in one graceful movement, pulled Mariah from the sofa and led her to the bedroom. This time he couldn't wait; he couldn't take the time to seduce her. He needed to be inside her *now*, needed to feel her soft, warm, tight around him.

But she didn't need seduction—she needed *him*. She welcomed him.

"I love you, Cody."

The soft whisper of sound came as he entered her, completely, fiercely, gently, with one stroke. His heat combined with hers, his hardness with her softness, his harsh groans with her sweet moans. The end came quickly, almost frantically, leaving them weary, sated and replete.

Cody sank down next to Mariah, covering half of her body with his. The perspiration that filmed his skin left him chilled as his heartbeat slowed to a more reasonable rate. Maneuvering carefully he tugged the comforter and sheet from beneath them and pulled them over their bodies.

Mariah lay still in the darkness, her face turned toward him, her eyes closed. In the moonlight shining through the windows, he could just barely make out the curve of her smile.

Had he really heard the words? They had been so soft, no more than a breath. No more than a figment of his imagination? Did he want to hear her say them so badly that he would imagine it?

I love you, Cody.

He heard it again in his mind, and he knew the answer. Yes, he wanted to hear her say it. He wanted her to love him.

Dear God, he *needed* her to love him.

Chapter 8

Mariah was awake, but she wasn't sure why. Had the sun, shining through the east windows with a brilliance that she felt on her closed eyelids, pulled her from a sound, restful sleep? Or had it been the shifting of the mattress as Cody left the bed, then came back? Or was it the realization that, when he came back, he didn't lie down again?

She opened her eyes to slits, shielding them from the light. Cody was sitting on the edge of the bed, his back to her, bent over and holding one shoe in his hands. She raised a hand to touch his back, bare and still warm from close contact with her body. "Cody?"

He looked over one shoulder and smiled. It was a rare, sweetly tender gesture. "Good morning."

"What are you doing?" Too tired to hold her hand up any longer, she let it slide down his back to the mattress. On the way, she encountered the jeans he wore. The change in texture, from the smooth silk of his skin to the rough denim, penetrated the sleepy fog that surrounded her. She blinked to clear her eyes, took a couple of deep breaths to clear her mind and raised herself up on one elbow. "You're dressed."

He glanced at the shirt draped over the end of the bed, at the shoe in his hands and the mate on the floor, and grinned. "I'm trying." He'd been trying for over ten minutes and had managed nothing but his briefs and jeans. He hadn't even found the energy to buckle the belt that dangled from its loop. He wanted nothing more than to undress, stretch out in bed beside her and stay there for the rest of the day. For the rest of his life.

"Why?" She slid her fingertip inside the waistband of his jeans in back and rubbed back and forth.

"It's morning."

"I see that."

"And Blake and Green will be coming up soon for breakfast."

She yawned, then pushed the covers away. Rising to her knees, she moved to the edge of the bed, directly behind him, and put her arms around him. "I know," she whispered into his ear. "But what does that have to do with you getting dressed?"

Cody could feel her breasts, small and warm, pressed against his back. He could smell her scent, could hear her breathing, could feel the warm, wet tip of her tongue in his ear. She was making it hard for him to think about leaving—to think about anything besides making love to her again. And again.

"You don't want them to know that I spent the night here, do you?" he asked, forcing himself to concentrate on that issue and not on the sweet feel of her behind him.

Mariah moved, causing her breasts to sway back and forth against his back. Her nipples were hardening with awakening desire, and she knew by his stifled groan that he felt it. "I don't care what they know," she said in a husky, enticing, sensuous voice. "I'll tell them myself, if you want."

"What I want is for you to put your robe on." Cody's voice was husky, too, warm and trembling. "Mariah? Please?"

She hesitated only a moment, then moved away. The white satin kimono had been discarded at the end of the bed the night before; she found it and slid her arms into the sleeves. Then she took up the same position, kneeling behind him, her arms draped around him.

The robe did no good, Cody thought with a grimace. She had left it unbelted, and he could still feel her breasts, her belly, the soft downy curls between her thighs. She was torturing him, and he couldn't find the strength to move away and stop it.

She added to the torment by gliding her hands across his chest. "It won't hurt if you stay a little longer," she entreated as her fingers found his nipples, small, brown and decidedly erect.

His shoe hit the floor with a hollow thump, and he grasped her hands in his. "Mariah," he warned. "I have to go." Lifting her arms over his head, he turned around to face her. He kept her hands firmly in his so she couldn't touch him. "I don't want anyone to know that I spent the night here," he said quietly. "It's no one's business but ours. Do you understand?"

The soft, sexy sleepiness disappeared, and she studied him, her lips pursed thoughtfully. "Are you ashamed?"

"No."

That left only one other explanation that she could think of. "My reputation doesn't need protecting."

"Yes, it does. I don't want them talking about you."

She stared at him for a long time, then pulled her hands free, piled the pillows behind her, sank back and pulled the comforter high enough to cover her breasts. "All right."

Cody put his shoes on, lacing them tightly, then his shirt.

"How do you want me to act?"

He paused in the act of tucking his shirt into his jeans. "What?"

"You want last night to be a secret. But I can't act as if it didn't happen, Cody. So how do you want me to act around the others?"

He sat down on the bed next to her. "Act normally."

She pulled him to her for a kiss, hungry and demanding. At the same time she guided his hand beneath the covers and inside her robe, molding his fingers to her breast. "This is normal behavior for me," she said when the kiss was over. "I want you to touch me. I want you to kiss me. I want you to want me so badly that you can't hide it."

He pulled his hand free. "I do. Believe me, honey, I do." After pressing a light kiss to her forehead, he stood up. "I'm going to have breakfast at my house, okay? I'll come back as soon as the others are gone, and we'll..." He let his gaze briefly touch her breast. They would probably spend the rest of the day making love, because he wouldn't have the strength to walk away from her twice in one day. "We'll talk then, all right?"

Mariah nodded solemnly. He kissed her once more, then left the room, closing the door quietly behind him. She waited until the complete silence of the house indicated that he was gone; then she slid down in the bed, pulling the covers to her chin.

She had told him that she loved him. She hadn't meant to, but she could clearly remember saying the words last night. She also clearly remembered that he'd had no response to them—no declaration of his own love, no smile, no frown, nothing. Had he heard her? Had he understood? Or had he chosen to ignore emotions that he didn't reciprocate?

She sighed, a forlorn, lonesome little sound. How was it possible to feel so right, so wonderful, with Cody, and so depressed and unsure without him? Easy, she scolded herself. She loved him, so of course she felt wonderful. And she didn't think he loved her, so of course she was depressed. It was so simple to explain—and so hard to accept.

Pushing the covers back, she rose from the bed. The men wouldn't want breakfast for more than an hour, but she couldn't sleep. After a shower, she put on the blue dress she had worn the night before and went to the kitchen to start a pot of coffee.

Breakfast was subdued. Cody didn't come, Philip had a hangover that kept him relatively quiet, and David wasn't in the mood for casual conversation. Mariah sat across from the two men and munched on a bacon and biscuit sandwich while she stared out the window at the buildings in the distance.

After little more than a cup of coffee, Philip left. Mariah watched him walk past the window, then looked at David. "You have problems?"

His mouth tightened into a frown. "Yeah. Big-time."

"With Suzanne?"

He nodded.

"Maybe I can help. I *am* a woman."

"Thanks, Mariah, but you've got enough problems of your own with the ranch and Daniels without taking on mine, too."

She smiled. "What's the saying—share your burdens with a friend and lighten the load? I've got broad shoulders, David. I don't think listening to you is going to weigh me down."

He was silent for a long time, considering whether he should confide in her. Finally he raised bloodshot brown eyes to her. "Suzanne is pregnant."

Mariah was surprised—and just a little bit envious. "You asked her to marry you." It wasn't a question. Of course he would accept responsibility.

He looked as if he couldn't get any lower. "I asked. She said no." He made an angry gesture, then clenched his fist. "Of course, she's been saying no all along, but I was stupid enough to believe that the baby might make a difference."

"So what are you going to do now?"

"There's nothing I *can* do. I can't kidnap her and carry her away and force her to marry me. I can't even force her to have the baby."

Mariah stared in shock. "She's not planning to have an abortion, is she?" She sounded incredulous. She didn't know Suzanne Fox well, but she found it impossible to believe that any woman David would fall in love with could even consider having an abortion.

"She hasn't decided. She just found out Friday, and she told me last night. She doesn't know what she's going to do." David tilted his head back and stared at the ceiling. "I don't know what to do, Mariah. If it weren't for my *crimi-*

nal past—'' he gave the words a twisted, mocking flavor ''—she would have married me months ago. But her dad doesn't want a convicted felon in the family, and she doesn't want to go against him.'' He laughed bitterly. ''I wonder what her old man's going to think about having a convicted felon's bastard in the family.''

Mariah reached across the table to take his hand. ''I'm sorry, David. If there's anything I can do to help...''

''Thanks.'' He squeezed her fingers tightly, then released her to carry his dishes to the sink. ''It's something for you to think about, Mariah. If things work out between you and Cody this time, you're going to have to seriously consider stopping what you're doing. I know you feel a moral obligation to help those kids—believe me, no one understands that better than I do—but you also have an obligation to him. If you get busted, it's going to affect him, too.''

The subject made her uncomfortable. She knew she should tell Cody about her work with the children, but she didn't know how. Their relationship was so new and fragile. She couldn't just say out of the blue, ''Hey, Cody, you know those trips I make with David that make you so angry? We're bringing orphaned kids into the country illegally. What can I say? Some women read in their spare time, some women sew—I smuggle illegal aliens.''

She didn't have the vaguest idea how he would react, so she pushed the dilemma into the darkest corner of her mind and smiled brightly. ''But I'm not going to get busted. I have my own little guardian angel watching over me.''

David refilled their cups from the coffeepot on the stove before he sat down again. ''I'm serious, Mariah. One of these days you're probably going to have to choose. It's not an easy choice to make.''

''I know. And it's not one I *can* make right now. It may never come to that for Cody and me. If it does, I'll deal with it then.''

''If it does for Suzanne and me...'' David dropped his gaze from Mariah's face. ''I'm thinking about getting out. If I can talk her into marrying me and having the baby, then . . . I'll have to quit. I can't be much of a husband or father from prison.''

She nodded once. "I understand." If he took on the responsibility of a family, he had to make a commitment to *them*, above everyone and everything else—even if that commitment meant giving up work that he fiercely believed in.

"So...how about a more cheerful topic? How are you and Cody getting along?''

Mariah leaned her head on her hand. "I'm not sure that is more cheerful.''

"You have problems?" he asked, mimicking her tone when she had asked the same question earlier.

She smiled faintly. "Yeah.''

"Maybe I can help. After all, I *am* a man. Come on, Mariah, share your burdens with a friend.''

"I wish I could. The trouble is . . . I'm not even sure what the trouble is. I think . . . Lord, David, I think I'm falling in love with him all over again.''

"No, you don't." He smiled gently. "You *know* it—and you're not falling, Mariah, you've already fallen. How does Cody feel about you?''

"He cares, but that's about it, and I don't think that's enough for me.''

"I'm sorry.''

"So am I." She gave a heavy sigh, then smiled at him. "All we can do is give them time. Sooner or later they're bound to realize just how lucky they are to have us, right?''

"Yeah, right." He sounded more confident than he felt. As he walked to the sink once more, he drained the last of his coffee. "They're having a rally in Phoenix today to protest the government's immigration policies. Want to go?''

"No thanks. I . . . I have plans.''

"I'll see you tomorrow, then." At the door he paused, grinning. "Have fun with Cody.''

Mariah was standing at the sink, washing dishes and lost in a daydream, when a pair of strong, hard arms wrapped around her from behind. "I thought he would never leave,''

Cody muttered, nuzzling her hair back to nibble the soft flesh of her ear.

"We were talking." She tilted her head to one side, allowing him better access.

"About what?"

"You and me and him and Suzanne and life and the world in general."

"Wide range of subjects. No wonder it took so long." He slid his hands over the soft blue cotton to her breasts, covering them completely with his palms. He felt her shiver, heard her breath catch.

"I thought..." She broke off as his fingers gently grasped one hard nipple, teasing it until it ached for his mouth. Until *she* ached. "I thought you might not come back."

He laughed huskily and disagreed with her. "You knew I couldn't stay away." Tugging carefully at the square neckline of her dress, he managed to slide one hand inside to her naked breast. She sank against his chest for support. "Do you still have that white quilt?" he whispered in her ear.

She knew instantly the one he meant. The one they had lain on for their very first time together. "Yes... it's in the laundry room."

"Do you have any ice?"

"In the freezer."

"I have an ice chest in my truck." He slid the hand that was inside her dress from her left breast to the right one, pulling gently at the hard nipple. "You get some ice and some of that turkey from last night...maybe some fruit...and something to drink, and I'll get the quilt and the ice chest, and we'll have a picnic. Okay?"

Even though it was close to a hundred degrees outside and guaranteed to get hotter, Mariah agreed. To be this close to him, she would have agreed to anything.

He turned her around and cupped his hand beneath her breast, gently forcing it above the distended neckline of her dress. Lowering his head, he touched the tip of his tongue to her nipple, then drew away. "I'll be back in five minutes."

Mariah gathered the food he had suggested, filled a couple of containers with iced tea and pulled a bag of ice from the freezer in the pantry at the back of the kitchen. Just as she finished, Cody pulled his truck to a stop near the back door. He put the food and the ice in the chest he'd brought, got the quilt from the top shelf in the laundry room and loaded the truck, while Mariah wrote a note to Bonita.

"Where are we going?" she asked when they left the house.

"Out." He indicated the desert around them with a sweep of his hand. "I know a place that's got everything we need. It's private—no one ever goes there—and it's even got a tree or two to give us shade."

Mariah knew the place he meant. "The canyon" they had called it in their youth. It *was* private. They had made love there literally dozens of times and had never been disturbed by anything more than a curious mouse.

Cody kept his eyes on the nearly non-existent road ahead of them. "Do you remember the first time, Mariah?" he asked softly. The question was intended to arouse her. He knew that she remembered, and he knew that, like him, remembering would fill her with desire. He wanted that desire.

With a smile, she slid across the wide seat until she was pressed against him and laid her hand on his thigh. "Of course I do. We rode out there separately, because you didn't want the other hands to see us leave together. When I got there you kissed me, and you asked me to touch you. You were so hard...." She moved her hand between his legs, cupping him gently. "Like now."

Her voice was no more than a breath in his ear. He had to force his eyes to stay open, had to force his hands to control the steering wheel. He felt weak, helpless to resist, wanting no more than to lie back and let her touch him, kiss him, stroke him, seduce him. Let her take whatever she wanted. He would be satisfied with whatever she gave in return.

He recognized the entrance of their private place and braked awkwardly. His legs were unsteady, and as they worked the brake and the clutch, the movement insinuated her hand more snugly against his aroused flesh. He shut off the engine, engaged the brake and laid his head back, his eyes fluttering shut. "Oh, Mariah," he groaned.

"Let me make love to you, Cody."

He didn't give her permission, but he didn't turn her down, either. She moved across the seat and climbed out of the truck, taking the quilt with her. A moment later Cody followed.

They spread the quilt in the shadow of an ancient wall of rock. Mariah removed her shoes, leaving them on one corner of the quilt, then turned to Cody. Sliding her hands beneath his green T-shirt, she lifted it, pulling it slowly upward, over his head, freeing his arms, and dropped it to the ground. Next she let her hands glide over the smooth softness of his chest to his waist. She unbuckled his belt and undid the cool metal buttons on his jeans.

"Mariah..." Cody raised his hands to her shoulders, capturing a handful of her hair.

Smiling, she shook her head. "Don't. Don't say anything. Don't do anything. I'm going to make love to you, remember?"

His brain was so overloaded with sensation that he could hardly remember anything as she finished undressing him. One moment he was standing, fully clothed, and the next he was lying on his back on the quilt, naked.

While he watched, Mariah removed her own clothing. Her dress landed in a pale blue heap beside his jeans, and her panties—also pale blue, soft, tiny, lacy—drifted down on top of the denim. Smiling, she knelt next to him, her hair falling forward to hide her body from him. He raised one hand to push it aside and reveal her breasts. "Beautiful," he murmured.

Slowly she leaned over him, touching him. The different textures overwhelmed him—the soft caresses of her hands, the wet kisses from her mouth, the erotic tickle of her hair, the sensual graze of her breasts. There wasn't a place that she didn't touch, kiss, caress, love, and there was nothing Cody could do but enjoy it.

"Mariah . . ."

She looked up. Her eyes were soft, drugged, full of emotion. "What do you want?"

"Make love to me. Take me inside you."

Smiling again, she moved slowly, until she was astride him. Her touch was as soft as a whisper when she guided him, gently, with care, until, with an easy thrust of her hips, she had sheathed him completely.

Cody stared at her. The sun was breaching the shelter of the canyon wall, turning her hair blue-black with its light. As he watched, it touched her face, then her shoulders. Beneath her, he was still in shadow, darker and cooler. She was beautiful.

She rocked against him in a slow, torturing rhythm, taking him easily, smoothly, setting the pace. At the same time, her hands moved across his body, stroking his eyes shut, accepting a nibbling kiss on her fingertips from his mouth, feeling the uneven pulse at the base of his throat, rubbing his nipples. When he grasped her hips to take control, she forced his arms to his sides and held them, her hands on his wrists.

She closed her eyes and tilted her face to the sun. It was hot. Beneath her hair, her back and shoulders were sticky and wet; perspiration was starting to bead on her forehead and along her upper lip. But she loved the sun. It warmed her body—her upturned face, the long column of her neck, her naked breasts, her back. Its heat on her skin was erotic, adding to the heat Cody was stirring in her belly.

Cody freed one hand and slid it between their bodies. One long slender finger worked through her black curls to find and stroke that most sensitive, most womanly part of her, sending a long, exquisite shudder through her. "Are you making love to me?" he asked in a hoarse, broken voice. "Or are you punishing me?"

Her black eyes glittered when she looked at him. "What do you want?"

"I can't stand . . ." He needed release, fulfillment. He needed to fill her. He was hurting, every nerve end tingling, crying for relief. His skin was so sensitized that her every touch was agony—the sweetest, most unendurable pain he'd ever felt.

Mariah laughed softly, bent over and drew her tongue over first one nipple, then the other. Her hair fell over her shoulders, swaying like silken fingers over his ribs, and Cody groaned.

The tempo of her hips' movement increased as she took his mouth with hers. Her kiss was ardent, fiery, to match her lovemaking, and Cody's response was equally ardent, equally fiery. When it ended in a burst of searing passion, they both cried out, both shuddered uncontrollably. Each clung to the other long after the cries and the shudders were gone.

Cody held Mariah at his side, his lips pressed to her hair. Their bodies were heated, slick with sweat, and exhausted. He could barely find the strength to move his mouth to form a kiss that she barely felt.

She was the first to move. Sitting up on the quilt, she pulled a rubber band from the pocket of her dress and began braiding her hair. When she reached the end of the long strands, she wrapped the band around and around, then flipped the braid over her shoulder. For a moment she simply sat there, absorbing the sun's rays, and Cody simply watched her, unable to touch her because her lovemaking had left him weak, unable to speak to her because his love left him without words.

She was beautiful. She was perfect—exquisite. And she was the woman he had always loved and always would love. The knowledge didn't thrill him. He had so many questions...so many doubts. Did she love him? Could he trust her? Could they make it work this time, or was he facing guaranteed heartache?

Mariah reached for her dress and pulled it over her head. It settled in a blue cloud around her hips. "I'm thirsty."

Her husky comment broke his solemn mood, and he smiled, rising up on one arm. "Is that a hint for me to get the ice chest?"

"Do I need to be more blunt?"

He stood up and tugged on his jeans, buttoning them as he stepped into his worn sneakers. "While I'm gone, why don't you move the quilt over there?" He nodded toward a shadier spot.

Mariah agreed. Making love in the sun was fine, even erotic, but she, too, preferred some protection from its brilliance while they ate their picnic lunch. When Cody had returned with the ice chest, she was sitting in the shade, languidly wiping away the perspiration from her throat.

"Was this a good idea, or what?" Cody asked with a wry grin as he sat down next to her. "It feels like it's about a hundred and ten out here."

"I don't mind." She pulled a plastic bag from the ice chest and removed a napkin to dry her face. "I've always liked the heat."

"Yeah, I remember." Heat, to her, was sexy and erotic. To him, it was just plain hot. He handed her a cup filled with iced tea. "After more than thirty years of living in the desert, I got mighty tired of it. When I was in El Paso, I wanted to head north—live someplace where it snowed for a while."

Mariah took a long, cool drink. "What happened?"

Cody stared at the quilt. The fabric was worn, and the intricate stitching done years ago by Mariah's grandmother had broken in many places, leaving tiny tails of thread dangling free. After a moment he looked at her. "I came here instead." Here, to lie to the only people who cared about him. Here, to deceive the only woman he'd ever loved.

"You didn't have to come back here."

Yes, he had—for reasons she knew nothing about and probably wouldn't understand. For reasons that he wished to God she would never have to find out. Maybe even for reasons that *he* didn't understand. He could have refused the orders—with his record, he was confident that he wouldn't have been fired if he hadn't accepted the transfer. But he *had* come, claiming an obligation to his job—a duty. Maybe someplace way deep down inside him—the same place where his love had hidden for eight years—he had wanted to come back.

Mariah watched a distant, faintly troubled expression steal across his face. Reaching out, she laid her hand on his denim-covered knee, wanting to remind him of her presence, to bring his attention back to her. "Talk to me, Cody."

"About what?"

She shrugged. "Tell me what you've been doing for the last eight years."

"Working. That's all."

"And moving to California and Texas. And almost marrying Andrea. There had to be more to your life than that. I could spend more time telling you about one *day* in my life than you've used to cover eight years."

"My life was very boring."

"All right." She conceded that he didn't want to discuss the past. It piqued her curiosity, but she let it go—for now. "The other night you told me a little about your father. Is he off limits, too?"

Cody stretched out on his side, supporting his head in one palm. He couldn't tell her about his past; she would know by the big gaps in his story that he was trying to hide something. But at least he could answer her questions about his father. "No, he isn't. What do you want to know about him?"

"Is he still alive?"

"Yes. He lives in Las Cruces, he's married, his wife is two years older than I am, and they've got three sons who are young enough to be *my* children."

Mariah daintily fished a chunk of ice from her cup and stuck it in her mouth. When it had melted to a manageable size, she asked around it, "Do you see them often?"

"I used to drive over occasionally when I lived in El Paso. It was kind of awkward, though. He's a different man—he has a different life, and I'm not a part of it."

There was a hint of loneliness in his voice that made Mariah long to comfort him, to tell him that he would always be a part of *her* life—the most important part. Would that matter to him? He didn't seem to have any objections to being lovers, but did he want anything more from her? Did he want her love? Did he trust her enough to accept it?

"Did you ever forgive him for leaving your mother?" The question came unexpectedly, although she understood its importance. If he'd forgiven his father for disappointing him, maybe he could forgive her, too.

He considered it for a long moment, his brow furrowed in thought. At last the frown eased. "It wasn't a matter of forgiving, Mariah, but of understanding. I was young when it happened—too young and immature and foolish to really understand."

Mariah hid a smile. She couldn't imagine Cody ever being immature—his maturity was one of the few things that had favorably impressed even her parents.

"I blamed him for not loving Mom enough, for leaving her, for never coming back. I could only see it from my point of view. She needed him—hell, *I* needed him—and he left. I didn't see him again from the day he walked out until the day of her funeral. He used to send us money, and he invited me to visit, but I always turned him down. I blamed him for leaving. I even managed to somehow blame him for her death."

He fell silent for a moment. His fingers moved back and forth over a broken seam in the quilt, tracing the faded design. "It took me a long time to understand what it had been like for him. He really loved Mom, but he had watched her throw away her life. She loved the alcohol more than she ever loved him or me. For almost twenty years he'd taken care of her, picking her up when she went out and got drunk, doing the housework and taking care of me when she got drunk and passed out at home. He'd lost jobs because of her, he'd spent every bit of money he ever made trying to get help for her—he had even forgiven her when she'd been with other men because she was too drunk to know or care. He just couldn't take it anymore. It got too hard for him to watch the woman he loved destroy herself like that."

"So he left her."

"Yes." He rolled onto his stomach, hiding his face. "But all I knew at the time was that he was gone. The last thing he said to me was, 'I love you,' but he still left."

Mariah wiped a tear from her eye with the tip of one finger. "But now you know that he truly did love you. Now you understand."

His response was an awkward nod.

She took a deep breath to steady her trembling. "And do you know that I truly did love you, too?"

In this vulnerable, emotional state, he didn't want to talk about Mariah's love—certainly not in the past tense—but he answered, "Yes." After a moment he made himself look at her. "But I wasn't sure then. I needed you to come back to the ranch and prove it—to me, to your parents and to everyone else."

"I'm sorry, Cody," she whispered.

He smiled grimly. "So am I."

They were silent for a long time, carefully avoiding each other's eyes. Finally Mariah opened the ice chest. "How about a sandwich?" she suggested, striving to sound as normal as possible. It wasn't easy with a lump the size of a baseball in her throat.

Cody took his cue from her. Normalcy. Forget for the moment that this entire conversation had taken place. They fixed their own sandwiches, with slices of turkey, cheese, onion and tomato, then settled comfortably on the quilt to eat.

"Can you believe we're out here in this heat, eating cold turkey sandwiches, when we could be at home, in an air-conditioned house, having Bonita's Sunday dinner?" Cody asked, wiping his face with his T-shirt.

Mariah's answering smile was worth one hundred and ten degree heat and cold sandwiches three times a day, he thought, swallowing his food with difficulty. "But we couldn't have made love like that with Bonita in the house," she reminded him. "She wouldn't have approved."

The mere mention of their lovemaking affected him. He felt desire curling, flaring, twisting inside him. He wanted her again, with a swiftness and an intensity that frightened him. He wanted to lay her down, lift her dress and take her, make her want, make her need, make her his.

Mariah knew what he was thinking, felt what he was feeling. She swallowed the last bite of her sandwich, washed it down with a drink of tea, then extended her hand to him. He took it slowly, his fingers wrapping around hers, and drew her to him. He kissed her greedily, never releasing her, while his hands dealt rapidly with their clothes. With no barriers between them, he entered her deeply, completely, and gave a low groan of pleasure, of satisfaction, of love, as she welcomed him.

"Tell me that you enjoyed it."

Mariah laughed huskily. "I enjoyed it."

He shivered as her hands tickled up and down his spine. Nuzzling her neck, he finally used his arms to lift himself from the warm refuge of her body. He lay down next to her, still sampling the soft skin of her throat and the sensitive curve of her ear. "Tell me that it was exquisite," he commanded.

She laughed again, then turned her head to look at him. Her movement effectively ended the enticing kisses that she was too tired to respond to. "It was exquisite. Absolutely, totally, completely exquisite."

Leaning on one arm so that he could see her better, he made one more demand. This time the teasing was gone. This time he was serious. "Tell me that you love me."

Mariah stared at him, her lips parted, her dark eyes wary. Her heart was pounding, echoing in her ears. Her mouth worked, her jaw moved, but no sound came out. No declaration of love, no denial of it.

Cody was embarrassed. He wished that he'd never spoken, but he needed to hear her say it again. He needed to know. "I heard you say it last night." He wet his lips nervously. "Did you mean it?"

With each second that she remained silent, his nervousness increased, along with shock. Pain. Finally he smiled a taut smile and said, "It's okay. You can't be held responsible for things you say in the throes of passion. I won't hold you to it."

For just an instant he looked so bleak that Mariah's heart ached for him. It gave her the courage to speak. "I said it . . . and I meant it. I love you, Cody."

His eyes were dark, shadowed and somber. He closed them for a moment, then looked at her again. "Do you know how long it's been since you've said that to me? Just stood there and told me flat out that you love me?" he asked hoarsely. "I've waited so long. . . ."

She laid her hand lightly against his cheek and smiled sweetly. "I *do* love you, Cody. I love you very much."

Suddenly he smiled and gathered her into his arms. He held her close, stroking her hair, occasionally kissing her, until it was time to get dressed and return home. It wasn't until they were halfway back to the house that Mariah realized something.

He had been upset when she hadn't said that she loved him, and pleased when she *had* said it. But not once, in all the hours they'd spent together, had he even hinted at his own feelings. Not once had he ever said that he loved her.

He made love to her as if she were the only woman in the world for him—but that wasn't love. He looked at her with such gentleness, touched her with such tenderness—but that wasn't love, either.

A little of her joy disappeared. A little of her pleasure in the day faded. What had she done?

What would she do?

Chapter 9

I see you're not planning to work today."

Mariah looked up as Cody caught up with her. He walked alongside her, his battered cowboy hat low on his forehead. "Good morning to you, too," she greeted him as they approached her office.

Cody grinned. They'd just had breakfast together, but it had been difficult to exchange more than a casual hello with everyone else around. He hadn't been able to touch her, speak to her or look at her the way he'd wanted. He waited while she unlocked the door. As soon as they were inside the small office, he closed the door, pulled her into his arms and kissed her, his tongue seeking the warmth of her mouth. "I missed you last night," he murmured when he raised his mouth from hers.

She had missed him, too, but it had been his decision to stay at his house instead of with her. Had he still been trying to protect her reputation, or had he wanted a little breathing room, a little distance between them? She had thought about it until early this morning and hadn't been able to find an answer.

"What's with the dress?" Cody asked, releasing her so she could go to her desk.

"I'm having lunch with Lissa today in Tucson." She seated herself behind the desk and started sorting through some files in the bottom drawer. "Then I'm meeting with my dad. I've got some legal papers that need to be taken care of." She also had some personal business to take care of with Jerry; she wanted to tell him that Cody was back at the ranch. She wanted to give him and her mother a chance to get used to the news, just in case... In case what? In case Cody miraculously fell in love with her and decided to stay? You're dreaming, sweetheart, she warned herself. Don't get your hopes up yet.

"Is Green going with you?"

She looked up from the jumble of papers she'd drawn from the desk. He was making an effort not to be jealous. After this weekend, how could he have any doubts about the nature of her friendship with David? "No, he isn't. If I wanted company, Cody, I would ask you to go. Unfortunately, I don't think you would enjoy spending the day with Lissa and my dad."

She was right about that. He didn't mind Lissa so much, but the last thing he needed was to see Jerry Butler. The old man would be livid when he learned that Cody was back—outraged when he learned that Mariah was seeing him again.

Mariah pulled a large envelope from another drawer and slid the papers inside it. Her hands shook just a bit. She was deceiving Cody, though not outrightly lying to him. She really was having lunch with Lissa, then meeting her father. But first she was going to San Benito and picking up three children and delivering them to Father Espinoza. Still, a lie of omission was a lie all the same, and she hated lying to Cody.

"Isn't it a little early to be leaving? Lunch is still hours away."

She rose from her desk, the envelope clasped in her sweaty grip. "I'm not going yet. I just wanted to get the papers for Dad, so I wouldn't forget them. And there are a few other things I want to do, too."

Cody slipped his arm around her shoulders. "I'm asking you a lot of questions that are none of my business, I know. You don't have to account for your time to me. It's just…" He drew her closer, until her breasts were flattened against his chest and her hair was falling over his bare forearm. "You are so beautiful, and you look so lovely, and I am so damn jealous of every minute you spend away from me."

Mariah squeezed him tightly. "I told you yesterday that I love you, Cody." *And you said nothing to me.* She pushed away the hurt, ignoring it. "Those aren't words I say easily. I meant them. You have nothing to be jealous of."

He raised her head for one kiss; then he put her away from him. "I've got to get to work. Enjoy your trip, and Lissa and your dad. And be careful."

"I will be."

"Save some time for me this evening, will you?"

She smiled warmly. "Of course I will."

Cody kissed her one last time, then left the office.

David was waiting for him outside, with two horses already saddled. He was impatient with Cody and annoyed with Mariah. He had wanted to go with her on this trip, but she'd said no. Until he and Suzanne reached a decision regarding the baby, Mariah had told him, she could handle the runs alone. He had argued with her for half an hour the night before, but she had refused to budge. Finally she had told him bluntly, "Cody is jealous. He doesn't like it when you and I disappear for most of the day, and I don't blame him. I can't even come up with a good lie to tell him. I can excuse *my* absence from the ranch, David. I can't explain yours."

David had suggested that she stay, letting him make the trip by himself. She had refused. In the end, all he'd gotten was a promise that she would be careful. In a few minutes she would be leaving, and he was staying behind. If anything happened to her…

Cody swung into the saddle, and they rode away from the stables. Both men were quiet for a long time until David spoke, simply to break the silence. "You and Mariah seem to be getting along better."

Cody fixed a narrow-eyed stare on him. "Yeah."

"Be careful with her. Don't hurt her."

Cody resented the interference and the implication that he would deliberately hurt Mariah. "I told you before that whatever goes on between Mariah and me is our business."

David wasn't offended by his harsh tone. "You don't like me much, do you?"

"No," Cody answered honestly. "I don't."

"Why not? Because of Mariah?" He paused for a beat. "Or because I have a record?"

Usually David was open about his past; today he seemed more than a little defensive. Cody wondered why. He answered in a lazy, unsympathetic drawl. "If you have problems with that, Green, you brought them on yourself. No one made you smuggle those people into the country. No one made you break the law."

"No one but my conscience," David quietly disagreed.

Part of his job, Cody reminded himself, was to get to know David Green. What was he like? How did his mind work? What was he up to now? He didn't have to like the man to question him, and since they were stuck together for the time being, this was as good a time as any to start. "Why did you do it? You knew you were committing a crime. You knew you would probably get caught. Those people meant nothing to you, so why bother?"

" 'Those people' have a right to live, the same as you and I do. They were being murdered, tortured, kidnapped and raped because they wanted a normal life. They wanted to provide for their families, to be allowed to work and to own land. They wanted freedom to speak out, to disagree with their government. They wanted to live."

The conviction in his voice had more effect on Cody than the actual words. He'd heard the words before, but David Green sincerely believed them. He had acted on that belief, risking his own freedom to bring refugees into the country. If, as the border patrol suspected, he was behind the smuggling of the Carta Blancans, he was taking an even bigger risk, that of violating his probation. If he got caught this time, it would almost definitely mean prison.

"So things are bad in their country," Cody said with a callous shrug. "That doesn't give you the right to break the laws of *this* country."

"Have you ever heard any of their stories?" David asked quietly.

Cody nodded again. He had once apprehended a group of Central Americans and the priest who had brought them across the border outside El Paso. They had told him a little about their life at home—about the poverty, the oppression, the horrors, they had faced every day. They had talked about the fear, the hunger, the dying.

"The things they've lived through..." David shook his head in dismay. "This is a big country—a wealthy country. We could take a lot more immigrants than we do. You know what the immigration quota is each year for Mexicans coming into this country illegally?"

Cody *did* know, but he caught himself before the answer slipped out. There was no reason for a ranch hand to know figures like that, he cautioned himself.

"About twenty thousand," David answered his own question. "Can you believe that? And for most people from Central America, it's just about impossible to get in legally, so we brought them illegally. And I'd do it again if necessary."

The silence between them was heavy and tense. Finally Cody looked at the other man. "Some people say you're *still* doing it—that you haven't stopped."

David was too quiet, too uneasy, for too long before he said awkwardly, "Some people will say anything."

Cody studied him—the flush of red in his cheeks, the nervous movement of his hands, the uneasy shifting of his weight in the saddle—and he knew, as surely as if the man had admitted it, that David Green was still involved with the smuggling. "Are you using Mariah's ranch to bring illegals into the country?" he asked in dismay. He was suddenly, coldly angry. Mariah had given Green a job as a friend, and this was how he repaid her? "Do you realize the trouble you could cause her?"

"I wouldn't do that! I would never do something like that behind Mariah's back!" David took a deep breath, trying to calm the flash of anger. His grin was weak, a failed attempt at normalcy. "Besides, that would violate my probation. If I did that, they could send me to prison. Believe me, I have several damn good reasons for not wanting to go to prison."

Suzanne Fox. Cody considered the woman while he let his anger cool. Could the love of a woman convince Green not to act on his moral convictions? It was possible, he admitted—for Mariah's love, Cody imagined he could do almost anything. But he didn't think it was likely in this case.

The conversation had accomplished nothing beyond convincing Cody of Green's involvement. But he had no proof, no evidence. He had no idea if Green was working alone, or if he had partners in Esperanza. He couldn't even make a guess about when Green was bringing the children across; most of his time was accounted for. If he wasn't working at the ranch, he was with Suzanne. Except for his occasional trips into the city to speak at political rallies, the only unexplained absences from the ranch were those trips he took with Mariah.

Cody forced himself to seriously consider whether Mariah could be involved. She and Green were close friends, he admitted. To some extent, she shared his beliefs. When Cody had referred to undocumented aliens as "illegals" that day, she had spouted out a question frequently heard from people like Green, "How can any human being be illegal?" On those days when Green was gone from the ranch on unknown business, he was with her. Could they be working together?

The idea was ludicrous. He'd known Mariah for more than nine years. She was as honest as the day was long. She had never cheated on a test, run a red light, shortchanged the IRS or kept a library book beyond its due date. She just wasn't capable of committing any crime, much less one of that scope.

But was that his head speaking? he wondered cynically. Or his heart?

* * *

Mariah's luncheon date with Lissa turned into soup, hot dogs and chips in the tiny kitchen at the church, seated at a table that barely reached her knees and flanked on each side by two of the children she had picked up from Efraín. The girl was eight years old, with a front tooth missing and her black hair untidily trimmed with a knife. She ate hungrily, rarely looking at the others. Enrique, seated on Mariah's left, was also eight. He was tall, skinny, solemn faced, shaggy haired. He only picked at his food, taking a few bites of each item and leaving the rest untouched.

"Aren't you hungry?" Lissa asked. *"¿Tienes hambre?"*

Enrique shook his head.

"He can't be full," Mariah commented. The boy looked more than half-starved, and Katy had told her that he'd eaten very little in the time he'd been at their house.

"He isn't. A lot of these kids come from very poor families. There was never enough food to eat, so they shared whatever they had. No one ate very much for fear that the rest of the family wouldn't get any." Lissa put her hot dog down and leaned closer to Enrique. In Spanish she explained to him that there was plenty of food; like Sara and Manuel, he could eat as much as he wanted. Unconvinced, he hesitantly picked up the spoon and took another mouthful of soup.

"David came to see Father Espinoza Sunday. He's thinking about quitting."

Mariah leaned back in the small chair. "I know."

"Are we going to hear you say that, too?"

"I have no plans to quit."

"But if you and Cody get married—"

Mariah laughed softly. "You're getting ahead of yourself, Lissa. Cody hasn't shown the slightest interest in marriage, at least not to me. Besides, marriage doesn't automatically mean I have to quit. Maybe I'll bring a new recruit to the business instead."

Lissa considered it, her brow wrinkled in thought. "Nah," she said finally. "I just can't see Cody Daniels smuggling kiddos across the border."

This time Mariah's laugh was strained. "Marriage doesn't automatically mean Cody, either," she reminded her friend.

"For you it does. You've been in love with him for all your adult life. It isn't going to change. If you can't marry him, you won't get married again, will you?"

It was no use trying to hide her feelings from Lissa. Besides, best friends were made for sharing confidences. "No," she admitted. "I won't. I'll say it, Lissa, so you can gloat, okay? You were right all along. I loved Cody when I married Chad. I still loved him when he came back. I never stopped. I think I have about as much chance of sprouting wings and flying as I do of not loving Cody."

"Me? Gloat?" Lissa asked innocently. "Why would I do a thing like that? Just because I was right and you were wrong—incredibly wrong?" She emptied a handful of potato chips from the bag onto her plate and ate one. "So... what do you do now? Does he love you, too?"

Mariah twisted the end of her braid around her fingertip. "No. He doesn't love me." Her eyes clouded with pain. Knowing it was bad enough; saying it aloud almost tore her heart in two.

"Has he told you that?"

She smiled sadly. "There are times, Lissa, when what a person *doesn't* say is more important than what they do say, and Cody..." Her sigh was soft. "Cody doesn't say anything."

"Well, he'll come around. Give him time," Lissa said briskly. She began gathering the dishes from the table, giving the children permission to go to the toy box in the next room. "Remember Raquel? The baby you brought last week?"

Of course she remembered the girl. She had half wanted to take the child home with her.

"She's already been placed with foster parents," Lissa continued when Mariah nodded in response. "The little ones like that are usually pretty easy to place. It's tougher for the older ones. Not too many people want a ten- or twelve-year-old who doesn't speak English."

A new voice answered Lissa, that of Father Espinoza— soft, calm, peaceful. "But even in a church orphanage, they're better off than they were at home. And these are bright kids, Lissa. They'll learn English in no time. Language won't be a barrier for long." He smiled fondly at Mariah. "How are you?"

"I'm fine. Keeping busy."

"We all are, I suppose. If there aren't any problems this week, we should bring in about twenty-two children. We appreciate your help with these three."

"Any time, Father. Lissa, I've got to be going. I have an appointment with Dad. I'll see you next week." She called goodbye to the three children, then left the church. It was a short drive to the building that housed her father's office. He was waiting when the secretary showed her inside.

"You look lovely," Jerry said, catching Mariah in a bear hug. "How have you been?"

She gave her standard answer. "Fine. Here are those papers I told you about."

Jerry accepted the envelope and laid it on his desk. "I don't suppose there's anything in here authorizing me to find a buyer for the ranch?" he asked with a hopefulness that made her laugh.

"Not a thing. How is Mother?"

"She's still beautiful—just like you." Jerry pulled two chairs close together and gestured to Mariah to sit down. "How have you been—really?" he asked seriously.

"I really am fine, Dad. Business at the ranch is okay. Everything's . . . fine." She shrugged expressively.

"Then would you mind telling me something?"

She waited.

"What is Cody Daniels doing back?"

Mariah stared, her mouth dropped open. "How—"

"Rosalie Chavez saw fit to let us know. Why didn't you tell me that he'd come back? And why in hell did you give him a job?"

She sank back in the chair, giving a shake of her head. "I was going to tell you today. I didn't want you to find out from someone else. I didn't want you to think that I was keeping it a secret, that I was ashamed...."

"You *knew* we wouldn't approve. For God's sake, Mariah, what were you thinking when you gave him a job? Have you forgotten what he did to you? How could you let him come back and just waltz right in?"

"Dad...the ranch is mine, isn't it? It belongs to *me* now. *I* get to make the decisions regarding it. That includes hiring the hands. Arcadio thought it would be a good idea to hire Cody—and so did I. He works hard, and he knows what he's doing. That's more than I can say about a lot of the men you've hired in the past."

"You're damn right he knows what he's doing," Jerry said angrily. "He realized what he gave up so long ago, and he's come back to see if he can get it back."

Mariah smiled sadly. "Me?" she asked with a sorrow-filled sigh.

"No," her father bluntly replied. "Not you. The land. That was what he wanted the first time, but he wasn't willing to wait until you inherited it. Now it's yours, free and clear."

"Mine, and about a hundred creditors'," she replied with a scowl. "Do you see why I didn't tell you sooner, Dad? Yes, I knew you wouldn't approve. I knew you'd be upset. But you're wrong. Cody wasn't after the land the first time—he loved *me*. But you could never accept that, could you? And he doesn't want the land now, either. He asked for a job, and I gave it to him."

"Is that all you've given him?"

"That's none of your business, Dad. Neither is this, but I'm going to tell you anyway. I love Cody Daniels. I have always loved him. If I thought he wanted the ranch, I would give it to him, if he would only stay with me." It was the simple truth. If Cody never said he loved her, she could live with that. But she couldn't live without him. She couldn't lose him again.

Jerry reached out to grasp her hands tightly in his, as if he could force his feelings, the certainty that he was correct, into her through the contact. "Don't you remember how he hurt you? It took you *months* to get over him. Your mother and I were so worried about you."

"I *never* got over him, Dad. But I wasn't the only one who was hurt. So was Cody. He thought—" She bit her lip. What he had thought was between them; she had no right to tell her father. "How long have you known?"

"About a week. Rosalie called your mother, and she told me."

Her mouth curved upward involuntarily. "And you kept quiet for a whole week? What would you have done if I hadn't come into town today to see you?"

"I don't know," he admitted. "Your mother made me promise not to call you or go to see you. She wouldn't even tell me about Daniels until I'd given my word."

Maybe she had an unexpected ally in her mother. She wouldn't count on it, though, until she had talked to her herself. Gently, she said, "You won't change my mind on this, Dad. You can't convince me to fire him. You can't make me stop loving him. So let's end the discussion here, all right?"

"You know we love you. I just don't want to see you hurt."

"I love you, too, Dad. But I'm twenty-nine. I can make decisions for myself. I can take risks myself. Okay?"

Grudgingly, he nodded. "Okay."

Mariah let her taut muscles relax. This was one battle won. But she didn't kid herself into thinking that the war was over. Her father never gave in so gracefully on something he felt was important. There would be more, but that was all right. She'd told the truth: he couldn't change her mind, and he couldn't make her stop loving Cody.

Nothing could do that.

The sun had set, and the evening was cool and bright, lit by a nearly full moon. Dinner had ended more than an hour earlier, and Cody was on his way back to the main house when he heard Mariah's voice through the open door of Antonio Chavez's house. He slowed his steps, then stopped completely as her words became clear.

"The next time you want to discuss my private life, I suggest that you come to me," she said angrily. "You had no right to tell anyone about Cody."

Rosalie's response was inaudible, just a short, low sound that only served to anger Mariah more.

"No, they didn't." Mariah's voice carried through the still night. "I don't have to answer to them anymore. *I* own this ranch, Rosalie—not my father and mother, but *me*. *I'm* the boss here. If I want to give Cody a job, that's no one's business but my own. If I want to move him into the main house with me, that's my business, too. I won't tolerate this kind of interference in my life from the wife of one of my employees. Do you understand?"

Rosalie's voice was a quiet murmur, joined by another murmur of sound from the house behind Cody. Glancing over his shoulder, he saw David Green and Philip Blake standing on the porch. Green looked serious; Blake was trying not to grin. Color flooded Cody's face in the darkness, and he silently cursed, then turned back toward his own house.

Mariah found him there over an hour later, sitting in the darkened living room. She stood in the entrance, the screen door gripped in her hand. "Cody?"

He didn't speak or move, but she could see his faint shadow in the darkness. "Cody, I thought you were coming back to the house." She had waited forty-five minutes beyond the time he'd said to expect him before she had come looking for him. Now he was sitting there so still and cold that she wished she hadn't found him. "What's wrong?"

In slow, deliberate words, he mocked her earlier statement. "The next time you want to discuss my private life, I suggest you come to me."

Mariah stepped inside and carefully closed the screen door so it didn't bang. "I ... I'm sorry. I ..." She couldn't think of anything else to say. "I'm sorry."

He rose from the couch and approached her. When he stood in the moonlight that came over her shoulder, she saw the anger on his face—cold, dark, dangerous anger. It made her shiver with fear—not fear that he would hurt her, but fear that she had unwittingly damaged their fragile relationship beyond repair.

"You had no right." He stared down at her, his hands clenched at his sides in tight, hard fists. After he had repeatedly told David Green that his involvement with Mariah was no one's business but theirs, she had recklessly shouted it to their entire little world. He was furious. *"You had no right."*

If he had yelled, she could have borne it better, but he **spoke** in a deadly soft voice. She raised her hand to reach out to him, but he looked as if her touch might make him ill. Choking back a sob, she let her arm fall again. "Cody..." There was almost no sound to her whisper.

He took a step back and began unfastening his shirt, one snap at a time. "So *you* own the ranch. *You're* the boss." The derision in his voice twisted inside her like a knife. "What you do with me is *your* business. Stupid me—I thought I had something to do with it. I thought *love* had something to do with it. But obviously I was wrong. It was business—*your* business. You hired yourself a stud." He spat out a foul curse. "I've been wrong about you all along, haven't I, sweetheart? But no more. By God, no more, Mariah."

Mariah was biting the inside of her lip, trying to keep the tears from falling, trying to keep the pain from taking her over. She couldn't speak, couldn't tell him how wrong he was, couldn't even explain to him what she had meant by her talk with Rosalie. All she could do was stare at him, horrified by the change in him—the change *she* had caused.

He pulled the shirt off and let it fall to the floor. Next he leaned back against the wall and tugged one boot off. It hit the floor with a resounding thud. The second one followed; then his socks floated down. "Why didn't you just announce it at dinner? That would have been easier, and that way you could have made sure that everyone heard. You could have given them the details over dessert, about how and where we did it, about every time I was inside you."

She shrank back, bumping her head against the door frame. If only her legs would respond, she could run away;

she wouldn't have to hear him talk like this. But she couldn't move.

He unbuckled his belt, then opened his jeans. The silver buckle jingled when the jeans hit the floor. A moment later his briefs landed there, too. He grasped her wrist and jerked her against him, holding her there with the cruel grip of his fingers. "Well," he said in a soft, silky, furious voice, "let's get down to business."

But he couldn't bring himself to do anything more. He couldn't take her in anger. He couldn't hurt her. He couldn't make her share the pain that was pumping through his body with every beat of his heart.

A fat teardrop rolled from her chin and landed on his hand. He pushed her away as if burned. "You may own this ranch, Mariah," he said in a curiously empty voice. "You may even own those other poor fools who work for you. But you don't own *me*. You'll never have me."

At last her muscles responded to her brain's frantic commands. Reaching out blindly, she pushed the screen door open and ran—down the steps, across the yard, to the safety of her house.

Cody stared at the spot where she had stood. Slowly he lifted his hand to his mouth and touched his tongue to the damp spot where her tear had landed. It was warm, salty. He knotted the same hand into a tight fist, closed the door and locked it, and walked through the dark empty house to his bedroom. There he finally unclenched his hand, allowing the cramping muscles to ease.

He wished it were that easy to heal the pain in his heart.

Kyle Parker drove through the open gate onto Butler property and turned his truck south, toward the border. He parked near the top of a hill, where the truck was out of sight from the border below, got out and climbed the hill. A dark green baseball cap that matched his uniform covered most of his black hair and shielded his eyes from the bright sun. He tilted it back as he lifted the binoculars he'd brought with him to his eyes.

He didn't look up at the sound of hoofbeats. Slowly he scanned the border, looking for anything interesting. He found nothing but continued to look until he heard the voice.

"I want a transfer."

Lowering the binoculars, he turned to Cody. His response was blunt and accurate. "You look like hell."

Cody wasn't offended. He *felt* like hell; he might as well look it, too. "I want a transfer," he repeated.

"Can't do that." Kyle gestured to Cody to join him on the ground so he wouldn't be so visible from below. "It would be too difficult to bring in someone new now. You're already there. Unless you have the proof we need to bust Green, you'll have to stay."

He didn't *have* to stay; they both knew that. He could quit. But they both also knew that he wouldn't.

"What's the problem?"

Cody needed someone to talk to. For six days he hadn't spoken a single unnecessary word to anyone—not even Arcadio. He had learned to look through Mariah, to shut out the soft sadness in her voice on the rare occasions when she had to speak to him. But he hadn't learned to hate her, hadn't learned to stop wanting her, to stop loving her, to stop needing her. He hadn't learned to stop waking up in the middle of the night, hard and aching for her.

"I started working here eleven years ago." He stared with sightless eyes at a nearby cactus. "I met her here. We were supposed to get married."

"I know." Kyle avoided looking at the younger man. He could hear the emotion in Cody's voice; he didn't want to see it in his face. "You were going to be married in June, after she graduated. But she didn't want to come back here, so...you left."

Cody looked at him. "You bastard."

Kyle didn't like the guilt that crept through him, but he knew it was deserved. "It wasn't my idea to bring you back, especially with her here. They thought you were their best choice. They figured that with your past relationship, you'd have a better chance than some stranger."

A better chance at what? he wondered bitterly. Seducing her? Using her to arrest Green? Gaining her trust and turning it against her? Betraying her?

But she had betrayed him first. And the border patrol and INS had gotten to him even before that. He was getting screwed all around.

"You guys are real bastards." And Mariah was a bitch, and *he* was a fool.

"Have you learned anything?"

A lot, Cody thought. He had learned how stupid he could be. How much he could hurt. But those lessons weren't important to Parker and the mysterious "they" who had sent him here. "Green says he's not smuggling anymore."

"Do you believe him?"

"No. He's still involved."

"Word around town is that Suzanne is pregnant. Has he said anything about it to you?"

"No." Nobody said anything to him anymore, because they knew he wouldn't answer. Mariah was especially quiet in his presence. She had never tried to speak to him, never tried to apologize, never tried to tell him that he'd been wrong. She had never tried to defend her love.

"He was at a political rally in Phoenix a couple of weeks ago. There's another one scheduled in Tucson next week. A lot of people active in the movement are supposed to be there." Kyle glanced at Cody, then back toward the border. "If Green's going, see if you can get him to take you with him."

Cody acknowledged him with a nod.

"I'm sorry, Cody," Kyle said quietly. "For whatever it's worth..."

"I'll get the information on Green. In exchange, I want something from you."

"Anything I can do."

Cody stared at the ground so hard that the rocks and sand faded into a blur. "I want a transfer to some place up north. The day I give you the evidence that Green is smuggling, I want out of here."

Kyle nodded once. "I think I can arrange that." He offered his hand as Cody stood up. He wasn't surprised that Cody wouldn't take it. Under the circumstances, Kyle couldn't place much value on his own handshake. "Keep in touch."

Cody moved gracefully into the saddle. "Be sure you close that gate when you leave."

Kyle frowned. The reminder was unnecessary. The law gave them access to border property, but he certainly wasn't going to abuse it by making the owners of that property angry with his carelessness.

Cody rode for hours, crisscrossing the ranch, without seeing another person. The solitude of the desert suited his mood today. He stopped to watch the sun set and found himself miles from the house. He didn't worry. It was never completely dark. Now the last rays of the sun lit his way. When they were gone, the first rays of the moon and the stars would do the job.

Back at the stables, he lingered with the horse, stretching out the brief time he needed to settle the animal for the night. He was delaying going back to his house. Nights were the worst. Nights were when he slept, when he dreamed, when he needed her the most. His sleep was so restless that, each morning when he awoke, he was more tired than the night before. Living without Mariah was enough to drive him to drink, he admitted grimly.

Finally there was nothing left to do. He passed the dark, silent houses of the other hands and entered his own dark, silent home, moving with confidence to the bathroom.

He showered away the day's sweat and grime, rubbed a towel briskly over his body, dried his hair and combed it back with his fingers. Shutting off the bathroom light, he opened the door, stepped into his unlit bedroom and froze.

For a moment he smelled her—the light, sensual scent of her perfume. Was he remembering? Or wishing?

Then he heard her—the uneven breathing, the sniffle that indicated tears, the whisper of sound as she moved.

And finally he saw her, standing in the doorway in a white skirt and a white blouse and white shoes. Even the big plastic clasp that held her hair in a graceful ponytail was white. He looked at her, and she looked back; then he spoke at last.

"The price has gone up, Mariah," he said in an insolent, mocking drawl. "You're paying me the wages of a hired hand. That doesn't include sex. You'll have to come up with a whole lot more to buy that."

Chapter 10

She had to struggle to speak. Hidden inside her skirt pockets, her hands were clenched into fists, her nails gouging deep half-circles in her palms. "What do you have in mind?" she asked in a quavering whisper. She would give him anything—anything to make him forgive her, to make him stop looking at her with such disgust.

"How about the deed to the ranch?"

Even though he couldn't make out her features, he could tell that his sarcastic response had struck her like a blow. Her voice was stronger, but so was the quaver when she sorrowfully answered, "That's what Dad always said you wanted. Not me. Just the land."

He exploded then, in anger and wounded outrage. "I never wanted your damn land!" he shouted. "You think this piece of land means anything to me without you?"

The thunder of his voice made her cringe, and the tears broke free. They left wide wet streaks down her cheeks and made it nearly impossible for her to swallow. "Cody, I'm sorry," she whispered. "I'm so sorry. Please...please don't hate me for this."

He dragged his fingers through his hair, tugging mercilessly at the ends. When he answered, he sounded so weary. "I wish I *could* hate you. I wish I could see you the way I see every other woman. Not beautiful. Not important. Not special. I wish I could pass you on the street and not even give you a second glance. I wish I could meet you and forget your name five seconds later and forget your face ten seconds after that. I wish..." He gave a deep sigh. "I wish to God I'd never met you."

But that wouldn't have made everything all right. Even if they had never met, he would have known in his heart that something was missing, some vital part of him without which he would never be whole. He wouldn't have known that that part's name was Mariah, or that she was the most beautiful woman in the world, but he would have known that it was gone.

She drew one hand from her pocket. Clutched inside it was a tissue that she used to wipe her cheeks. "I'm so sorry," she said yet again as she turned to go.

"Wait." Once more his fingers tugged at his hair. Her apology was soft, barely audible, but it clawed at his heart. He should feel nothing for her, but he did. He should hate her, but he didn't. He should send her away... but he couldn't.

Hadn't they both suffered enough for what he knew rationally had been no more than a careless display of anger? She hadn't meant to hurt him last Monday night—his head knew that, although he'd had trouble getting through the pain to convince his heart. And he didn't want to hurt her tonight. He didn't want to hurt her ever again. "Stay with me, Mariah."

At his quiet request, she turned back. The moonlight shining through the window touched her face, revealing the faint hope his words had given her. "Can you forgive me, Cody?" she whispered.

He moved toward her. "I've been so miserable this past week." His fingers skimmed over her hair, then rested against her cheek. "I've missed you. I've missed looking at you and touching you. I've missed talking to you and making love to you. I've missed lying next to you and hearing you say, 'I love you.'" His thumb moved back and forth over her skin, wiping away the dampness left by her tears.

"I *do* love you. Let me explain—"

His thumb slid down to cover her lips, stopping the eager flow of words. "I don't need an explanation. I need you." His lips replaced his thumb, his tongue sliding neatly inside her mouth. With the gentlest of touches, he drew her to him, cradling her close to the hard, naked strength of his body. As the intensity of his kiss grew, so did the fullness in his loins. He swelled against her, hot and heavy, and deep in his throat, he groaned with hunger.

Mariah rubbed him, her hands gliding firmly over hard muscles and hard need, while she returned his kiss with matching passion. He wanted her. Even as tears once again filled her eyes, she told herself that it was enough. He hadn't said he loved her; he hadn't said he had forgiven her. All he'd offered was need.

She closed her eyes, but the tears squeezed out and inched down her face. Cody tasted the saltiness when one reached the corner of her mouth, and he raised his head to kiss them away. Why was she crying again? Feeling bewildered and totally helpless, he held her and kissed her. He didn't know what to say to erase her sadness. He didn't know how to ease her sorrow.

He lifted her into his arms, his muscles straining with the burden, and carried her to the bed. Gently he undressed her, and tenderly he made love to her. At some point—he didn't notice when—her weeping stopped, and she gave herself fully, completely, to their loving.

"I love you."

Her whisper reminded him of a cool breeze on a hot, dusty, dry day, bringing relief, comfort, pleasure. It also brought him guilt. He should be telling her the same thing. He *did* love her. He had always loved her. He always would. Even this last week, when he'd been hurting so badly that he'd wanted only to crawl into himself and never come out again, he had known that he loved her.

But he couldn't say it. Not yet. So he pulled her even closer, so that their skin touched and their breath mingled, so that he could feel her heartbeat, and she could feel his.

His silence made her smile sadly. His wanting was enough. His lovemaking was enough. She pressed a kiss to his strong, stubborn jaw. "Do you want me to leave now?"

His arm tightened around her. She made it sound as if he had used her and, now that he was finished, would discard her. He wasn't ever going to let her go, and someday he would find the courage to tell her so. For now, he just held her tighter. "No. Stay with me."

"All night?"

The silence was heavy for a moment; then he shut his eyes, kissed her forehead and answered, "Always."

Monday morning Mariah rose early and dressed, while Cody lay in bed, his hands folded beneath his head, watching. "You don't have to sneak back to the house," he drawled.

She smiled faintly. She remembered this conversation from another time, only then Cody had been the one leaving, and she had remained, warm and snug in bed. "You don't want everyone else to know that I spent the night here, do you?" She injected a teasing note into her voice and put on a smile to match, but she didn't find much humor in the subject. Last week's argument had made Cody's feelings on that matter painfully clear; he wanted their affair kept secret. He didn't want to acknowledge his involvement with her to anyone.

"I don't care what everyone else knows. I'll tell them myself, if you want."

She sat down on the bed, smoothing the sheet over his chest with slow, even strokes. "Do you really mean that? You're not . . ."

"Not what?" Hooking his finger beneath her chin, he raised her head. "I'm not what, Mariah?"

"Ashamed," she whispered.

Cody stared at her. "Why would I ever be ashamed of you?" He waited a moment, but she offered no reasons. "I

wanted privacy, Mariah—that was all. I don't want to hear
from Philip or David about their lovers, and I don't want
them knowing about mine. But I was never ashamed of you.
Never.'' He kissed her gently for emphasis.

"Thank you, Cody." She was smiling when she rose from
the bed and began searching for her shoes. "I'm going to
Tucson today, so I won't be here for lunch. Any chance that
you and I could have dinner together tonight? Just the two
of us?"

"Sure. Is David Green going with you?"

"No, he isn't. I told you before, Cody, that if I wanted to
invite someone along, it would be you."

"I *hope* it would." He got up and walked naked to the
dresser as Mariah slipped her feet into the shoes she had
discarded at the door the night before. "What do you find
so interesting in Tucson that you have to go there every
week?"

Mariah turned away so he couldn't see the tension that
lined her face. She hated lying to him. How much longer
could it go on? But what choice did she have? She could quit
her work with the movement, or she could tell him about it.
Neither option was very appealing. She didn't want to quit,
but she was quite certain that Cody wouldn't approve of the
risks she was taking every week. Since she couldn't make a
choice, she would continue to lie—and continue to hate it.

"It's just a city, Cody," she said lightly, pushing her
hands, folded into fists, into her pockets. "I usually see
Lissa, and sometimes I go by Mom's or Dad's office, de-
pending on what their schedules are like. It's no big deal."

"But it's important enough for you to do it every week."
He turned toward her, his face set in stern lines. "Why can't
you be satisfied with what you've got here, Mariah? Why
isn't the ranch enough for you?"

She clearly heard the real questions, the ones that remained unasked: *Why can't you be satisfied with me? Why
can't I be enough for you?* Eight years ago she hadn't been
satisfied, and she had lost him. Now she went to him and
wrapped her arms tightly around his middle. "I love the
ranch, and I love you, Cody. I *am* satisfied here. It's just

that sometimes I like to see Lissa and Mom and Dad. It has nothing to do with you or the ranch or being dissatisfied. It's just . . . friendship. Family.''

"And what am I?" If Lissa was "friendship," and Jerry and Helen were "family," that didn't leave much for him, did it?

It did.

"You're love," she said simply. She kissed his cheek, then left the house, closing the door quietly behind her.

It was chilly, the sky a dull, lifeless blue. Soon the sun would be rising, and it would be another gorgeous summer day. But Mariah didn't take time to enjoy the quiet of the dawn. She was too deep in thought.

Obviously her trips to the city bothered Cody. She thought she had eased his worries this morning, but how much longer would he accept her flimsy excuse of visiting Lissa and her parents? The time would come when he would demand to know exactly what she did in Tucson, and she didn't know if she could tell him. She didn't know how he would react, and that frightened her. After so many years, she couldn't bear to lose him again—not for any reason. Not even for those lovely, sweet, innocent children whom she met every week.

David had warned her a few weeks ago that someday she might have to choose between Cody and the kids. At the time, she hadn't wanted to face it, so she had pushed it from her mind. Now she knew that he was right. She would have to make a choice, and God help her, she didn't want to do it.

Mariah smelled the coffee as soon as she entered the house. Bonita was in the kitchen, cooking and humming along with the radio on the windowsill. "Good morning," she called over her shoulder. "You're up bright and early."

"Hmm." Mariah poured herself a cup of coffee, then took a deep breath. "What is that I smell?"

"Cookies, for the children." Bonita gestured to a wire rack on the counter, laden with hot, fresh-from-the-oven chocolate chip cookies.

"They smell wonderful." She sneaked one from the rack, breaking it in half, then taking a bite. "Oh, Bonita, these are delicious. I love chocolate chip cookies."

Bonita playfully slapped her hand as she reached for another; then she suddenly grew still. "Listen."

Mariah turned the radio louder, listening intently to the news story being broadcast. She stared out the window, her expression somber, aware that Bonita was watching her. When the story ended, she turned the volume down again and met the older woman's gaze. "It happens," she said with a simple shrug.

"'It happens'?" Bonita echoed. "Did you hear what he said? That woman was caught with six children from Carta Blanca! She's going to be charged with smuggling and conspiracy! She's going to go to prison, Mariah!"

"Probably not. They don't like to send people in the movement to prison. It makes martyrs of them." She tried to sound unconcerned, but there was a knot the size of a baseball in her stomach. No one in their group had ever been caught before. Of course they'd all known it was a risk, but somehow it hadn't seemed as real before as it did now.

"Do you know her?"

Mariah nodded. "Lela? I met her a couple of times. David knows her better than I do. She has three children, and she's divorced. I wonder what will happen to her kids."

Bonita turned back to the stove. "Don't go today, Mariah. Tell the Father that something came up, that you couldn't make it."

Her laugh was sharp and humorless. "I'm already lying to Cody. Now you want me to lie to a priest, too?"

"Don't go. It's too risky. You can't afford to get caught. You have too much to lose."

"Lela Groves has three children," she said quietly.

"At least let David go with you," Bonita persisted.

"Let David do what?" David had entered the kitchen unnoticed by the two women. Mariah said a prayer of thanks that it wasn't Cody who had overheard them.

"Mariah's going to San Benito. I don't want her to go alone."

Mariah handed David a cup of coffee. "Lela Groves was picked up by the border patrol yesterday, David. She had six kids with her."

He looked sick. "Oh, God, no… How did you find out?"

"It was just on the radio." Mariah sat down at the table, her fingers linked around her coffee cup.

"Was she arrested around here?"

"They didn't say. She usually crosses closer to Nogales."

"Maybe Bonita's right. Maybe I should go with you."

Mariah shook her head. "There's no reason for two of us to go. What could you do to help if we got stopped? Nothing but get yourself arrested. I can handle it alone."

They fell silent for several minutes; then David said, "I wonder what will happen to Lela."

"*I* wonder what will happen to the kids—both Lela's and the six she had with her. If I had any money, I'd get her the best lawyer in the state. She's going to need it."

"Who needs a lawyer?"

Three heads turned toward the door, where Philip and Cody were standing. It was the younger man who had spoken.

Under the table, David's foot pressed lightly on Mariah's, signaling her to remain silent. "A friend of mine," he replied. "She was arrested for smuggling illegal aliens."

Cody looked from David to Mariah. She was staring down, her expression as somber as David's. He went to stand behind her, laying his hands on her shoulders. His action didn't go unnoticed by the other two men. This was the man who had pretended not to notice Mariah's existence for a solid week—the same man who had treated them all as if they were some deadly form of the plague—simply because she had admitted their involvement to someone else. This was the first time they had seen him so much as touch her in front of anyone else.

"Smuggling on a Sunday?" Cody asked, trying to sound only mildly curious.

David answered hesitantly, "A lot of people believe that the border patrol has fewer agents out on Sundays than the rest of the week."

Cody had heard that, too, although he couldn't say there was much truth to it. He had worked his share of Sundays over the years.

"If you people would get out of my kitchen, I could get breakfast fixed a lot faster," Bonita said, interrupting the awkward conversation. "I don't know how you expect me to work with all of you hanging around in here."

They went into the dining room, carrying their coffee cups with them. Mariah set hers down while she gathered place mats and silverware from the hutch in the corner of the room. Cody helped her set the table, then sat down next to her. For the first time since she'd mentioned her plans to travel to Tucson, he was glad that she was going. He planned to ask Arcadio for a few hours off—to take care of some business. He wanted to talk to Kyle Parker about this arrest, to see if they knew how this woman was connected to David Green, and he didn't want to have to lie to Mariah—again.

Both David and Mariah remained subdued through breakfast. Cody watched each of them alternately. He knew David was concerned over the arrest; Mariah's worry was harder to figure out. She'd said nothing about knowing the woman. Maybe it was the visit to Tucson that bothered her—maybe she was planning to see her parents.

After breakfast he kissed her goodbye before heading outside to work. Quietly he arranged with Arcadio to take a couple of hours off at lunch. The old man accepted his explanation of "business" without question. Why should Arcadio question him? Cody wondered bleakly. He had never lied to the foreman in the past; Arcadio trusted him— another trust that he was betraying.

In the kitchen, Mariah helped Bonita with the dishes, then packed the still-warm cookies in a bag. "I'll come straight back, okay?"

Bonita nodded somberly. "If anything happens . . ."

Mariah forced a smile. "If anything happens, someone will let you know."

* * *

Efraín and Katy had heard the news of Lela Groves' arrest. They looked as worried as Mariah felt. "It's kind of a shock, isn't it?" Katy asked softly. "We all know it's a risk, but it doesn't seem so real until it happens to one of us. Have you heard anything about what will happen now?"

"Father Espinoza will probably know."

"Poor Lela. You know, the maximum penalty for smuggling is five years per count. She could be sentenced to more than thirty years in prison." Katy shuddered at the thought. "It's almost enough to make you think about quitting."

Mariah smiled faintly. She didn't tell her friend that she *was* thinking about quitting. It seemed such a cowardly thing to do, even though she'd begun considering it before hearing about Lela.

She had chosen a different crossing place for today's trip. She couldn't guess what the border patrol's response to their first success in the crackdown on Carta Blancan smugglers would be—whether they would increase their patrols or possibly relax their vigilance slightly—but following her normal routine wouldn't be wise. Once she was certain that Efraín knew where to meet her, she left San Benito and headed back to the border.

The customs agent was the same man she usually saw sweating in the heat and bored by the job. "Visiting friends again?" he asked when she stopped next to him.

Hidden behind her smile, her teeth were clenched. It didn't please her that the customs agent remembered her *and* her reason for being in Mexico. She shifted uncomfortably and couldn't quite meet his eyes.

"You make pretty regular trips to visit this friend."

She coolly replied, "I do whatever I want."

"Do you live around here?"

"My name is Mariah Butler," she said instead of answering. "My father is Jeremiah Butler, and my mother is Judge Helen Butler."

The agent took a step back. He'd been assigned to the Esperanza crossing long enough to know who the Butlers were and to recognize the power that they wielded, not just in Esperanza, but in the entire state. "Have a nice day, Miss Butler." His voice and expression belied the friendly nature of the words.

By the time she reached the agreed-upon spot, her fingers ached from gripping the steering wheel so tightly. Each border patrol truck that passed made her nerves tense even more. She was going to be a nervous wreck by the time she returned home this afternoon; she was sure of it.

She and Efraín approached simultaneously from opposite directions. The transfer of the children from his truck to her car was made quickly and smoothly; less than two minutes after stopping, she was on her way again.

She had never been so glad to see Father Espinoza's little church as she was that day. The children had ridden quietly, munching on Bonita's cookies and rarely speaking, not even when Mariah spoke to them. Her head ached, her hands were cramping, and her muscles throbbed.

"You look terrible," Lissa commented as they followed the children into the church.

"I have a headache."

"I guess you heard about Lela."

Mariah nodded.

"She's in jail here in town. She was arraigned this morning, and the judge set her bail at fifty thousand dollars." Lissa shook her head in dismay. "Nobody I know has that kind of money."

"Except your parents," Mariah said with a grin. "And my parents. And an awful lot of our friends."

Lissa smiled ruefully. "Let me rephrase that. Nobody I know is willing to spend that kind of money to help Lela. My parents would die if I asked them for it, and your parents would probably have me arrested."

"What about the children?"

"Father Espinoza said that lawyers for some Central American rights group based in Phoenix have already filed the necessary papers to allow the children to remain in the United States. It could take months for their cases to come before INS—but at least they won't be deported right away."

Mariah found little comfort in that. "Do you know how few Central Americans who request asylum are granted it?" She didn't need to ask; of course Lissa knew. She knew the figures better than Mariah did.

The estimates ranged from two to four percent—discouraging, Lissa admitted. "But these are children. They have no one to return to—no families to take care of them. Technically, INS can't even prove that they came from Carta Blanca. The oldest one is five. Are they going to deport a five-year-old orphan based on nothing but his word?"

"It wouldn't surprise me," Mariah said dryly. "What about Lela's children?"

"Her mother's taking care of them for now. We're still hoping to get her out on bail." Lissa studied her friend for a moment, then suggested, "Let's run down the street and get a hamburger. You look like you need a friendly shoulder."

Mariah agreed. She wasn't sure Lissa could offer any advice, but just talking to someone who knew what she was doing might help.

"Judging from the look in your eyes," Lissa began when they were seated in a booth at the restaurant, "I'd say you want out."

Mariah stared at her. "Is it that obvious?"

"Yes."

She took a bite of her hamburger and swallowed without tasting it. "It isn't that I *want* out," she said slowly. "I don't think I have much choice left."

"Because of Cody."

She nodded.

"Does he know what you're doing?"

"No. I can't tell him. I don't think he would approve, and I can't bear arguing with him." She gave a deep sigh. "I know we have an obligation to the kids, Lissa, but . . . what if carrying out that obligation hurts our families? Is it all right for me to hurt Cody and my parents in order to help those children?"

"I can't answer that for you. It's your choice."

That was the only answer Lissa could give; Mariah realized that, but she was still disappointed. She didn't want advice, she decided. She wanted someone to tell her that it was all right to quit. That she wasn't being selfish in choosing Cody over the children. That she wasn't being cowardly, or avoiding her obligation as a human being to help those who needed help. That it was all right to be afraid of going to prison, of living the rest of her life without Cody.

"Don't you ever worry, or get scared?"

The blonde lifted her shoulders. "I'm scared most of the time. I guess I've just gotten used to it. Maybe I just don't feel that I have as much to lose as you do. I've never been that close to my parents, and I don't have anyone else in my life. Just the kids."

Mariah looked at her friend for a long time. She had never considered that Lissa might feel lonely. She was such a pretty, intelligent woman, and she had more friends than she could count. Mariah hadn't realized that, since the breakup of her marriage, there had been no one special in Lissa's life.

"Do what you have to do, Mariah. Follow your conscience. If Cody is that important to you, your obligation to him supersedes your obligation to anyone else." Lissa smiled gently. "Maybe you ought to be talking to David. I think he understands your dilemma better than I do, since he's going through the same thing himself. Any change there?"

Mariah shook her head. "Suzanne's still refusing to marry him. I don't have that problem. If Cody asked me to marry him, I would say yes so fast that his head would spin." The wistfulness in her voice softened her black eyes as she rose from the table. "We'd better go," she said softly, aware that further conversation wouldn't solve anything for either of them.

"They picked her up yesterday afternoon a couple of miles east of Nogales." Kyle Parker pointed to a place on the map, then turned back to Cody. "There were six kids. The youngest is about nine months, the oldest probably five or six.''

The ages stunned Cody. He'd known all along that they were smuggling children, but he hadn't given it much thought. These were *babies*. "Are they going to deport them?"

"Where would we deport them to? We can't even prove that they're from Carta Blanca. The kids are too scared to talk, and they weren't traveling with passports or ID cards. All we know for sure is that they're Latino."

"What do you know about the Groves woman?"

Kyle gave him a brief rundown. She'd had no prior arrests. Although they were aware of many people in southern Arizona who sympathized with the Central Americans, they hadn't suspected that Lela Groves was one of them.

"She's a friend of David Green's," Cody said flatly. "He seemed pretty upset when he heard the news."

"Almost all their crossings are made during the day. Is he ever gone without explanation?"

"Only twice since I started working there, and both times he was with Mariah." Cody scowled jealously. "They had 'business' in Tucson."

Kyle left his desk and paced the small office. After seeing Cody yesterday, he hated to make this suggestion, but he had to. "Look, I know you're pretty heavily involved with Mariah Butler, but . . . is it possible that she—"

"No."

"Are you sure?"

Could she be the smuggler they were after? Was his love blinding him so that he could see only what he wanted to see? Was she lying to him, deceiving him the same way he was deceiving her? "I'm positive. You'd have to know Mariah to understand. She's just so damn honest."

"That puts you in a hell of a position, doesn't it?" Kyle asked bluntly. "When she finds out that you've lied to her . . ."

"We'll work it out." Cody stood up, unwilling to sit still any longer. "How much more time do I have? This can't go on forever."

Kyle grinned. "Don't count on it. The government doesn't like being outsmarted by a bunch of priests, nuns and housewives. The war in Carta Blanca might end before INS is willing to give up on this."

That would be a pleasant surprise. "How's it going down there?" he asked. The only news he heard was on the radio; he didn't have time to watch television, and he rarely saw a newspaper.

"The government has requested peace talks with the *contra* leaders." Kyle paused to light a cigarette. "Of course the last time they did that, when the *contras* showed up at the meeting place, the army executed most of them. These wars tend to drag on for years, Cody. We'll probably be old and retired before this one ends."

"I'd better get back to the ranch."

"I'll let you know if anything happens. The U.S. Attorney might be willing to make a deal with Groves—to drop the charges if she'll give the names of the others involved. If she's as dedicated as most of them, she won't say a word. But she's got three kids of her own. She might decide that keeping them is more important than going to jail for a cause."

"That's blackmail."

Kyle shrugged. "When she picked up those kids yesterday, she knew the risks. Women in prison can't take care of their children on the outside."

"How many of these women have been sent to prison?"

"Offhand, I only know of one, in Texas. But it's going to happen sometime. Most of the people convicted in these refugee cases have gotten off with suspended sentences or probation. That's not a deterrent—it's a slap on the wrist. Sooner or later the courts are going to have to give someone a *real* sentence, if for no other reason than to make an example of him—or her."

"And Lela Groves, with her three children, seems like a good place to start, doesn't she?" Cody asked sarcastically. "Especially since the majority of people smuggling refugees are women."

Kyle shrugged. He sounded callous, and he knew it. "It will make them choose between their high ideals and the law. Between some stranger's kids and their own children—the ones that they're morally, legally and ethically responsible for."

Cody walked to the door. His shoulders were rounded with weariness. "Sometimes...I don't like this job much."

"I know." Kyle sounded tired, too. "Sometimes I don't either."

When he left the border patrol station, Cody drove straight back to the ranch. He had a full afternoon of work to put in before dinner—dinner with Mariah. Despite his somber mood and the guilt he felt over his lies, the prospect of an evening alone with Mariah was enough to put a smile on his face. This was what he wanted: to work with her; to live with her; to spend every evening of the rest of his life with her. He wasn't going to lose her.

This time he wasn't going to let her go.

Chapter 11

On Friday morning Arcadio sent Cody and David into town to pick up supplies for the ranch. It was the first chance Cody had had to question Green about Lela Groves, and he took advantage of it as they drove away from the ranch. "Have you heard anything about this friend of yours who got arrested?"

David shrugged. "She's still in jail. They're trying to raise the money to get her out."

"Why did she do it?" Cody asked suddenly, bluntly. "What makes a divorced woman with three children to support risk everything she's got for six kids from another country she doesn't even know?"

"Conscience. Religious beliefs. Humanity." David turned slightly in the seat to look at him. "If your child—or better yet, if Mariah's child—was playing in the road, and a truck was coming toward him at eighty miles an hour, would you risk your life to save him?"

Cody's muscles grew taut. Mariah's child would be *his* child. He wanted children with her—wanted them so badly that he couldn't consider the possibility of not having them. But he blocked the vision of a pregnant Mariah from his mind and answered David's question. "Sure, but that's different."

"Different how? Because you'd know the kid? Because it would be Mariah's child, and not some stranger's son or daughter?"

"You're talking about saving a kid's life. This is about breaking the law."

David shook his head in exasperation. "This is about saving a kid's life, too—or in this case, six kids' lives. People are dying in Carta Blanca every day—men, women, children and babies. Those six kids that Lela had were probably orphans. More than likely they saw their families murdered right in front of them. A lot of them have been wounded themselves. She was trying to give those six kids a chance to live."

"What about her own kids? How can she justify what she's done to them? Why aren't her own kids more important to her than some stranger's children?" That was probably the one thing that Cody truly couldn't understand. These people risked more than their freedom; they put their families at risk, too. If Lela Groves went to prison, her children would lose their mother. Green was risking a lifelong separation from Suzanne and his unborn child. They chose their beliefs, their convictions, over the people they claimed to love, and as much as he was beginning to sympathize with their work, Cody would never, in his entire life, be able to understand that.

"How could she stand by and do nothing while innocent children are being slaughtered?" When Cody didn't offer an answer, David hesitantly extended an invitation. "There's a rally in Tucson Sunday. They're going to try to raise some money for Lela's defense, and there are going to be a lot of people there who work with refugees—legally and illegally. Maybe they can make you understand. Do you want to go?"

Cody was reluctant to accept. Sundays were the only days he could spend with Mariah. He was working six days a week as it was; couldn't they have one day for themselves? But he knew he couldn't turn down the invitation, not when Parker had specifically told him to go along if he could.

That was why he was here—to find out what Green was up to. "Yeah, sure. Just don't expect me to be easily impressed."

David smiled wryly. He already knew that. There wasn't much beyond the boss that impressed Cody Daniels at all.

"I don't understand," Mariah said cautiously. "What's your sudden interest in the refugee movement?"

It was Sunday morning, and they were settled comfortably on the sofa in Cody's living room. She had been more than a little stunned earlier when he had announced that he had already made plans to spend the day in Tucson with David Green. It was so totally unexpected that she didn't know what to make of it.

"I'm curious."

"About what?"

He chose an answer that he knew would convince her, and he hated it, because it violated her trust in him. "This friend of Green's, the woman who was arrested last week, she's got kids of her own, but she chose those illegals—" Remembering how she disliked that word, he grinned. "Excuse me, those undocumented aliens over her own children. I want to know why. I want to know how she could betray her own flesh and blood like that."

Mariah sighed softly. She should have known Cody would see it that way. How could he view things differently, when his own parents had betrayed him? She couldn't even argue the point with him. There were jobs Lela could have done that wouldn't have entailed actually smuggling the children, jobs that wouldn't have taken her from her two sons and her daughter.

"You have to admit that these people are something of an oddity," he continued. "From what I understand, for the most part they're a fairly religious bunch—priests and ministers, nuns, lay workers. But they're criminals. They're breaking this country's laws left and right. I'm curious."

"These are good people, Cody. They see a problem, and they do what they can to help. How can they stop and discuss right or wrong, legal or illegal, when a child's life is in danger? The government, INS, the border patrol—they see things from a different point of view. They want to see proof, then they'll make studies, and they'll consider taking action, and eventually they might change the laws or apply them more fairly. But the proof they need is bodies, and for those people, it's too late—they're dead. Why should anyone have to die to prove that his life is in danger?''

She realized that Cody was staring at her, his blue eyes wide with surprise. She smiled ruefully. "I've spent a lot of time in the last seven months or so listening to David," she offered in explanation.

Cody hugged her closer, pulling her head down on his bare chest. "Come with us," he invited. "We can still spend the day together."

"No thanks." If Lissa, Father Espinoza and her other friends saw them together at the rally, it was possible that they might say something about her work in front of Cody. "But if you don't mind, I'll meet you afterward. I can go see my mom and dad, then we can meet for dinner this evening."

"All right." He kissed her forehead. "I'll drive up with you, then. We can follow Green."

There was a large crowd in the park that David led them to—four or five hundred, Cody estimated. He made arrangements with Mariah to meet her in a few hours, gave her a quick kiss and climbed out of the car.

David was greeted by almost everyone they passed, or so it seemed to Cody. He followed Green while he scanned the crowd for familiar faces. After the first speech began, given from a hastily constructed platform in the center of the park, he found one: Lissa Crane.

She stood next to a priest, a handsome man not much older than Cody. When she realized she was being watched, she looked up. Surprise rounded her eyes when she recognized him. Weaving her way through the crowd, she reached his side a moment later. "Hi. Where's Mariah?"

Cody's gaze was cool and thoughtful. "What makes you think Mariah's here?"

Lissa mentally bit her tongue. "Well...it's no secret that you loathe the city. I figured Mariah was the only incentive that could get you here. My apologies if I'm wrong."

"She's at her parents' house. We're meeting when this is over."

"So you're interested in Central American refugees?"

He shrugged. "I'm interested in a lot of things. How are you connected to this?"

"I'm interested in a lot of things, too." Lissa combed her fingers through her blond hair, then folded her arms across her chest. She looked as if she were ready to challenge him.

She knew she had met the enemy, Cody thought with a humorless grin. He wasn't surprised that she felt that way. Mariah's parents hadn't been the only ones to disapprove of their engagement eight years ago; every one of her friends, including Lissa, had also spoken out against Cody. "You sympathize with these people?" he asked in a sardonic drawl.

She met his gaze evenly. "How can anyone with an ounce of compassion *not* sympathize?"

She would be surprised, he thought, by how compassionate he could be. She probably still thought he was too common to have feelings. "So compassion makes it all right to break the law?"

Lissa shrugged. "The immigration laws are unjust, and they're unfairly applied, based on the Administration's prejudices. Is it wrong to break an unjust law?"

"A law is a law. Who are you to decide its justness?"

"Who are you to judge what we're doing?" she countered.

Aware that they had gained an audience, including the priest who had been next to Lissa, Cody raised one hand in self-defense. "I'm not judging. I'm just here to learn."

"I see we have a cynic in our midst." The priest extended his hand. "I'm Julio Espinoza."

Before Cody could introduce himself, Lissa did it for him. "This is Cody Daniels." She gave him a sly smile. "He's one of Mariah Butler's employees."

Cody had enjoyed the brief exchange with Lissa, but her emphasis on his proper place in Mariah's life erased the pleasure. For just an instant he hated her for it. He shook the priest's hand and said easily, "I'm not a cynic, Father. I'm just curious."

"Feel free to ask any questions you'd like. That's the best way to learn about us. Knowledge can be a powerful tool."

It could be a more powerful weapon, Cody silently admitted. A little more knowledge, and he could probably bring charges against most of the people here.

He kept an eye on David throughout the afternoon, listening to his conversations, making note of who he talked to, and he learned nothing. The day would have been better spent alone with Mariah. Finally, after several hours, he left David and found a spot under a shady tree nearby. From there he could see Green but still be alone to think about Mariah.

"You look troubled."

He was surprised to see the priest. Had he been so deep in thought that he hadn't noticed the man's approach?

"I've been told that I'm a very good listener," Father Espinoza joked.

"I'm not Catholic."

"That's okay. We speak the same language."

After a moment Cody shook his head. He couldn't discuss his problems with this man. "Do you know Mariah?" he asked idly, wondering why Lissa had made a point of mentioning Mariah when she had introduced him to the priest.

"We've met. She's a lovely woman."

"Yes. She is."

"Have you learned anything new from your few hours with us?"

Cody shrugged. He had listened to a lot of conversations, had asked a few questions and had received relatively satisfactory answers. But no one had explained to him why Lela Groves had betrayed her children. There was no explanation, he decided. There couldn't be one.

"Would you like to join us?"

"No." He didn't need time to consider it. Although it had been done before by INS-paid informants, there was no way Cody was going to infiltrate this movement. He was lying to enough people in his life as it was; he wasn't going to add the priest or anyone else to the list.

And he wasn't going to lie to Mariah anymore.

That certain knowledge brought him a sense of well-being, of peace, that had been absent from his life for too long. If he loved her, he had to trust her. If he trusted her, he had to stop deceiving her.

"Thanks, Father," he said with a pleasant smile.

"For what?"

"For making me think. It was good meeting you." He shook hands with the priest and crossed the park to the place where he had agreed to meet Mariah. She would be there soon, and he wanted to be ready.

"Are you sure you can't stay longer?" Helen asked as she walked to the door with Mariah. "Your father will be home soon."

Mariah shook her head. "Sorry, Mom, but I told Cody I would pick him up in half an hour. What is Dad doing working on a Sunday, anyway? Doesn't he know that this is supposed to be a day of rest?"

"He's got a murder case starting tomorrow. He wanted to go over some of the details again with the detectives involved. He'll be sorry he missed you."

"I'm sorry I missed him, too." Mariah hugged her mother, then stepped back, grinning. "But I'm not sorry I missed his usual lecture about selling the ranch, and I'm certainly not sorry I missed whatever he's got to say about Cody. I know he's convinced that I'm crazy where Cody's concerned."

"Crazy in love," Helen murmured with a faraway smile.

"What?"

The smile deepened. "That's what your father used to say—that he was crazy in love with me. He shouldn't be surprised that it's happened to you." She pulled her daughter closer for another embrace. "Be careful."

"I will."

"And be happy."

Mariah answered in a husky, hopeful voice, "I'm trying. I've got to go now, Mom. Cody will be waiting."

Helen leaned against the door, watching until the Grand Am was out of sight. She had just straightened to close the door when another car turned into the driveway, Jerry's steel-gray Mercedes.

He looked grim when he climbed the steps to kiss his wife. "Is Mariah gone?"

"Yes, you just missed her. What's wrong?" Helen took his briefcase and led the way inside to the small, informal family room.

"I ran into Sergeant Shepard today." At the bar, Jerry fixed himself a drink. With a raised brow, he offered one to his wife, but she refused. "I had asked him to run a check on Daniels."

Helen frowned sternly at her husband. "You didn't." Yes, she sighed, he did. She should have expected it. "And what did you find out?"

"Cody Daniels isn't a cowhand," he said tersely. "He's a border patrol agent—and he has been for nearly eight years."

Cody glanced at Mariah, who was still sitting close enough for him to touch if he reached out—close enough for him to smell her perfume if he breathed deeply. She was so relaxed, so comfortable, next to him. Everything about her felt so right, and it reinforced the decision he'd made earlier.

He wanted to be honest with her. Completely, totally, unquestionably honest. Once she knew his secrets, then she would know his love. Once he had ended the lies between them, he could ask her to marry him. He could build a life with her, a future. One that would last forever.

Her head was tilted back, her eyes closed. When he looked at her again, he caught her in a delicately covered yawn. The moonlight, silvery and bright, bathed her face with its softness. She was beautiful.

Feeling his gaze on her, Mariah laughed throatily. "Sorry about that. It's been a long day."

"I know," he agreed softly. They had both been too tired during dinner to sustain a conversation, so they had eaten quietly. Most of the trip back had passed in silence, too. "How is your mother?"

"She's fine."

"And your father?"

"He wasn't there, but he's fine, too."

He reached out to touch her hair, smoothing an unruly strand back into place. "When are you going to tell your parents about me?"

Mariah blinked, trying to bring herself completely alert. "They know. That's what Rosalie and I were arguing about last week. She'd taken it upon herself to call Mom and tell her that you were back."

Cody sat silently for a moment. He could imagine Jerry and Helen's reaction to the news. They must have been furious with their daughter—and then *he* had taken his own anger out on her, too. "I'm sorry," he said softly. "I was wrong to say..." He remembered how nasty he had been to her and winced. "I'm sorry."

Mariah shrugged off his apology with a smile. "It's all right."

"No, it isn't. I said—"

She interrupted him. "I remember what you said." And the memory could still hurt her. "You wouldn't have gotten angry if I had handled the situation with Rosalie better. And none of it would have happened if Rosalie had minded her own business." She reached across to lay her hand on his thigh, wanting the physical contact with him.

Cody lifted her hand to his lips, placing a warm, open-mouthed kiss in her palm. "When we get home...can we talk?"

"We can talk now."

"No. This isn't the sort of thing we should be discussing in a car." He smiled, just a bit nervously. "I want to tell you something."

Mariah felt a quiver of excitement deep inside. Love? Was he finally going to tell her that he loved her? Making a vow of love definitely wasn't the sort of thing he should do on the highway; she would be so thrilled, she would probably cause him to have an accident. And it would explain that brief glimpse of nervousness that she had seen.

The more she considered it, the more sure she was. Eight years of waiting were going to end tonight. After a lifetime of believing that she would never again have Cody's love, she was finally going to hear him say the words tonight.

"All right," she agreed softly.

At the ranch, Cody parked his truck next to his own house; then they walked, hand in hand, back to the main house. "Come into the living room," Mariah invited, leading the way down the tiled hall.

While she turned on several lamps, Cody sat down at one end of the sofa. Mariah took her seat at the opposite end, facing him without touching him, waiting expectantly.

He had made the important decision earlier—to tell her the truth—but he didn't know how to start. How did he tell the woman he loved that he had been deceiving her from the start? How could he convince her that he had lied only about his job, that it had absolutely nothing to do with her?

For a moment he regretted not telling her sooner that he loved her. At least that would have given her something to hold on to. It would have given her a reason to have faith in him when she found out that everything else had been untrue.

On the other hand, tonight's confession could give her a reason to doubt everything he'd ever said or done. If he had told her that he loved her, she could doubt that, too. It was better this way. He tried to convince himself of that.

Wiping his damp palms on his jeans, he cleared his throat, took a deep breath and spoke. "There's something I want to tell you, Mariah." It was an awkward way to start, but the entire confession was awkward. All he could do was hope and pray for the best. "I told you I was living in El Paso before I came back here, which was true, but...I wasn't working at a ranch there. In fact, I had the same job there that I had in California...the same job I have here."

Jobs? She was expecting a declaration of love—maybe even a marriage proposal—and he was talking about *jobs*? That sickening sensation that swept over her was disappointment crushing her hopes, Mariah realized. She struggled to hide it, to present a blank face. She felt so incredibly let down that for a long moment she couldn't understand what he was trying to tell her. If he wasn't going to tell her that he loved her, exactly what did he want to say?

She concentrated on his words, replaying them in her mind. *I had the same job there that I have here.* Yet he had just said that he hadn't been working at a ranch, which was obviously his job here...wasn't it? "I don't understand," she said in a soft, unsure voice.

Cody tried to gauge her response from her expression, but he couldn't tell anything. She looked stunned. Was she surprised, disappointed, angry—or just plain confused?

"Why are you here, Cody?"

"I got transferred back."

Transferred. He hadn't returned because he'd wanted to, and he hadn't stayed because he liked it. He was here only because someone had ordered him to be here. "By whom?"

Cody could see that it was beginning to sink in that he had been less than honest with her. There was a flash of emotion in her eyes; then they went blank again. He hated that emptiness. Even more, he hated knowing that he was responsible for it. But once he got through this confession, he could make it up to her. He could tell her how much he loved her, how much he needed her. He could make her forget that he had lied.

"The border patrol."

Mariah's body went rigid. She had expected love; she was getting a nightmare. The border patrol. The enforcement arm of INS—her enemy. And Cody was one of them. He was a border patrol agent. He was...a skilled, accomplished liar. He had lied to her. He had used her. God, he had made love to her.

She shook her head slowly, numbly. "No," she whispered.

"I've worked for them since right after I left Esperanza."

Mariah stood up. For the first time in his life, Cody saw her move clumsily, as if she couldn't quite control her body's actions. She looked down at him for a long time before asking in a sad little voice, "Did you ever care at all about me, Cody?"

He stood, too, clutching her hands in his. "Don't, Mariah," he commanded sharply, anxiously. "Don't do this."

"You asked me so many questions. You seemed so interested about everything in my life. I thought it was because of *me*. I thought you really wanted to know." She wiped away a tear. "I didn't know you were looking for information. Who are you spying on? David? Arcadio? Antonio? Me?"

He pulled her unresisting body into his arms, holding her close while his hands stroked her hair. "It's a job, Mariah. It has nothing to do with you, I swear."

"Nothing to do with me," she repeated miserably against his chest. "You came to *my* ranch, you asked *me* for a job, you slept with *me*—yet you say it has nothing to do with me." She raised one hand to wipe her cheeks, then pushed against his chest. Cody let her step back, but he still held her tightly. "Why are you telling me now?"

"Because I'm sick of the lies between us. I never wanted to deceive you, Mariah. I never wanted to hurt you." He touched her face, willing her to look at him, pleading with her to believe him.

"Why are you telling me *now*?" she asked again. "Does this mean that your . . . investigation is over?"

"No." He looked away from her. "It's not over."

She looked at him, at the lines etched into his face and at the deep weariness that darkened his eyes. He wasn't supposed to tell her this, wasn't supposed to confide in her. She understood what it had cost him to tell her, the tremendous amount of faith he had put in her. Did he understand what it was costing her to hear it? Did he understand that it wasn't David or any of the others that he was after, but that it was her?

"I . . . I don't want any secrets between us, Mariah," he said with a helpless shrug. "That's why I'm telling you."

She leaned against him, letting him bear the burden of most of her weight. Now he thought they had no secrets. He didn't know that the biggest secret of all was still between them, and would stay between them. If she'd had trouble discussing her involvement with Cody Daniels, ranch hand, how could she ever find the courage to reveal it to Cody Daniels, border patrol agent?

When she said nothing, his heart sank. He had thought this would solve all their problems; telling her about his undercover assignment would ease his guilt and clear the way for their future. Instead it had done nothing but hurt her, doubling his guilt and leaving their future a hazy question.

For a long time he held her close, wishing he could force love and acceptance and understanding into her through the contact. His hand moved tenderly over her hair, offering a wordless comfort that she gratefully accepted.

"I *am* sorry." His voice broke the silence and sent a tremor through her, causing her to stiffen in his arms. "Do you want me to go home?"

Mariah hesitated. It would be the first night in a week that they hadn't been together. One part of her wanted desperately to keep him here, close enough to touch for reassurance, but one part needed distance, time apart to assess the effects of his admission.

He took her failure to answer as a yes. Bending, he kissed each of her cheeks, then her mouth. "I'll go," he said quietly. He released her and started to walk away, then turned back. "Don't let this ruin it for us, Mariah. We've got something too important, too special, to lose it now. Please . . ."

She managed to give him a faint smile. "I—I'll see you tomorrow."

He had gone a few feet when she spoke again. "I love you, Cody."

His eyes met hers once more. Both sets, his blue and hers black, were tinged with sadness. Then he left.

Mariah stood where she was, unmoving. She heard his footsteps fade away; then the back door closed, leaving the house in silence. She still didn't move, except for the flutter of her lids, closing over eyes filled with tears.

It wasn't supposed to be like this.

Cody lay on his back, staring into the darkness with dry, gritty eyes. He had known that telling Mariah the truth would make a difference in their relationship—but this wasn't quite what he had expected. He'd expected . . .

He hadn't thought it through enough to know what to expect. He should have known that she would be angry, hurt and disappointed. He could deal with her anger and soothe her hurt, but he couldn't bear the disappointment. He couldn't bear knowing that he had let her down.

At least, when he was leaving, she had said that she loved him. It was more than he deserved, but he was grateful as hell for it.

The phone startled Mariah out of her statuelike pose. She stared at it for a moment, wondering who could be calling her at this hour on a Sunday night. She decided she didn't want to know. She didn't want to talk to anyone.

Numbly she left the living room. She locked the doors, turned out the lights, took a shower, dressed for bed and slid beneath the covers—all without thought, without feeling. There, in the quiet, dark warmth of her room, she let function return to her brain, let herself feel again.

She thought of the border patrol agents she had met— Kyle Parker and a dozen others. They were dedicated men and women in dark green uniforms, wearing badges and guns. She tried to imagine Cody in that uniform, carrying a gun, but the image refused to form. She simply couldn't accept that he was one of *them*.

"Them?" She choked on tearful laughter. Was that what it had come down to? "Us" versus "them"? Good against bad, right against wrong, the border patrol against the movement? Cody against Mariah?

She couldn't even confide in him. If she did, he would have to arrest her. She needed help, but she couldn't turn to the man she loved to get it.

She couldn't turn to anyone. She couldn't tell him that she and her friends were smuggling illegal aliens, and she couldn't betray him by warning David or Lissa or anyone else about his real job.

Tears, hot and stinging, spilled over, rushing down her cheeks to soak the soft fabric of her pillowcase. Feeling more lonely and alone than she'd ever felt before, she let them fall, until, finally exhausted, sleep claimed her.

Cody came to the house early the next morning, hoping to talk to Mariah before any of the other hands showed up for breakfast. Bonita was in the kitchen, but there was no sign of Mariah. When questioned, she lifted her shoulders in a shrug. "Sometimes she sleeps a little late."

"I need to talk to her, Bonita."

"You two have another fight?" She smiled fondly at him. "You go on. But be sure you come when breakfast is ready."

His knock at her door went unanswered, but he went inside anyway. She *was* still asleep, one hand curled beneath her cheek. Cody sat down on the mattress next to her and gently brushed a lock of hair from her face before he kissed her.

She woke slowly, smiling warmly at him. "Good morning," she greeted him, her voice husky and soft.

It wouldn't be, he guessed, as soon as she woke up enough to remember their talk the night before. Even as he watched, the light disappeared from her eyes, and she withdrew from him. It was subtle, nothing more definite than a faint sense of loss, but Cody felt it just the same. "Good morning," he responded sadly.

Mariah longed to take him in her arms and tell him that everything was going to be all right, but she couldn't lie to him. Until she was free of the movement, nothing would be all right for them.

Both Lissa and David had told her that quitting the movement for Cody was a choice *she* had to make. But she had thought she had time to make such an important decision. Last night, though, Cody had taken that time away from her. From now on, any contact that she had with the children or her co-workers was, in effect, a betrayal of *him*. She had to quit—had to quit *now*—and until that decision was effected, she had to stay away from Cody. When she was completely free of the group, with nothing to compromise her love, they could start again. And this time it would be forever.

She looked up at his dear, handsome face. He looked so anxious, worried by what he saw in her expression. How could she possibly keep him at arm's length for the few days it would take to sever her ties with Father Espinoza and the others?

"Cody..." Her courage almost fled when she saw the fear that flickered in his eyes. It would be so easy to pull him down to her, to make love to him, to pretend that everything was all right while she made the arrangements with Lissa and the priest—so easy and so wrong. Then *she* would be deceiving *him*. "I—I need a little time to...to think...."

To decide if she could forgive him for lying to her? He started to reach out, but she hastily pulled her hand back, out of reach. Her action hurt, and it showed in the brusqueness of his voice. "How much time?"

"Just a few days. Please, Cody..."

He walked to one of the windows to stare out. "Last night you said you loved me. I thought that meant it would be all right. But love isn't much without forgiveness, is it?"

She looked at the proud, straight line of his back and said in a faintly accusing tone, "That's more than you've given me."

He whirled around angrily to protest, but the words, along with the anger, died before he could speak them.

"What have you done that needs forgiveness?" he asked softly, making it clear that, in his eyes, she couldn't have done anything wrong.

"What I've done needs love."

He stared at her for a long time. At his sides, his hands formed fists, relaxed, clenched again. Finally he pushed them into his pockets, out of sight. "Would you believe me if I said it now? After what I told you last night, *could* you believe me?"

Mariah folded her hands in her lap. "I believe you without you saying it," she admitted quietly. "Maybe I'm fooling myself. Maybe I just want it so damn much that I have to believe in it, whether I have it or not."

"You've always had it," he nearly whispered. His eyes damp and bright, he turned away for a moment, then came back to kneel at the foot of the bed. "When I left here, this job saved me. It was all I had. I couldn't have you, so I made it the most important thing in my life. I worked like hell to be the best damn border patrol agent that ever existed, because it helped the pain. It helped me live without you."

He took a deep breath to strengthen his voice. "When they transferred me to Esperanza, I didn't want to come. When they told me to get hired on here at the ranch, for the first time ever I considered quitting. I had to decide if the job was important enough to me to face the pain of working here again."

"And it was."

He nodded once. "I had a duty, an obligation. This job got me through eight years without you, Mariah. Don't make me pay for that loyalty by sending me away now. I don't want to lose you."

"I'm not sending you away. I'm just asking for a little time to accept what you told me—what you are."

"What I am," he said deliberately, "is the man who loves you. That hasn't changed. Whether I work for you or for the border patrol, I'm still *me.*"

"And I still need some time."

He knew he couldn't change her mind; he accepted that ungraciously. "All right. I don't have much say in the matter, do I? What do you want me to do? Leave here until you decide that it's okay for me to come back? Or do you want me to pretend that I'm just another hand, and that you're just the boss and not my lover?"

She moved to the foot of the bed and clasped his hands. "Don't be angry, Cody. A couple of days...that's all I need."

A couple of days. It seemed like a lifetime to him.

Chapter 12

Cody needn't have worried about how to act around Mariah for the next few days: he rarely saw her. She ate her meals separately and never set foot in the office, where she might run into him. It was frustrating as hell to need her, to want her, and to know that he had to stay away from her.

He wanted to tell her that this was wrong. He had lied to her, he had shaken her faith in him, but sending him away wasn't the way to deal with it. She needed to work through it *with* him, not apart from him, and he needed to help her. But he had agreed to give her "time"—long, empty, lonely days without her. That promise kept him from her.

Mariah drove into Tucson on Monday afternoon to talk to Father Espinoza and Lissa. Reluctant to lose another worker so soon after Lela's arrest, the priest hadn't been above a little arm-twisting. He could be pushy and manipulative, he admitted good-naturedly, but only for the best causes. But Mariah held out against his pleas. She had to quit, she told him, without saying a word about Cody's job. Without giving a warning about Cody's job. She would make her last scheduled trip to the border on Wednesday, and then she was out.

When she arrived home, Bonita met her at the door with a grim smile. "Your father's on the phone."

Mariah rolled her head in a slow circle to loosen the muscles. "You say that as if it's a warning."

"It is. He says he called last night, and he's called three times already today. You'd better talk to him."

"Thanks." She picked up the receiver on the hall table, fortified herself with a cheery smile and said, "Hi, Dad. How is your court case going?"

"Where have you been, young lady? I've been trying to get hold of you since last night. I need to talk to you, and I'd rather not do it over the phone."

She leaned back against the wall. "I had some errands to run today. What is it we need to discuss?"

"Cody Daniels."

Mariah rubbed her eyes wearily. She should have known that her father wasn't going to let the subject drop. He had given in too easily when she'd seen him in his office. "What did you do, Dad? Call some of your buddies over at the police department and ask them to run a check on him?"

"You know me too well." He sounded pleased, not in the least ashamed of what he'd done.

"Okay. I'll be in Tucson Wednesday. Can we meet then?"

"I'll be in court all day. How about dinner?"

"That's fine. Why don't I meet you at your office."

She hung up after a few more minutes. The meeting with Jerry didn't worry her; on the contrary, she was starting to look forward to it. It would be a pleasure, when he broke the news of Cody's real job, to tell him that she already knew. He would be disappointed that Cody had confided in her.

She missed Cody, she admitted as she went to her room. She hadn't had even a glimpse of him all day. Only two more days, she counseled herself. In two more days she would be free.

Wednesday morning she made her last trip into San Benito. Lissa had volunteered to take it for her, but Mariah had refused. Her friend, along with another worker named Cheryl, was scheduled for Thursday and it would be too risky for Lissa to make two trips in two days. When she delivered the children to the church that afternoon, her commitment to the movement was fulfilled.

"Are you sure this is what you want?" Lissa asked, walking to the car with her.

She nodded.

"I don't understand. Last week you were talking as if this was something you planned to do in the future—not now."

"Circumstances changed. Maybe someday I can explain it all to you."

"If you ever change your mind . . ." Lissa let the words trail off. She didn't think Mariah would change her mind. Her friend was in love; Lissa fully expected her to be married and pregnant within a month. "You've been a lot of help and a good friend."

Impulsively, Mariah hugged the blonde. "I hope I'll always be a good friend."

"Send me a wedding invitation."

She laughed as she climbed into the car. "I will—as soon as he asks me."

"He's done that before. Why wait for a second time? You ask him."

"I just might." Mariah started the car, then looked back at her friend. "Be careful."

After she had waited for more than an hour in his office, Jerry showed up to escort her to a restaurant nearby. "Your mother can't make it," he explained as he scanned the menu. "Her schedule's fouled up again."

"Sometimes I wonder how you two ever manage to get together. You work the oddest hours."

"It can be tough." Jerry looked up at her and smiled. "You know, I think you get prettier every time I see you."

"Flattery isn't going to get you out of this one, Dad, but thanks anyway."

"Am I in trouble?" he asked innocently.

"Yes, you are." She gave her order to the waiter standing next to her, then folded her hands on the tabletop. "Why don't you tell me what you found out about Cody, then I'll tell you what I think of your methods," she suggested.

Jerry sobered. "Honey, you know I wouldn't ordinarily dream of interfering in your life—" he ignored her choked laughter "—but Cody Daniels has never been anything but trouble for you from the first day you met him. Do you know that he's lied to you? Do you know what his real purpose for being in Esperanza is?"

Mariah interrupted before her father could continue. "He's a border patrol agent," she said quietly. "And he's investigating a smuggling ring."

He looked surprised as he slowly relaxed back into his chair. He reminded her of a deflating balloon. "You know," he said in an accusing tone. "How did you find out?" His eyes narrowed suspiciously. "Have you been talking to your mother?"

"No. I've been talking to Cody. He told me himself." She didn't try to disguise the proud note in her voice. Jerry had never believed that Cody cared for her, so he'd never expected him to confide in her. She was glad she had proven him wrong. "Now it's my turn. What right did you have to check up on him? If I had wanted a background investigation, I would have asked for one."

"I just wanted to be sure that he wasn't lying to you."

She shook her head sadly. "No, you didn't. You were hoping for proof that he *had* lied, weren't you, Dad? You've never liked Cody. You've never thought that he was good enough for our family."

Jerry had the grace to look both guilty and apologetic. "He's a cowboy, Mariah. He doesn't fit in. You need someone better, someone who was raised the way you were raised."

"Someone like Chad?" she questioned dryly. "A lot of times when people fall in love they have to make choices, Dad. I've made a few choices already, and the most important one is that I'm going to marry Cody Daniels if he'll have me. And that means *you'll* have a choice to make. You can either accept Cody...or forget me. I won't subject my husband or my children to your prejudices. You'll have to choose."

They stuck to neutral topics while they ate, and after dinner, she leaned across to kiss Jerry's cheek and stood up. "I've got to go home now. Give Mom my love."

She walked out of the restaurant, leaving her father staring blankly after her.

The trip back to the ranch seemed to take forever, although she knew that was just her impatience. She wanted to see Cody, to tell him that everything was all right, that she loved him. Maybe, she thought with a carefree grin, she would take Lissa's advice and propose to him. After all, he *had* asked the first time. Now it was her turn.

It was already dark when she reached the house. She parked her car and walked straight to Cody's house, rapping lightly at the door.

"He's not home," David Green said from behind her.

Mariah's smile faded. "Where did he go?"

"Into town with Philip."

"On a Wednesday night?"

David shrugged. "Sometimes a person needs to relax and have a little fun."

Disappointment tugged the corners of her mouth downward. "I was hoping to talk to him."

"Why don't you try me instead?"

She smiled in spite of herself. "I don't think you'd want to hear what I was going to say to him."

"Try me. You might be surprised."

Pushing her hands into her pockets, she walked back to his house with him. "All right. Will you marry me?"

David burst into laughter. "You're right. You'd better save that question for Cody. He'll probably jump at the offer."

"Do you think so?" She smiled sheepishly. "I've never proposed to a man before."

"Half the time he's so happy he can hardly stand it, and the rest of the time he's so miserable he can hardly stand it." David smiled, too, giving her a hug. "I think he'll drag you off before you can change your mind."

"How's Suzanne?" Mariah sat down on the steps of David's house. They were still warm from the day's heat.

"She's still saying no. But I can wait. I'm stubborn."

They sat there and talked quietly for several hours, but there was still no sign of Cody and Philip. At last Mariah returned to the house so David could get to bed. She waited impatiently until midnight; then she, too, climbed into bed.

She had expected the evening to end in bed, she thought sadly as she snuggled beneath the vividly colored comforter; she just hadn't expected to be there alone.

It was after one o'clock when Cody drove past the main house. He was tired, but not too tired to notice that her car was there and the lights were off. She was probably in bed. As tired as he was, he wished like hell that he could join her there.

It had been three days. How much more time did she need? What was there to think about that took three entire days? The secret of his job hadn't been so important that it should take her this long to accept it.

He shouldn't have gone into town with Philip tonight. He was too old to be staying up late in a smoke-filled bar listening to loud music and louder customers. He'd known that spending a few hours there with Blake and his friends couldn't ease his loneliness. Only Mariah could do that, and she needed "time."

Another day. He would give her one more day, but that was all. Then they would have to settle things between them, once and for all.

The next morning after breakfast, Bonita gave Cody a brief message from Mariah. "Mariah said to tell you that time's up, and she'd like to have dinner alone with you this evening, here in the house, about seven o'clock. Can you make it?"

His swift, broad grin was answer enough. "I'll be here," he drawled. "Where is she now?"

"She's sleeping in, then she's got a few things to take care of for tonight."

Cody was still grinning when he left the house to work. Things were finally looking better, and tonight they would be better still: tonight he was going to ask Mariah to marry him.

"Mariah!"

In all her life, Mariah had never heard Bonita shout. Quickly fastening the pink clasp she was holding around her hair, she hurried down the hall to the front door. There stood Bonita, surrounded by five frightened youngsters, one of whom was sobbing as if his heart would break. "Who are they?" she demanded.

"This lady dropped them off. She said her name was Cheryl—she said you know her." Bonita bent to pick up the crying boy, drying his cheeks with the corner of her apron. "She said that Lissa has been arrested with seven other children, and she thinks the border patrol is looking for her. She left them here and took off."

Mariah stared at the children in dismay. "No," she whispered. "Bonita, they can't do this to me. I quit! I told them I can't help anymore!" She glanced quickly at her watch. "Lord, the men will be here for dinner in less than an hour, and Cody—" Her eyes formed large black circles. "If Cody finds them here . . ."

"I'll put them in the guest room. You find Cody and tell him that you want to go to dinner in the city tonight."

Mariah looked down at herself. She had been dressing for dinner; she was wearing a red knee-length robe over soft white silk lingerie. "I—I guess I'd better change. Thanks, Bonita."

The older woman shepherded the children to the bedroom farthest from Mariah's, closing the door behind them. As Mariah closed her own door and disappeared into the closet to find a pair of jeans and a shirt, the phone began ringing. Arcadio was probably in the office by now, she thought; he could get it. She shed her robe and tugged the fragile silk camisole over her head. She replaced it with a plain cotton T-shirt, then stepped into a pair of faded jeans. After the luxurious, sexy silk, the denim and cotton felt rough and ordinary against her skin.

She had just started down the hall when Cody rounded the corner. "Cody!" she exclaimed, sneaking a glance over her shoulder. Please, Bonita, keep them quiet, she prayed silently. "I was just coming to find you."

He laid his hands on her shoulders. "I need to talk to you."

"Can't it wait until dinner?" She managed to maneuver him back around the corner without seeming to push him away, but there he stopped.

"No. It's about Lissa Crane." Cody put his arms around her, pulling her close. "She was arrested just a little while ago," he said softly. "She was picked up with a bunch of kids—kids from Carta Blanca. I'm sorry, honey."

Her face was burning red. She tried to look surprised or shocked, but she knew the attempt was an awful failure.

She was rigid and unbending in his arms, Cody realized. He took a step back and looked at her, reading the guilt that shadowed her eyes, and he remembered Kyle's words, "The second woman got away with some of the kids, but we're looking for her. We should be able to pick her up before this evening."

Dread made him stiffen, and he stared down at her with dismay. "Mariah, where were you this afternoon?" His voice was hard and cold with the anger growing inside him.

"I—I had to pick up some things in town," she stammered. "Cody, I wasn't anywhere near the border!"

"How did you know Lissa had been picked up before I told you? How did you find out?"

Her sigh made her shudder against him. She was going to tell him the truth—everything—and pray that he would help her. But even as she opened her mouth, a door slammed down the hall; then came the sound of running feet.

The little boy skidded to a stop when he saw them. He looked from Mariah to Cody, then flung himself against Cody, wrapping his arms around his legs. *"¿Dónde está mi hermano?"* he cried. *"¿Dónde está?"*

The look Cody gave Mariah would have broken her heart if it hadn't been frozen solid in her chest. He released her and knelt in front of the boy, lifting him into his arms. *"¿Cómo te llamas?"* he asked softly.

The boy clung to him. "Rico."

"Me llamo Cody." He asked about Rico's brother in Spanish. The boy's answer was mumbled, but Cody understood the last three words, *"la otra mujer."*

The other woman. Lissa Crane. Cody glanced at Mariah, but she wasn't looking at him. *"No tengas miedo, Rico. Tu hermano está seguro."*

Mariah crossed her arms over her chest and leaned against the wall. She hadn't known Cody spoke Spanish, but, with his job, she supposed it was necessary. Don't be afraid, he had said. Your brother is safe. Rico's brother might be safe, but she knew *she* wasn't.

"Is Bonita back there?"

His voice changed from gentle with Rico back to hard when he addressed Mariah. She nodded.

He sent Rico back to the room, then stood up to face Mariah. "It was you."

She bit her lip.

"You knew I was investigating Green, and it was you all along." There was such disgust in his voice that it made her wince. "You've been putting me off for four days, to punish me for lying to you, when you've done nothing *but* lie to me. How do you do it, Mariah? How can you be so damn self-righteous?"

"Cody—"

"I want those kids out of here," he demanded. "I'll give you until noon tomorrow to get rid of them and to cut your ties to that group. If you haven't done it, I'm turning you *and* the kids over to INS. I'll be back then for your answer." He swung around to leave.

"Cody! Wait a minute! Let me explain...." Her voice faded as the door slammed behind him. Tears filled her eyes, and she angrily wiped them away. She had cried enough tears over Cody Daniels; she wasn't about to start again. By refusing to listen to her, he had shown how much he loved her. He had called her self-righteous when he wouldn't even give her the benefit of the doubt.

"Mariah, I'm sorry."

She wiped her cheeks again before facing Bonita. "It's all right. It's not your fault." She took a deep breath and managed a sorry smile. "Let's feed the kids. They must be hungry."

Mariah sat in the children's room all night, too unhappy to go to her room, too full of self-pity to sleep. It wasn't fair, she repeated over and over. Cody could have caught her all those times that she had actually done something illegal—then she wouldn't have felt so wronged. But she had *quit*! She had quit for *him*. Didn't that count for something?

At nine o'clock Friday morning, she and Bonita loaded the five children into her car. "Do you think it's safe?" the housekeeper asked as she tightened the seat belt over Rico's stomach.

Mariah lifted her shoulders in a shrug. "I don't have any choice. I have to take them today. Could you call Father Espinoza? Tell him that I'll get in touch with him when I get into town. He might not want me coming to the church."

Impulsively, Bonita folded her arms around the younger woman. For a long moment she simply held her; then she stepped back. She watched as they drove away from the house.

The children were quiet. In the mirror, Mariah could see that the littlest, only about three, had fallen asleep again, with the tiny rag doll Bonita had given her clutched in her hand. Two of the others, four- and six-year-old sisters, clung to each other. The two boys, Rico in front and Martín in back, stared out the windows at the desert.

"Oh my God."

Mariah took her foot from the accelerator, and the car's speed began falling. Rico looked up curiously, but he couldn't understand the sign they passed that read Stop Ahead—U.S. Officers. Less than a half mile ahead, she could see the makeshift roadblock set up across the highway, with several border patrol vehicles and uniformed agents on foot. For an instant she considered turning the car around and heading back toward Esperanza, but the sight of a border patrol truck parked on the shoulder just a few yards ahead effectively changed her mind.

She whispered a prayer as she slowly applied the brakes. There were three agents ahead, two in the center of the road next to another sign and one on the right. The cars ahead of her slowed, then picked up speed as the agent motioned them on. When she reached the three men, though, one of them bent down. "Would you pull to the side of the road, ma'am?" he requested politely, gesturing to an area on the sandy shoulder marked by brightly colored traffic cones.

All five children craned their necks, looking at the agents and the green and white trucks and vans parked next to the road. When Mariah brought the car to a stop and two agents approached, Rico's eyes grew so wide that his face seemed to disappear. *"¿La migra?"* he whispered. Suddenly he wriggled free of his seat belt and leaned over Mariah. *"¿Dónde está mi hermano?"*

The man ruffled his hair, giving him a smile. *"No sé. Espera un momento."* Then he turned to Mariah. "Could I see your driver's license?"

Rico wasn't satisfied with the agent's response; he didn't want to wait a minute. *"Pero—"*

"Siéntate, Rico," Mariah commanded in a whisper, motioning to him to sit down. Her hands were trembling as she removed her license from her purse and handed it to the man.

He glanced at it, then passed it on to the agent with him, this one a woman about Mariah's age. "Are you a U.S. citizen?"

She looked up at him. Kyle Parker had introduced her to him once before, but the only name she could remember was Montez. "Yes, I am."

"What is your place of residence?"

She haltingly gave her address.

"When were you last in Mexico, Miss Butler?"

It occurred to her to lie, but she didn't see that it would serve any purpose, other than getting her in deeper. It wouldn't be too difficult to prove her wrong. The customs agent at the border more than likely remembered her. "Wednesday."

"What was the purpose of that trip?"

"I was visiting friends in San Benito."

Montez bent a little lower and looked for a moment at each of the five children; then he turned his cool, dark gaze on her. "Are these your children, Miss Butler?" he asked softly.

The trembling in her hands was spreading through the rest of her body. She had to try twice to get the answer out; even then, it came out in a tiny, frightened little whisper. "No."

"If they're not your children, what are you doing with them?" His voice was even softer.

"I—I—" She quit trying. She couldn't tell him that she was taking them to Father Espinoza; they would have him under arrest before she finished speaking.

"Who are their parents?"

"I don't know."

"How did they get into this country?"

"I don't know."

"What is their citizenship?"

She looked at the children, laying her hand gently on Rico's head. They didn't understand what was going on. Rico was excited—she assumed that he recognized the uniforms as the same ones that the men who had taken his brother had worn—but the other four were frightened. Again she murmured a silent prayer, then looked back at Montez. "They're from Carta Blanca."

Montez straightened and opened the door. "Would you step out of the car, please?" With a nod, he signaled to another agent, who went to the passenger side. In Spanish, he asked the children to get out and follow him to the van parked nearby.

Mariah stood next to her car, turning her back to the bright morning sun. The metal was warm through the soft cotton of her clothes. She liked the car, she thought with a sigh. As of this moment, though, it was no longer hers. The border patrol might get to keep it, or some other government agency might preempt their claim, but she would never get it back. She was just grateful that it was her car and not her land.

"Linda, you want to search the car?" Montez called to the lone female agent before he turned back to Mariah. "You have the right to remain silent..."

She listened to the rest of his words without looking at him. The drivers of the cars being waved through the checkpoint gawked, curious about what was going on. She didn't look at them, either. And when another agent, tall, black-haired and handsome, joined them, she didn't look at him, either.

Kyle Parker just stared at her. When one of his men had told him in the van that they'd gotten the five Carta Blancan kids, he hadn't been surprised. But *this*—this surprised him. When Montez finished reading her the Miranda warning, Kyle said, "Mariah Butler. Just what the hell do you think you're doing?"

She looked at him at last and gave him a wry, strangely empty smile. "Going to jail, I'd say."

"I'm afraid so. At least for the few hours it will take your mother and father to persuade the judge to bond you out."

"Do my parents have to be notified?"

"Do you think we can keep it secret?" Kyle scoffed. "The daughter of County Attorney Jeremiah Butler and Judge Helen Butler arrested on ten or twelve felony charges? Everybody in the state's going to know by tonight."

Including Cody. What would he think when twelve o'clock came and she wasn't there to tell him that she had chosen him? He would probably think terrible things about her, until he heard the news of her arrest. She winced slightly. And he would probably think terrible things about her after he heard, too.

"Mike, when you take her to Tucson, I want to go along," Kyle said to Montez.

That was it, Mariah thought with grim satisfaction. His first name was Michael.

"I'm ready whenever you are," the agent answered.

"Aren't you going to handcuff me?" Mariah asked, her voice taut.

Kyle gave her a reproachful look, then took her arm and led her to the nearest truck. As she climbed into the cramped back seat, she thought somberly of her favorite childhood game, Monopoly. "Do not pass Go. Go directly to jail."

"Is Mariah back?"

Bonita shook her head. That must have been the tenth time Cody had asked that question in an hour. "You aren't getting much work done today, are you?"

He didn't respond. He had told Arcadio this morning that he couldn't work, and the old man had calmly accepted that. Since eleven o'clock he had divided his time between the house and the office, waiting for Mariah to return. "She took those kids, didn't she?"

"Yes."

"When will she be back? How long does that usually take?"

"A few hours."

"Then she should have been back by now. It's noon. I saw her drive away around nine o'clock. Was she planning to come straight home?"

"I suppose. She didn't say."

Cody sat down at the kitchen table. He'd given her until noon; it was ten after now. He didn't know what to do. What if she wasn't coming back? What if she'd decided not to quit? What if she had chosen the children over him?

Abruptly he stood again and began pacing the length of the room. He had given her an ultimatum, and time was up. Now he had to tell Kyle Parker. He had to find the strength to do what he had threatened: to turn her in. He stopped pacing in front of the telephone, stared at it, then turned away. He would give her another hour. One more hour wouldn't hurt.

That hour passed, too, and then the next one. At two-thirty he walked to his house, climbed into his truck and drove into town. He drove with the air conditioning off and the windows down, but the summer heat couldn't warm him. He was cold with dread, with fear and disappointment. Mariah hadn't come back, and she hadn't called him.

That could mean only one thing: she hadn't chosen him. She hadn't loved him enough to give up the children.

Kyle Parker had returned only a few minutes before. He was pouring himself a cup of coffee when Cody walked into the office.

"I need to tell you—" Cody broke off. What he was about to say could sentence Mariah to prison. How could he do that? So she didn't love him enough to want to be with him; he still loved her. Could he be the one to condemn her to prison?

"Close the door," Kyle quietly requested. When that was done, he motioned to Cody to sit down. "I just got back from Tucson. We found those five kids—with Mariah Butler. She's being held in the city. Her arraignment's set for Monday morning."

Chapter 13

Mariah stared out the bedroom window. Beneath her was the swimming pool, surrounded by her mother's garden. It was lovely and colorful, but it made no impression on her. All she could see in her mind was the ranch—the ranch and Cody.

Her arraignment had taken place this morning. Her parents had offered to use their influence to get her released Saturday, but she had refused. She didn't want any special favors because of Jerry and Helen. She had spent the weekend in jail, meeting once with Mitchell Wilson, the attorney her parents had chosen for her. The rest of the weekend she had been alone—and very lonely.

Eleven felonies—that had been the final total. Five counts of smuggling undocumented aliens; five counts of transporting undocumented aliens; and one count of conspiracy to violate the immigration laws of the United States. The judge had set the bond at fifty thousand dollars, and her father had promptly paid it. Mitchell Wilson had brought her here, to her parents' house, while Jerry returned to his own courtroom down the hall.

She couldn't see Cody, Mitchell had stressed. He would be called as a government witness to testify against her, and contacting him could only harm her case. But his warning didn't stop her from reaching for the phone and dialing the ranch number.

"Bonita?"

"How are you?" the housekeeper demanded.

"Okay. I'm out of jail—for the time being." She hesitated a moment. "Bonita, is Cody there, or...has he...?"

"He's gone, Mariah. He moved out Friday."

Mariah panicked. "He's still in town, isn't he?"

"Yes, he's living in town, but he's not supposed to come to the ranch or have anything to do with any of us." Bonita didn't add "especially you," but she didn't need to. That was another thing Mitchell had made clear. "Did you know, Mariah?"

"That he worked for the border patrol? I found out just a few days ago."

"Was he investigating you?"

"No. I just happened to be the one they caught." She wasn't surprised at the tears that were filling her eyes. "I want to come home, Bonita. I don't want to stay here."

"Can't you come back until your trial?"

"No, I have to stay here. I hate it here."

"If I should see Cody..."

"Tell him I was coming back. Tell him I'm sorry." She wiped her cheeks. "I've got to go, Bonita. Tell Arcadio I'll be in touch with him about the ranch. Take care of everything for me, will you?" She quickly hung up, before she broke down completely.

The judge had set the date for the preliminary hearing this morning—two weeks away. Then, according to her father, it would be another two to four weeks before her trial. Four to six weeks before she could see Cody, before she could know if he blamed her, if he hated her. She didn't know if she could stand it. She could endure anything in the world as long as she knew she had Cody's love, but not knowing—that was unbearable.

She sank across the bed, hiding her face in her arms. It was all right to cry, she told herself sorrowfully. She had lost those five children; she had spent three days in jail; she was sure to be convicted on those eleven charges; she faced more than fifty years in prison; and she just might have lost Cody. If those weren't good reasons to cry, she didn't know what would be.

But her eyes remained only slightly moist; the tears wouldn't come. It figured, she thought with a self-pitying sniff. Nothing else in her life was going right; why should this be any different?

The United States Attorney was a pretty, slim brunette named Sarah Johnson. She sat behind a desk so massive that it made her look like a child playing at being grown up, but the stare she was directing at Cody was strictly adult— cold, hard, appraising. "I assume you're here to discuss the Butler case."

Her voice was cultured, refined, rich. It reminded Cody of Helen Butler's voice. Other things about Johnson reminded him of Judge Butler—her efficiency, her killer instinct, her reputation for toughness, her air of superiority.

It bothered him to hear Mariah referred to as "the Butler case," but he didn't comment on it. Instead he shifted uneasily in his chair. The uniform that he'd worn for eight years seemed suddenly uncomfortable, more confining than jeans and boots, and the gun belt around his waist was heavy and awkward.

"You're one of the people who chose me for this job, aren't you?"

Johnson nodded once.

"Why?"

She smiled faintly. "Because of your past relationship with the Butlers."

"With the Butlers?" he echoed. "Or with Mariah?"

"Both."

"I thought you were aware of that. I just wanted to make sure before I tell you why I'm here."

She waited patiently, refusing to ask him to explain. When he was ready, he continued. "I was sent to the ranch to investigate David Green. No one ever told me that Mariah was a suspect."

"She wasn't."

"Well, while I was keeping an eye on Green, I was . . . doing a lot more than that with Mariah." He forced himself to hold Sarah Johnson's gaze, even though his face was flooded with heat. He wasn't ashamed of his involvement with Mariah, but he hated having to discuss it with this stranger, this woman, who was determined to send Mariah to prison.

"You're saying you had an affair with her." Johnson's voice was cold and tinged with derision.

"I'm saying that Mariah and I . . . picked up our relationship where we had left off." He shifted nervously again.

"You were intimately involved with her."

He nodded once. "Being *intimate*" with Mariah sounded much better than "having an affair."

"How intimate?"

He stood up and walked to the shelves that lined the wall. Running his finger over a long shelf of law books, he shrugged. "I was going to ask her to marry me."

"Are you still planning to ask her to marry you?"

He looked at her. "Yes."

"Then I guess you'll be handing in your resignation soon."

He hadn't given it much thought, but he realized that she was right. If Mariah was convicted, he would be forbidden, as a federal agent, from even spending time with her, much less marrying her. "Yeah," he said with a grim smile. "I guess I will."

Johnson swore softly. "You know, you've substantially prejudiced our case against Mariah with your conduct. If this gets out, Jerry and Helen Butler will be screaming 'impropriety.' You could lose your job."

He nodded. He had already been aware of that fact, and Kyle Parker had reminded him, too.

She was silent for a long time, considering how much damage Mariah's attorney could do with this information. Cody's credibility would be severely affected, making his testimony practically worthless. She could refuse to call him, but Mitchell Wilson would know that something was up when the government's undercover agent didn't testify, and he would call Cody himself. That would put her case in an even worse light. "Right now, I'm still planning to call you as a witness," she said warningly. "We'll see if we can work around this."

Cody looked at her for a moment. He didn't want her to "work around" it. He wanted her to drop the charges against Mariah. He wanted to be free to see her, to tell her that he loved her.

"If you've hurt my case, Daniels, I'll turn you over to the Office of Professional Responsibility for investigation, and I just might bring charges against you myself."

"What charges?" He knew he had used poor professional judgment in getting involved again with Mariah. In smuggling cases such as these, when the defendants received so much support from the people, the government's case had to be solid, with no room to question the charges, or the evidence and the means by which it was obtained. But criminal charges?

She thumbed through the file in front of her, then pulled out a thick sheaf of papers. "According to your investigative report, you discovered the children in Mariah Butler's house at approximately four-thirty Thursday afternoon, yet you failed to report that fact to Parker until Friday afternoon—almost twenty-four hours later. You gave her a chance to remove the children and to avoid arrest."

He sat motionless. She was talking about withholding evidence in a major investigation—a felony in itself. He hadn't realized it at the time, but he had let his concern for Mariah, for keeping her out of trouble, color his judgment. He had handled the situation in the only way he could, but he had broken the law.

He had to clear his throat to make a response. "I could say that I was changing the scope of my investigation. I *had* been concentrating on David Green, then the focus changed to Mariah." It was offered simply as an excuse, one that he didn't give much merit. Neither did Sarah Johnson.

"You *could* say that," she agreed, "and, under most circumstances, I would believe you. But these aren't the usual circumstances. Do you think a jury would believe you after I told them that you were having an affair with Mariah Butler, that you wanted to marry her?" She shook her head. "All they would see is a federal agent, a man sworn to uphold the laws of this country, breaking them to protect the woman he loves."

Knowing she was right, he said nothing. There was nothing he *could* say.

"I'm not being vindictive, but your future depends on the outcome of this trial. This investigation cost the government a lot of money, and if we lose because of you . . ." She let the threat trail off, then continued in a businesslike tone.

"Butler's attorney is Mitchell Wilson. He's one of the best in the city—in the state. You'll be hearing from him soon." She made no effort to hide her sarcasm when she continued. "Try not to mention any of this to him, all right?"

He nodded once more. He wouldn't volunteer the information, but if he were asked, he wouldn't lie, either. He left the office without another word.

"Everything okay?" Kyle asked, rising from a seat in the hallway.

"Yeah."

"What did she say?"

"My future depends on the outcome of the trial." After a moment, he added quietly, "She's considering bringing charges against me for withholding evidence."

They walked outside to Kyle's truck. "At least you told her about Mariah now," he remarked. "If she hadn't found out until the trial, you'd be in serious trouble."

Cody smiled wryly at that. He was already in serious trouble. The best he could hope for was getting fired, if he hadn't already quit. The worst was a possible jail sentence. "I didn't go near her after I found out about the kids," he said quietly, almost to himself. "I didn't talk to her, didn't touch her, didn't kiss her.... One of the reasons they chose me for this job was because I had worked for the Butlers before, because I had been involved with Mariah before. She was never a suspect, but because I got involved with her again, I could go to jail. Somehow, it just doesn't make sense.''

"What are the chances that her attorney won't find out about you two?''

Cody smiled again, remembering their argument because she'd told Rosalie Chavez and everyone else at the ranch about them. He didn't think she would risk that again. But her father... "I imagine Jerry Butler has already told Mitchell Wilson. Jerry's a damn good attorney, and he knows the only way to get Mariah off is to discredit the government.'' He sighed deeply. "And Sarah Johnson thinks I'm one hell of a discredit.''

Kyle drove in silence for a while before asking quietly, "Do you still want that transfer?''

He was surprised when Cody laughed. "You're an optimistic bastard, aren't you? Kyle, I'm quitting, if I don't get fired first. I just might end up in jail alongside Mariah.''

"What will you do?''

"Assuming that Johnson decides not to prosecute me and that Mariah will have me, I plan to go back to the ranch.'' If she wouldn't have him... well, nothing he did would matter much without her.

"And what will you do if she goes to prison?'' Kyle asked quietly.

Cody stared out the window, his sigh inaudible. "I'll wait.'' For the rest of his life.

"Why don't I just plead guilty and save everyone a lot of time and money?'' Mariah asked, folding her hands on the gleaming mahogany table that filled the conference room next to Mitchell Wilson's office.

"Hush,'' Helen said. "You're not going to plead guilty.''

"But, Mom, I *am* guilty. We don't need a trial to prove that.''

"Nobody pleads guilty.''

"Maybe some of us should. I committed a crime, Mom—eleven of them. And a whole lot more that I didn't get caught at. It's pretty simple, Mom. I broke a bunch of laws, and I got caught."

Helen frowned darkly at her daughter. "There are extenuating circumstances, such as moral, ethical and religious convictions."

"You never cared about extenuating circumstances before. How many times have I heard you and Dad say, 'The law is the law'?"

"That was before my daughter got herself arrested." Helen reached across to lay her hand over Mariah's. "Honey, let us handle this, okay? All you have to do is sit at the defense table and look—"

"Sorry?" Mariah interrupted. "Properly chastised? Repentant?" She gave a humorless laugh. "Mom, I want to go home. I don't want to drag this out. The sooner I get sentenced, the sooner I can go home."

"And the sooner you can see Cody Daniels."

The door opened as Jerry, Mitchell Wilson and Wilson's assistant, a young man named Troy, came in. "Oh, you'll be seeing Daniels soon enough," Jerry said. "He's going to testify against you at your trial. He's going to help send you to prison. That says something about just how much he loves you."

"Stop it, Dad," she snapped. "Cody isn't the one sending me to prison. I committed the crimes I've been accused of—me, Dad. No one made me do it. I made the decision to smuggle those kids, and I can damn well accept the penalty for doing it."

"I'd like to talk to Mariah alone," Mitchell Wilson said, sliding gracefully into a chair near her. "Why don't you two get a late lunch, then come back?"

Jerry started to protest, but Helen took his arm and led him away. When they were alone, Mitchell smiled at Mariah. "As officers of the court, they technically can't help you at all. As parents, it's hard for them to remember that."

Mariah relaxed in her seat. She liked Mitchell, even if he was siding with her parents in insisting that she plead not guilty. He was in his forties, not too handsome, but charming and intelligent and just plain nice. On meeting him, she'd had a hard time believing that this nice, pleasant man was one of the toughest criminal lawyers in Arizona, but her father had lost more than a few cases to him.

"I need to ask you a few questions about Cody Daniels, Mariah," Mitchell said.

She dropped her gaze to her hands. So far, in her few meetings with Mitchell, she had managed not to discuss Cody. She didn't know much about law, but common sense told her that revealing their relationship in court wouldn't present Cody in a very good light. "What do you want to know?" she asked, her expression and voice guarded.

"You were engaged to him eight years ago, weren't you?"

"Yes."

"But things didn't work out, and he left Arizona."

She nodded.

"What happened when he came back?"

She sat in silence.

Mitchell and Troy waited patiently for some answer, but she stubbornly said nothing. Finally Mitchell continued, his voice gentle. "Your father tells me that you were once again planning to marry Daniels."

"This has nothing to do with my smuggling," she said at last. "It has no bearing on it whatsoever."

"Cody Daniels is a border patrol agent who was sent to your ranch under cover. His actions while he was there *do* have a bearing on this case," Mitchell explained. "Your father and your mother have already told me about him. Troy's going to interview the other employees at your ranch about him, and I'm going to talk to Daniels himself tomorrow. Why don't you make it easier on all of us by answering my questions?"

"Because I don't like your questions." She pushed her chair back from the table and walked to the windows. They were on the top floor of the building, with Tucson spread out below. She had been in the city for three and a half weeks now. Her trial was scheduled to start in another week. That would make it four and a half weeks since she had seen

Cody. Four and a half weeks since she had talked to him, or touched him, or even simply looked at him. "I don't suppose you'd let me be present when you talk to Cody." Her wry smile said she knew that was impossible, but she had asked anyway.

"The U.S. Attorney would have my head if I did that," Mitchell admitted. "Are you in love with him, Mariah?"

She folded her arms over her chest and bit her lip.

"I'm trying to help you, but I can't do it without your cooperation. Do you *want* to go to prison?"

"Of course not. But I don't want to talk to you about Cody, either." She sat down again, leaned back and crossed her legs. In a pale blue summer dress, she looked cool and lovely, completely at ease. "I suggested to Mom that I plead guilty."

"And she told you no." Mitchell didn't have to ask; he knew that Helen Butler would never let her daughter plead guilty to anything.

"What do you think about it?"

"You've got a chance, Mariah."

She looked skeptical. "How? I was caught red-handed by practically the entire contingent of border patrol agents assigned to Esperanza. What chance do I have?"

"Of course we'll present character witnesses, who can support your reasons for smuggling the children into the country. Our best bet, though, is to try to impeach the credibility of the government's witnesses."

Mariah considered the government's witnesses—Cody, Kyle Parker, Michael Montez and the others—and she smiled faintly. "I wouldn't put much money on it. How can you impeach someone who's unimpeachable?"

"You're taking this very lightly, Mariah."

Suddenly serious, she shook her head. "I'm not taking anything lightly. I'm facing reality. I'm not going to live with false hopes of an acquittal that isn't going to happen. I committed a crime, I got caught, and I'm going to have to pay for it."

But, please, she added silently, don't let the cost be too high. Send me to prison, but don't take Cody from me.

* * *

Mitchell Wilson, Cody had been told, was a highly respected lawyer. That was good—Mariah needed the best. Just as Sarah Johnson had predicted, Wilson had called, asking Cody to come to his office "for a talk." He had been both dreading and looking forward to this meeting—dreading the questions he knew Wilson would ask about Mariah and looking forward to meeting the man who was defending her.

When he walked into the suite of offices with its dark paneling, priceless Oriental rugs and original works of art, Cody knew the meaning of "understated elegance." Wilson was a good attorney, and he was apparently well paid for his skills.

A secretary showed Cody into the inner office, where Mitchell Wilson greeted him with a handshake. "Sit down, please," he invited after introducing himself and Troy Andrews. "Thank you for coming."

Cody said nothing. He had come willingly, but both him and Wilson knew that he'd had no choice; if he had refused, the lawyer would have subpoenaed him.

Mitchell wasted no time. "I have a copy of your report on your investigation at the Butler ranch. It all seems pretty straightforward. I have no questions about that." He sat down behind his desk, placing himself in the position of authority. Cody hid a smile at the simple, but effective, technique. "I do have some questions, however, about a few things that weren't in your report. Let's start with your relationship with my client."

Your client, Cody wanted to retort, is *my* lover, but he remained silent.

"I know that you and Mariah were...involved."

"Did she tell you that?" Cody asked. He found the thought of Mariah discussing their relationship with anyone unsettling.

"No," Mitchell answered honestly. "Her father did. Mariah has refused to answer any of my questions about you. Is she trying to protect you?"

"I don't know what she's trying to do. I haven't seen her in almost a month." And it had been the longest month of his life.

Mitchell studied him for a minute before quietly asking, "Do you need protection, Agent Daniels?"

"Apparently you think I do."

He nodded. "Yes, I do. I think Mariah's willing to go to prison if that's what it takes to keep your affair a secret. I don't want to see that happen, and frankly, I don't think you do, either."

Cody held his gaze for a long time before softly murmuring, "No...I don't." And Mitchell Wilson knew as well as Cody did that he had only one chance of preventing that: to use their affair, as he called it, against Cody in court. He was going to accuse Cody of unprofessional conduct, of being untrustworthy, of displaying a lack of good judgment. He was going to represent Cody as immoral, unethical and unprincipled, as a man who cared so little about his job that he would have an affair with one of the principals in his investigation; as a man who cared so little about Mariah that he would lie to her, use and betray her. It wouldn't change the facts of the case, that she had been caught with five undocumented aliens in her custody, but it would certainly make the jury skeptical of everything that Cody told them and far more sympathetic toward Mariah.

It just might work. It would undoubtedly mean the end of Cody's career, but he didn't mind, since he had already decided to resign. It would also mean charges brought against him—jail for him. But if she went free, wasn't that all that mattered? He was strong; he could deal with imprisonment more easily than Mariah could.

He relaxed in his chair, his fingers twined loosely together. "What do you want to know?"

Thursday morning Mariah rose early, showered, dried her hair and dressed in a simple pale blue skirt and white blouse. She needed makeup, she thought, staring at herself in the mirror. As tan as she was, she somehow managed to look pale, and her eyes were huge and shadowed. She would look sorry and repentant, she had teased her mother last week, but all she looked was scared. Talk about guilty pleas and prison and paying for her crimes had been easy in Mitchell Wilson's plush, elegant office, but today wasn't going to be so easy. Today her trial was going to start. Today she was going to see Cody.

She had never been so afraid in her life.

"You look lovely," Helen said, greeting her with a kiss on her cheek when she entered the living room.

"I look terrified," she retorted, her voice quavering a bit. "I don't know what's worse—going on trial for all those crimes, or seeing Cody again."

"You won't be able to talk to him," Helen warned. "Don't forget that he'll be there as a witness against you."

Mariah nodded, sitting down and folding her hands. As soon as her father was ready, they would go to the courthouse. Her parents spent most of their working days in courtrooms, but Mariah had only been inside one twice—for her arraignment and her preliminary hearing. To her, they were big, cold, frightening places.

The trial was expected to last about two days, Mitchell had told her when he called yesterday. Two days, and her fate would be decided. If she was convicted, the judge would then set a sentencing date, several weeks to a month away. Mitchell had told her that, too, because she had insisted on knowing what she had to look forward to. He seemed to have faith that he could get her off on all charges, but she wanted to be prepared for the worst.

Jerry came downstairs at last, and they left for the courthouse. Mitchell met them there, Troy at his side, as usual. Together, with the men and Helen surrounding Mariah, they went to the room where the case would be heard.

In a small office down the hall, Cody checked the thumb-snap strap, a wide strip of leather that held his gun securely in place in his holster, then unhooked his gun belt and handed it to the waiting U.S. marshal. He could wear the gun belt in court, Kyle had told him, or leave it in the marshal's safekeeping. Since this would be the first time Mariah had seen him in uniform, Cody figured that would be a big enough shock without her also seeing the items he wore on the wide black belt—the .357 magnum revolver, the handcuff case, the cartridge carrier loaded with a dozen shiny bullets, and the speed loader case that enabled him to reload his gun in seconds. Then he went to the witness room where the other agents were waiting.

Since Mariah's arrest, he had met the other agents who were scheduled to testify. There was Michael Montez, who had actually arrested her; Kyle, the supervisory agent; Linda Stevens, who had searched her car; Gerald Isaacs, who had questioned the five children; and John Maxwell, the agent at the checkpoint who, by singling Mariah out from the other drivers on the road that morning, had decided that she was suspicious enough to warrant questioning. Maxwell would testify first, Sarah Johnson had informed them, and Cody would be last. She hoped to present her good witnesses and impress the jury with the facts before Mitchell Wilson had a chance to get hold of *him*, Cody guessed.

A few minutes after nine, John Maxwell was called from the small room. Mariah watched with curiosity as he took the witness stand at the front of the courtroom. She didn't remember seeing him the day of her arrest, but she had been pretty shaken then.

Maxwell explained the criteria used to select cars for closer inspection at the checkpoint that day. Because a woman with five Carta Blancan children had eluded arrest the day before, they had been double-checking all female drivers with Hispanic children. Mariah had been a match.

"Well, they just showed probable cause for stopping you," Troy Andrews murmured to Mariah, who was sitting between him and Mitchell.

Maxwell left the courtroom, to be replaced by Michael Montez, then the others. The time each witness spent on the stand was brief; their testimony was straightforward, with little for Mitchell to challenge.

During Kyle Parker's testimony, Mariah shifted uncomfortably in her chair, turning slightly toward Troy. The young man was doodling on a yellow-lined pad, drawing loops and circles around neat block letters that spread across the line.

Mariah watched Troy while she listened with half a mind to Mitchell's questioning of Kyle Parker. Mitchell had seemed so sure that he could get her off with probation at the very least; he had even believed that the charges might still be dropped. How? she wondered, wishing now that she had taken a more active interest in the defense he had prepared for her. So far, no one had said anything that could possibly sway things in her favor. Every one of the border patrol agents had been serious and convincing, giving an impression of complete professionalism. She was certain that Cody would be no different.

At last Kyle was allowed to leave, and the U.S. Attorney called Cody. Mariah sat straighter in her chair, folding her hands together in her lap. She had waited over a month for this moment, to see him again. She hated not being able to speak to him or touch him, but at least she could look at him and hear his voice.

He was sworn in before he took a seat in the witness stand. For just an instant his gaze met Mariah's; then he quickly looked away again, focusing instead on Sarah Johnson.

He looked even more handsome than ever to Mariah's eyes. The dark green uniform he wore, complete with shiny badge, fitted snugly, as if it had been custom-tailored, and the color complemented the dark gold of his hair. She had tried before to picture him in uniform, but she hadn't succeeded. She hadn't known he would look this handsome.

Sarah Johnson walked around the table and stopped, facing Cody. "Would you please state your full name and occupation?"

"Cody Daniels, patrol agent, United States Border Patrol." There was a quiet strength in his voice that held Mariah's gaze on him, but he still carefully avoided looking at her.

"Agent Daniels, how long have you been employed as a patrol agent with the U.S. Border Patrol?"

"Eight years."

"Where are you currently assigned?"

"At the border patrol station at Esperanza, Arizona."

"How long have you been assigned there?"

"About two and a half months."

"Allow me to call your attention to this past June. What duties were you assigned at that time?"

"I was working in the El Paso district when I received a transfer to Esperanza. It was believed that a smuggling ring was bringing children from Carta Blanca into this country in and around Esperanza, and I was assigned to work the case under cover. The suspect in the case was employed at the Butler ranch outside Esperanza, so I was instructed to get a job there to gather information."

"During your investigation, did you find evidence of this individual's involvement in smuggling?"

"No."

"Did you find evidence of smuggling taking place at the Butler ranch?"

Mariah finally dropped her gaze to the table as he answered quietly, "Yes, I did."

"And what evidence did you find?"

"On July fourteenth the border patrol arrested Lissa Crane as she was smuggling seven Carta Blancan children across the border. Another woman, with five other children, evaded arrest at that time. A short time later on that same day, when I went to the ranch house to talk to the defendant, I found her there with a juvenile Hispanic male named Rico, who was approximately five years of age. I believed that he was one of the children who had escaped arrest."

"Why did you believe that?"

"Because Mariah Butler has no children. Also, she and Lissa Crane have been best friends most of their lives. They were roommates in college, and Lissa had visited the ranch since I'd begun working there."

Mariah gave a slight shudder as she sat back in her chair. Cody's testimony had probably just sealed her conviction. She shut out the annoying sound of the attorney's voice and the lower, quieter rumbling of Cody's and stared into the distance.

She didn't mind him testifying against her—she truly didn't. He'd had no choice—just as she had had no choice in accepting those five kids into her home. The only thing about his testimony that bothered her was his use of the word "defendant" to refer to her. It made her feel less than human.

"Our turn," Mitchell said in a low whisper, smiling reassuringly at Mariah. "This is where we get you off."

She realized that the courtroom was quiet. Sarah Johnson had returned to her seat, and Cody was still on the stand, his head lowered. Frowning, Mariah looked from Mitchell to Troy, who was also smiling, then at Cody again. Had he stiffened since the prosecutor had finished her questioning, as if he were dreading the questions Mitchell Wilson would now ask? Her thoughts about the other agents flashed through her mind—serious, convincing, complete professionalism. Then she looked at Troy's legal pad again. The words inside his doodle hadn't registered when she saw them earlier, but now they jumped out at her: professional misconduct.

"I want to talk to you," she whispered, catching Mitchell's hand as he stood up.

"Not now, Mariah. Let me question Daniels, then we'll talk."

She tightened her grip. There was no way he could get away from her without causing a scene. "I want to talk to you now!" she whispered.

Mitchell looked beyond her, to where her parents were sitting in the first row. She squeezed his hand to bring his attention back to her. "My parents may be paying you, Mitchell, but *I'm* your client, and I want to talk to you now!"

The lawyer looked down at her for a minute, then sighed, nodding. "All right." Facing the judge, he said, "Your Honor, I request a thirty-minute recess so that I may confer with my client."

Finally Cody was looking at her, Mariah noticed with some satisfaction. He guessed that something was wrong. Did he have any idea what Mitchell Wilson was planning to do to him?

"All right, what's wrong?" Mitchell asked as he and Troy escorted Mariah out of the courtroom. He directed her toward a conference room down the hall where they could talk privately.

She waited until they were in the room. Her parents had followed, and she turned a cool gaze on them. "Would you wait outside, please?"

"Mariah—"

She cut her father off. "This is between Mitchell and me. Please wait outside."

Grumbling, Jerry left the room. Helen followed, stopping at the door to smile worriedly at her daughter. "Remember, *no one* pleads guilty," she said softly, then closed the door.

"What is it, Mariah?" Mitchell asked impatiently.

"What is professional misconduct?"

He and Troy exchanged glances; then Mitchell said, "It's nothing that concerns you."

She folded her arms stubbornly across her chest and asked the question again.

"It's a dishonest act, dereliction of duty, unlawful behavior, improper or wrongful behavior, mismanagement, impropriety." Mitchell rattled off the definitions, then lifted his shoulders in a shrug. "Take your pick."

She sat down in the chair behind her, feeling suddenly numb. Now she understood why Mitchell had been so optimistic. "It was...improper behavior for Cody to sleep with me, wasn't it?" she asked in a low voice.

"Yes."

"Improper enough for him to be punished for it?"

"Daniels had knowledge that you were committing a crime, but because of his relationship with you, he failed to act on it. His affair makes him guilty of professional misconduct. His failure to arrest you makes him guilty of withholding evidence. He could be fired, or...the U.S. Attorney could charge him, or both. His relationship with you taints her entire case."

Mariah sat quietly for a long time. Both Mitchell and Troy also remained silent, watching her, waiting for her to respond. Finally, Mitchell touched her arm. "We've got to go back in a few minutes."

"I want to change my plea."

"Mariah, don't be a fool—"

"I wanted to plead guilty all along, but no one would listen to me. That's why you never told me about this."

"We knew you would object."

She stood up, pacing around the table. "I want to change my plea. I'm not going to sit there and let you destroy him for me. I won't let you do that to him."

"He knows." Mitchell said it softly, hoping to sway her.

Instead she looked shocked. "He what?"

"I talked to him. He knows the questions I'm going to ask, and he knows the effect it's going to have on his career. He's willing to go through with this, Mariah, to help you."

She had always wondered if Cody loved her. He was willing to give up his career and to risk going to jail for her; if that wasn't love, it was enough. She wiped a tear from her eye. "No. *I'm* not willing to let someone else pay for what I've done—especially Cody. We're going back in there, Mitchell, and you're going to tell the judge that I'm changing my plea to guilty. Then you can't question Cody anymore, can you?"

Grimly he shook his head.

She smiled faintly. "All right. Let's go."

By the time the judge returned to the courtroom, everyone else was in place—Mariah, Mitchell and Troy at the defense table, Sarah Johnson at the prosecutor's table, the jury in their seats, and Cody on the witness stand.

Mitchell turned to Mariah. "Are you sure?"

She nodded.

Rising from his seat, he faced the judge. "Your Honor, I request to see you and the government's attorney in your chambers on a most urgent matter." He touched Mariah's shoulder, signaling her to rise, also. With Sarah Johnson and the court reporter close behind, they followed the judge to his chambers.

"What do you want?" the gray-haired man asked as soon as he was settled behind his desk.

"My client wishes to change her plea to guilty," Mitchell reluctantly replied.

"Do you understand what you're doing?" the judge asked, turning his sharp gaze on Mariah.

"Yes, I do."

"Has Mr. Wilson explained the consequences of such an action to you?"

"Yes, he has."

"And you still want to plead guilty?"

"Yes."

The judge looked at Sarah Johnson and shrugged. "All right, let's go."

Mariah could feel Cody's eyes on her as she walked back to the table and sat down. She kept her head up, but her eyes couldn't quite make contact with his or anyone else's.

The judge gave Mitchell a nod. "Mr. Wilson, are you ready to make your motion now?"

"Yes, Your Honor, I am." Mitchell rose to his feet. "At this time, my client wishes to amend her plea and enter a plea of guilty to the government's charges against her."

The hallway outside the courtroom was filled with people, but Mariah ignored them all, until Jerry caught her shoulders and gave her a little shake. "Why?" he demanded. "Why did you do it?"

She looked from her father to her mother, her eyes pleading for understanding. "I had to. Listen, I don't want to talk about it now. I want to go home."

Helen nodded sympathetically. "When you do feel like talking, call us."

She nodded, too, then turned to find Bonita and Arcadio in the crowded hallway. She knew they had been at the trial, and she wanted to get a ride home with them. She could pick up her clothes from her parents' house later.

She made contact with a pair of intense blue eyes down the hall. Cody was standing between Kyle Parker and Sarah Johnson, his attention riveted on her. His face was a cold, expressionless mask, but his eyes were filled with emotion. She took a step toward him, but the attorney noticed her. Grasping Cody's arm, Johnson pulled him away.

Kyle waited until they were out of sight before he approached Mariah. "He's resigned from the border patrol," he said.

"Then...why...?" She blinked tear-filled eyes. "Doesn't he want to talk to me?"

Kyle shrugged. "He has another week to work. Until then, he can't come around you. You're a convicted felon, Mariah, and you almost took him down with you. Leave him alone for now, okay?"

She looked at him for a long time before nodding and whispering a soundless, "Okay." Turning away, she found Bonita and Arcadio waiting for her.

Bonita hugged her tightly, then offered Mariah a tissue to wipe her eyes. "Let's go home now," she said softly, still holding on to her.

"Yes," Mariah agreed sadly. "Let's go home."

The ranch was lonely and empty. There was little for Mariah to do, proof of how well they got along without her. She spent her days in the office anyway, making work, straightening, rearranging—anything to keep her busy. A hundred times a day she reached for the phone to call Cody, but every time common sense stopped her. As long as he was working for the border patrol, he couldn't talk to her. He might not even want to. She had been placing so much importance on the fact that he had been willing to sacrifice himself to help her in court, but that might not mean anything. As Kyle had so bluntly said, she had almost brought Cody down. He might hate her for it.

She walked to the window and stared out. She couldn't shake the depression that had hung over her since her return from Tucson. She had thought that coming home would cheer her, and she *was* glad to be back at the ranch, but without Cody, it just didn't seem worthwhile. Nothing did.

Outside she heard the voices of the men as they returned from the day's work. As soon as they'd had a chance to clean up, dinner would be served. Mariah didn't have much of an appetite, but if she didn't put in an appearance, Bonita would send Arcadio after her, as she had done for the last week.

When the door opened behind her, she smiled without turning. "I know, I know, it's almost dinnertime. You go on. I'll be there in a few minutes."

"I'm not really hungry. I'd rather wait for you."

She whirled around, her mouth hanging open. Cody stood in the doorway, wearing faded jeans, a dark green shirt and his old, scuffed, worn-out cowboy boots.

He looked at her for a long moment before a little smile curved his mouth. "On second thought, I think I am hungry—hungry for you." He opened his arms, and she rushed across the small room, throwing herself against him. "I missed you," he whispered against the soft silk of her hair.

"I thought you hated me," she whispered back, tears running down her cheeks to soak into his shirt.

"I love you."

She raised her head to look at him. Her eyes glistened. "What?"

Cody smiled. It was sweet and tender and full of love. "I love you."

Touching his mouth with one finger, she laughed joyously. "It's been years since you've said that to me."

"I'll say it every day."

A sudden sadness stole over her face, and she pulled away from him. "I don't have every day, Cody. I have to be back in court in two more weeks." She tried not to think of her sentencing too often. She could get probation, as David had gotten, or she could go to prison for a very long time.

He very gently drew her back into his embrace. "I'll be here," he assured her. "I'll always be here." He lowered his head to kiss her, and his body responded hungrily to the contact with hers.

"Make love to me, Cody," she whispered, twining her arms around his neck. "Help me forget all these weeks we've been apart."

"Everyone's at your house for dinner," he murmured, tracing her ear with his tongue, "and I don't have a house anymore."

"I know a place in the desert...."

He smiled at his memories of that place. "And I've still got your quilt in my truck. Let's go."

"What's been happening lately?" Cody asked, nuzzling her ear.

Mariah gave a soft, sleepy yawn. "Lissa's trial starts next week."

"Uh-huh." His kisses moved lower, to the elegant line of her throat.

"Suzanne still won't marry David."

His lips reached the swell of her breast. "Hmm." The sound vibrated around her nipple as he took it into his mouth.

"The ranch is doing fine."

"Nice."

Mariah slid her fingers into the thick gold of his hair, holding his head to her breast. "And I've missed you so much that I could have died."

Cody's response to her fierce whisper was a tightening in his loins. He wanted her again, but not here. There was a distinct chill in the air that made the canyon floor increasingly uncomfortable. He rolled away and handed her clothes to her.

"Let's stay here," she protested.

"Let's go home. I want to make love to you for the rest of the night, and soon it's going to be too cold here." He quickly pulled on his own clothes, then helped her with hers. They returned to the truck and made the long drive across the desert to the house.

Dinner was long since over; they had the place to themselves. Cody led the way to Mariah's bedroom, quickly undressing her as soon as he'd closed the door behind them.

He laid her gently on the bed and joined his body with hers. Supporting his weight on his arms, he stared down at her. "Marry me."

Mariah's smile was both happy and sad. "Cody—"

"You love me," he interrupted, "and I love you. Marry me. Now. Right away."

"I ca—"

He kissed her before she completed the word. He didn't want to hear "can't" from her, not ever. Still kissing her, he made love to her fiercely, passionately, gently, lovingly, until he finally collapsed on the bed next to her.

"I love you," she whispered.

"Then marry me."

She smiled drowsily. She couldn't accept his proposal, not when she might spend the rest of her life in prison, but she loved him dearly for asking. "I love you," she repeated.

Cody was tired, too, and half-asleep. "I love you, too. And I'm going to marry you, Mariah. I swear I am."

The last two weeks had passed quickly, Mariah thought as she stood next to Mitchell, in court for the fourth time. The judge was beginning to seem like an old friend, but the U.S. Attorney was definitely still an enemy. Mariah got the impression from the looks Sarah Johnson was giving her that the lawyer resented Mariah's guilty plea; she had gotten a conviction, but she hadn't earned it herself.

Mariah glanced over her shoulder. Cody was seated in the front row, next to her mother and father. He smiled faintly when he caught her eye, and she returned the smile. They had spent most of the last two weeks together, neglecting the ranch and everything else, simply talking, loving, creating memories. He had told her about his eight years with the border patrol, and she had told him about her work with the movement—how she had gotten involved, why she had taken the risks, why she had quit and, most importantly, how she had gotten dragged back in. Knowing that he had felt betrayed by his father and let down by his mother, she had wanted him to understand that *she* hadn't betrayed him, hadn't let him down.

And he *did* understand. He told her often that he loved her, and, in the fifteen days that he had been back at the ranch, he had asked her to marry him at least fifteen times. She had repeatedly refused, but he had promised her that he would never stop asking. She hoped he wouldn't.

Mitchell called her attention back to the proceedings with the nudge of an elbow. She looked at the judge, listening to the end of his quiet little speech.

"Mariah Butler, upon your entering a plea of guilty to the charges contained in the government's information, and after careful consideration of the presentencing investigation report, it is the opinion of this court that you be sentenced to a term of six months' imprisonment, less time served, at the Federal Correctional Institution at Pleasanton, California. Therefore, you are remanded into the custody of the United States Marshal's Service until transfer can be arranged with the Federal Bureau of Prisons. Do you need time to get your personal affairs in order?"

She bit her lip. In the event of a prison sentence, she had given Cody power of attorney to run the ranch in her absence; he also had the authority to handle her personal affairs. There was nothing else she needed to do. "No," she said, her voice low but firm.

She looked over her shoulder again. Her mother was in tears, and her father, for the first time that she could remember, looked badly shaken. Cody was motionless, his eyes dark, his face just a little pale.

She turned to the neatly dressed man in the dark blue suit who had approached her. "Do I get to say goodbye to my family first?" she asked with a nervous smile.

The marshal nodded. "You can use the conference room down the hall."

Cody stood near the door of the small room while Mariah spoke quietly to her parents. He didn't try to understand their words. Six months. He closed his eyes tightly. It seemed like forever. It wasn't really so long, not when the alternative could have been more than fifty years. But every one of those six months would last a lifetime.

He opened his eyes when he heard the door open, then close. Turning, he saw that Jerry and Helen were gone. He was alone with Mariah. He walked to her, reaching up to brush his hand lightly over her hair. "California's a long way off." His voice was husky, thick with emotion.

She tried to smile. "It's right next door."

"When I see you—"

She shook her head, laying her fingers over his mouth. "No. I—I don't want you to visit me there. No visits, no phone calls, no letters."

He stared at her, dismay darkening his eyes. He had, she thought, the most beautiful eyes. "Mariah, I can't stay away from you for six months."

"You have to, Cody. Please. I don't want you to see me there."

He blinked at the hot stinging in his eyes. "I should have made you marry me."

She smiled again. "I wouldn't have let you tie yourself down like that. What if I had gotten a longer sentence? What if you meet someone else while I'm gone?"

"It'll never happen. I love you. I'll always love you."

Closing her eyes, she stepped into his embrace, wrapping her own arms tightly around his waist. "I love you, too, Cody," she whispered. She hugged him, then raised her face to kiss him. She tasted the tears and didn't know if they were his or her own.

At last she stepped away. For a moment he refused to let go. He couldn't do it. He couldn't let them take her away. He couldn't spend the next six months of his life without her. But she pushed at his restraining arms, and finally he had to let her go.

She walked to the door, then paused there. "I love you, Cody," she whispered. Quickly she walked out, knowing that she would never forget, as long as she lived, the look of anguish on his face.

Mariah stood in front of the mirror, her eyes searching her image intently for changes. Her hair was still long, smooth and straight. She was still tanned, though the months inside showed in the slightly lighter tones of her skin. She had lost a little weight, but not enough to matter. The biggest change, she decided, was in her eyes. Just like on the day of her trial, they were huge, unsure and frightened.

Taking a step back, she dropped her gaze to her clothes. The dress Helen had sent her to wear today was enough to make her smile, something she hadn't done much lately. After six months of wearing slacks and shirts, the white dress with its camisole-style top felt heavenly. The neckline and the hem were scalloped and edged with heavy white lace, and it belted at her waist with a lavender satin sash. For the first time since she had walked out of the courtroom in Tucson, she felt feminine and pretty. Too bad Cody wouldn't be there to see her.

Her expression sobered. How many times in the last six months had she regretted telling him that he couldn't visit, call or write to her? How many times had she lain in bed at night, aching with loneliness that only he could ease? Her parents had visited, but they had never mentioned Cody. They had told her about Lissa's conviction and sentence to one year at a federal prison in West Virginia; they had mentioned David's marriage to Suzanne Fox; they had even told her about the end of the civil war in Carta Blanca, with the brutal regime ousted once and for all. But they had never said Cody's name once, not even last week when Helen had written to finalize their arrangements to meet Mariah today.

Was he still at the ranch? she wondered sadly. Had he missed her the way she had missed him? Did he still love her?

Processing out didn't take long. When it was finished, Mariah stood still for a long time. She was free, she realized. She could walk out and go practically anywhere, do practically anything. She could meet her parents and catch the first plane home. To the ranch. To Cody.

She was free—and she was scared. What if he didn't want her? What if his feelings for her had changed? What if he had gotten tired of waiting?

She took a deep breath, forcing air into her aching lungs. She unfolded her fists and pressed her palms together, making her fingers lie flat and unclenched. When she looked at her hands in the prayerful pose, she almost smiled. That was what she should do—pray. All the way from here to the ranch.

At last she walked into the room where her parents and the relatives of other newly released inmates were waiting. She scanned the room quickly for her mother and father; then her search came to a sudden halt.

Standing at the window, staring out, was a man dressed in a sky-blue shirt, faded jeans and worn boots. His hair glinted dark gold in the sunlight shining through the dusty glass. For a minute he continued to look out; then he stiffened, feeling her stare. Slowly he turned to face her.

Mariah's black eyes met Cody's blue ones across the room. For what seemed like ages they simply looked at each other until, at last, the corners of his mouth lifted in a welcoming smile. Mariah smiled, too. It came slowly, like the blossoming of a rare flower, and it transformed her face into radiant beauty. She took a step toward him, then another and another, until they were close enough to touch.

She raised one hand to his face, the tips of her fingers brushing his mouth; then a tear escaped from the corner of one eye.

Her prayer had been answered. Cody had waited.

Epilogue

From his position near the patio door, Cody watched Mariah, his mouth curved into a soft, loving smile. She was beautiful—so incredibly beautiful. Just looking at her made him want and need and ache. But he didn't mind the ache. He didn't mind sharing her with her parents, his family and a few close friends. Today was their wedding day, a time to share with the people who meant the most to them. Tonight . . . tonight, though, would be theirs alone.

The wedding had been a small affair, held in the desert garden behind Jerry and Helen's house. But small, to Helen Butler, didn't mean informal. She had bullied Cody into a tux, had convinced Mariah to wear the loveliest gown she could find, even if it *was* white. What did it matter that she'd already had one wedding? Helen had asked, disregarding convention. This was going to be her daughter's *last* wedding, and it should be perfect.

And it had been—the music, the flowers, the champagne, the cake. Even the weather had been absolutely perfect.

Across the patio, Mariah looked up and smiled at Cody. He couldn't remember ever seeing her look lovelier, or happier. Her wedding dress was white linen, lavished with lace at the hem that brushed gracefully over the red-tiled floor. The off-the-shoulder bodice was covered with a wide, lace-edged ruffle, and around her slim waist was a sash of blue satin—the color of your eyes, she had laughingly told him.

His eyes were filled with love and dark with desire. Even from a distance, Mariah could see it. When he pushed himself away from the wall he'd been leaning against and started toward her, she felt a tingle of excitement begin inside her.

His touch was as soft as a whisper, feathering over her bare shoulder. A slight tremor shivered through her body, increasing with the sudden tickle of warm, moist breath in her ear. Mariah raised her chin to look up at him.

"I think it's time you and I said our goodbyes and got out of here," he murmured in her ear.

She nodded, reaching up to take his hand from her shoulder and clasping it tightly in hers. Together they made the rounds, speaking softly to each of the guests. When they had finished, they left the house.

Mariah's parents had offered a wedding gift of a honeymoon at one of Arizona's luxury resorts, but they had politely turned it down. They wanted to return to the ranch, to their home.

The house was quiet. Mariah listened to the click of their shoes on the tile as they went to the bedroom. Inside, Cody turned her to face him and laid his hands on her shoulders. For long, silent moments, he simply looked at her before saying softly, "You're beautiful, Mariah."

With a touch so tender it made her want to weep, he removed the lovely white gown, laying it on the corner chair before turning to discard her filmy, silky lingerie. When she was naked before him, he studied her intently. "I love you," he said hoarsely.

Now it was her turn. Her movements were slow, measured, agonizing. It seemed like forever before he, too, was naked. Like him, she studied him for a long time before she whispered, "And I love you."

He laid her gently on the bed and followed her down, and in the stillness of the house, they made love—gently, tenderly, wondrously.

Cody held Mariah close in the warm security of his arms. "Today was the most perfect day of my life." His voice was low so it didn't intrude on the quiet that surrounded them.

"Was it." She said it as a statement, not needing to question. She pressed a kiss to his chest, then tilted her head back to see him.

"What more could I want?"

"Children, maybe?"

Cody pushed her onto her back and leaned on one arm to look down at her. He spread his fingers across her flat belly and tried to imagine her pregnant. "Do you want children?"

She nodded, a wistful look in her eyes. With a grin, he rolled over, settling comfortably between her thighs. "What are you doing?" she asked, stifling a laugh.

"You've given me everything I've ever wanted—your smile, your laughter, your body, your joy, and your love," he explained. "Now I'm going to give you what you want." His grin faded as he found his place inside her with one sure stroke. For a moment he closed his eyes, just savoring the feel of her around him; then he looked down at her. "I'm going to give you a baby."

His words were a husky promise, one that made Mariah shiver with anticipation. He had been right—today *was* a most perfect day. What more could she possibly want?

*　*　*　*　*

Silhouette Intimate Moments

COMING
NEXT MONTH

#261 SMOKE SCREEN—Emilie Richards

Paige Duvall had come to Waimauri, New Zealand, to forget a
painful past, not embark upon a future. But then she met handsome
sheep farmer Adam Tomoana, a man who held the secret to her
heritage, and quite possibly her heart.

#262 FLOWER OF THE DESERT—Barbara Faith

Strong-willed Princeton coed Jasmine Hasir had always been able to
take care of herself. But that was before she was kidnapped by a
nomadic horseman in the lawless Sahara sands. Then only the
power of love—and Raj Hajad—would be able to rescue her.

#263 CROSSCURRENTS—Linda Turner

Mitch Flannery had never trusted anyone; his work in the Secret
Service had taught him that. But his prime suspect, Serenity Jones,
had too much integrity to be a criminal. And when she became a
killer's prime target, Mitch had to learn a new lesson. Only his faith
could give them a future—together.

#264 THE NAME OF THE GAME—Nora Roberts

Television game show producer Johanna Patterson knew the larger-
than-life people of show business were just that: unreal. But she
soon realized that actor/contestant Sam Weaver wasn't playing a
game. He *really* was determined to gain her trust—and win her love.

AVAILABLE THIS MONTH: